Below the Surface, Vol. 2

By

Megan Reiffenberger

I want to dedicate my second novel to everyone who has
ever believed in my dream of being a published author.
It's been a long journey, and I still have a long way to go,
but I've loved every second of it! Thanks for all the
encouragement, love, and support.

Chapter One

Charlie

"You won't get away this time, you stupid little bitch."

I had to get out of there. Find Brody and make sure he was alright. I tried running, but my feet wouldn't move quickly enough. It was as though I was running through a pool filled with maple syrup. I was stuck.

"Gotcha!" A hand reached out from behind and grabbed me by the arm, whipping me back around to face its owner. Camila Hale stared back at me, her hair strewn in every direction, teeth bared, and dark eyes buried under a deep frown.

"Leave me alone!" I shouted, trying to break free from her grip.

"You'll pay for what you did," she growled, reaching behind her.

Next thing I knew, I was staring down the barrel of a gun. My breath caught in my chest. "Don't! I didn't do anything!" I cried.

Camila's lips widened into a devilish grin. "Say goodbye, Charlie."

I opened my mouth to scream, but nothing came out.

Then I felt my body being shaken, and I heard someone shouting my name. After the second 'Charlie' I realized it wasn't Camila speaking anymore.

"Charlie! Charlie, wake up!" It was Brody yelling.

My eyes shot open, and it took me a minute to realize where I was. I was staring at the ceiling in our bedroom. Brody stopped shaking me, and he was now watching me with concern, propping himself up on one elbow.

"I think you were having a bad dream," he said. He placed his hand on my shoulder and massaged it gently with his thumb. "Whatever it was, Charlie, you're safe. It was just a nightmare."

I covered my face with my hands and rubbed my eyes. My cheeks felt sweaty under my fingers. "I thought these Camila nightmares were over," I groaned.

"It was a Camila dream?" Brody asked, his frown deepening. "You stopped therapy over a month ago. I thought you said things were better?"

"I thought they were too."

I'd been having crazy nightmares about Camila for the last six months. Ever since that night in the warehouse where Brody, Landon, and I had tried to stop Camila and Landon's dad—who we just called Mr. Davis—from kidnapping American Swimming's highest paying sponsor, Roman Howard. Camila had tried to fake a relationship with Roman so that she and Mr. Davis could attempt to hack into his company, Roman Enterprises, and steal his money. And while they were successful once, it wasn't enough for them, and they had to come back for more. We found out about their plan, and attempted to stop them.

While we did end up being successful in our attempt, it had been a close call for Brody and me. Camila and Mr. Davis' helper, Victor, had shot at Brody, hitting him in the shoulder, and Camila had tried to strangle me. If Brody hadn't summoned the strength to pick up Victor's gun and shoot Camila, I probably wouldn't be here today. And even though I knew Camila was gone, and I was lucky to walk away mostly unharmed, I still suffered mentally every time I closed my eyes.

After a few weeks of constant nightmares, I finally decided to go see a therapist. I was referred to Dr. Hannah Stevens, who diagnosed me with PTSD. She practiced several exercises with me to combat the dreams, and she helped me through a lot. I truly owed her a debt of gratitude for all she did for me.

"Do you need to go back to Dr. Stevens?" Brody asked.

I shook my head. "No, she said the nightmares could come back randomly, especially if a particular event triggers the memory." I rolled over towards him and buried my face in his chest.

Brody wrapped his arms around me and held me close to him. "Has anything happened that you didn't tell me about?"

"I don't think so," I sighed. "I'm not sure why the dream popped into my mind tonight."

"Well, if they continue, I hope you consider going back to Dr. Stevens." He smoothed my hair out of my face and kissed me gently on the top of my head. "I worry about you."

Tilting my head back, I looked Brody in the eyes. "I'll keep it in mind. I just really want to be over this and get my life back to normal. It doesn't feel normal if I have to see a therapist."

"I get it, I do. Unfortunately, we've been through some pretty abnormal shit. If I could go back in time, I would've done everything differently. Sure, I'm glad we stopped them, but at what price? We're all still recovering from that night. I'm not sure we'll be fully back to normal anytime soon."

"I hate to admit it, but you're probably right." I made a face. "How does your shoulder feel?"

Once the police had finally arrived on scene that night in the warehouse, Brody was immediately taken to the hospital for surgery. The bullet had lodged in his shoulder, but thankfully didn't hit any internal organs. He had lost enough blood though that the doctor rushed him in as soon as the ambulance arrived.

Fortunately, he's been recovering nicely ever since, but he wasn't adjusting well to the almost six months of not swimming at full capacity. He couldn't swim at all for two months, and even now, he still had to cut back on workouts to allow for his shoulder to ease back into it—something much easier said than done for a professional swimmer. He complained often about how sore it was, but he still went to physical therapy three days a week, which he said helped.

"It isn't bugging me too much right now," Brody said, shrugging his shoulder a few times to test it.

I pulled away from him to check the time on my phone. "Ugh, it's already almost five," I whined, and plopped my head back down on the pillow. I was hoping I would have had more time to go back to sleep.

"Happy Monday, babe." Brody chuckled. He then got out of bed and proceeded to pull all of the covers off me. "Time to get up!"

"I hate you," I said, despite the wide smile on my face.

"I'll whip us up some breakfast." He laughed as he walked out of the bedroom. "I'm sure Landon is up and hungry already."

"Poor kid probably can't wait to move out with all the nightmares I've been having," I groaned. Brody didn't respond, so he may not have heard me.

Shortly after the incident, Brody and Landon met with a lawyer at the courthouse to determine where Landon would be staying since his father was put in jail. Mr. Davis had not only been working with Camila to steal from Roman, he was also a horrible father. He hadn't been officially sentenced yet, but he was being charged with attempted murder, grand theft, kidnapping, and physical and emotional neglect of a minor. The chances of him seeing the light of day again were pretty slim—at least, that's what we hoped.

Brody didn't want Landon to have to live with a foster family, and even though Brody himself was only twenty-five-years-old, he gave a solid argument to the judge, and the court agreed to let Landon stay under Brody's care until he turned eighteen. I moved in around the same time, and ever since, the three of us have been living together in Brody's house. It's honestly been great, and I'm glad the living situation turned out like it did.

Finally dragging myself out of bed, I went into the bathroom to get dressed and brush my teeth. I threw Brody's and my swim bags together and went downstairs to join the boys for breakfast.

When I entered the kitchen, they were already seated at the table eating scrambled eggs and bacon.

"Morning, Landon," I said as I joined them. "Have you been up long?"

"Not terribly long." He shrugged. "I heard you screaming. Brody said you had another nightmare."

I grimaced. "I'm sorry. I didn't mean to wake you."

"Don't worry about it. My alarm was going to go off soon, anyway."

"On the bright side, less than a month until you can move out!" I said, trying to make a joke. I often teased Landon about when he was going to move out of the house, especially when he complained about Brody and me kissing outside of our bedroom. It was all in good fun. I didn't actually want him out of the house, but if he was going to dish it, I was going to give it back.

Landon gave a half-hearted laugh. "Yeah, I suppose." He stood from the table and put his plate in the sink. "We should probably get going. I'll go grab my bag."

"Should I not have said that?" I asked Brody when Landon left the room. "He knows I'm still joking, right?"

"He knows you're joking," Brody assured me. "I made breakfast. Eat quick, and we'll get going."

The boys piled into Brody's truck, and I followed shortly behind them in my own car. Landon had school after our morning swim practice, and Coach Tanner still wasn't letting Brody swim more than one practice a day, so he usually came home sooner than I did.

By the time we arrived at the pool, and I had changed into my suit, I still had plenty of time to get on deck and stretch before practice started. Our branch of the American Swimming organization only had four professional swimmers on the team, and our fourth and final teammate, Allison, was already changed and stretching when I came out of the locker room.

"Good morning!" she said cheerfully when I walked up to her.

"How are you always so chipper this early in the morning?" I chuckled. "I'd love nothing more than to go back to sleep."

She laughed. "I don't know. I just love knowing it's a new day! Anything can happen."

"That's a great way to look at it," I said, smiling.

Coach Tanner walked out of his office then, followed by a short blonde woman. Her straight hair was pulled back in a ponytail, she had an athletic build—but nothing compared to Allison and me—and she looked very young. She couldn't have been older than twenty.

From here, my initial thought was that she looked like Camila, and my breathing instantly became heavier. Deep down, I knew it was impossible, but the irrational side of my brain was taking over.

"Who's that?" I asked Allison, trying to focus on my breathing. My eyes went straight to the floor.

"I don't know," she said. She continued to watch them approach. "Coach Tanner would have mentioned something already if we were getting a new teammate."

I stayed rooted to my spot and forced my gaze back towards the pair. The closer she got, the more I relaxed.

It's not Camila.

Taking a deep breath and shaking my head, I mentally kicked myself for thinking such a ridiculous thought.

"Charlie?" Brody suddenly appeared at my side, making me jump. "Are you okay?"

"Yeah." I nodded too quickly and plastered a smile on my face. "I ... I thought I saw something. False alarm."

He narrowed his eyes, suspicious, but let it drop.

Was every new blonde woman for the rest of eternity going to send me into a near panic attack? Maybe Brody was right: I *should* go back to Dr. Stevens.

I let out another long, frustrated sigh.

When was my life going to get back to normal?

Chapter Two

Brody

"Good morning team." Coach Tanner slapped his hands together when he and the blonde woman reached us. "Before we get started, I'd like to take the time to introduce you to this young lady over here." He motioned for the mystery woman to come forward. "This is Ellie Wyatt. She's a student at Jacksonville University, and dreams of joining the American Swimming executive team someday. She's asked if she can get involved with the organization, and I've happily agreed to have her join us. She'll be my coaching assistant for the remainder of the semester."

She smiled at us. "I'm excited to get to know each of you a little better."

Allison gave her a small wave and a smile. "What are you studying?"

"Criminal justice," Ellie said.

"But you want to work for American Swimming?" Allison asked, looking confused.

She shrugged, but her smile was still in place. "A girl needs a backup plan, right?"

I silently wondered why she would choose criminal justice as her backup plan instead of another business-related field of study. Wouldn't something like marketing or accounting be a bit more useful if she wanted to work for a professional sports organization? But since I never went to school and never had a backup, I kept my mouth shut on the matter. I was in no position to judge.

"Where are you from, Ellie?" I asked instead.

"All over," she said. "I've never lived somewhere long enough to call any one place home."

"Military brat?"

She nodded. "Pretty much."

"Well, we're happy to have you."

"Thanks." She smiled.

"Alright, let's get started." Coach Tanner turned and went for his marker board. "Allison and Landon in lane one. Charlie, lane two. And Brody, Ellie is going to give you your modified workout in lane three."

I tried like hell to hide my annoyance, as I didn't want Ellie to think it was because of her. The problem wasn't because she was going to give me my workout, it was because I still had to be doing these modified practices. I wanted more than anything to get back to training full-force and compete, but that wouldn't happen until my physical therapist cleared me.

Before Charlie could slip away to her lane, I grabbed her by the arm. "Hey, are you sure you're okay?" I asked again. I saw the color drain from her face when Ellie had first walked out of Coach's office. She looked a lot better now, but I still wanted to know what was up.

"I'm fine." She avoided my gaze.

Putting a hand on each of her shoulders, I held her in place and made her look at me.

"It would just sound silly if I said it out loud," she huffed. "My brain was playing tricks on me. I'm fine, I promise."

"If you're sure."

"I am." She smiled and threw her cap over her head. "Hope you have a good practice."

"You too." I watched her until she disappeared into the water and then put my goggles on and jumped in my own lane.

I took it easy, and did a long and smooth swim to stretch my muscles. Ever since my shoulder surgery, I had to ease into practice a bit slower to avoid getting sore halfway through. My warmup was a touch longer than everyone else's, and by the time I stopped, they were already working on the first set.

"What's on the agenda for today?" I asked Ellie when I came to the wall. She was standing on the deck towering over me, but crouched down to my level before she spoke.

"He wants you to do ten 100s on the 1:30," she said, reading from the set list Coach Tanner must have given her.

I groaned. "Ugh, that interval is ridiculously slow."

She shrugged and turned the piece of paper around so I could see. "I'm just telling you what he wrote down."

"No, I know," I assured her. "I need to apologize in advance because it's going to sound like I'm frustrated with you, but I'm not. I'm going to be a grump until I can swim normally again."

"Hmm, wonder if that's why he hired me," she laughed. "He doesn't want to deal with the unruly swimmer."

"I wouldn't put it past him." I chuckled.

"Well, as long as I know it's nothing personal, I can deal with it."

I gave her a thumbs up and then slipped my goggles back on and started the set. The interval was way too easy, and I was getting a lot of rest in between each 100. At some point during the set, Ellie took my kickboard from my equipment pile and sat on it. It was something swimmers did a lot rather than sit on the hard ground. Although not much, the kickboard offered some cushion.

When I finished the ten 100's, Ellie told me I had a nice, long kick set next. "He wants you to give your shoulder a rest, I guess," she said.

I nodded and expected her to hand me my kickboard, since, you know, she was sitting on it. When she didn't move, I cleared my throat. "Can you hand me my kickboard?"

"Oh, this?" She pointed to it and winked. "You'll have to come get it."

"Uhh," I said, caught off guard. Now that most people knew I was off the market, I didn't really have random girls trying to flirt with me anymore. A year ago, I would have milked it and flirted back, but now I was just uncomfortable. I pretended not to notice and decided I'd kick without my board. "I'll do streamline kick instead."

"Brody!" she said before I could take off. "I'm only joking, lighten up."

Even though I didn't really believe she was joking, I gave her a pity laugh anyway. "I knew that."

She handed me my kickboard, and I took off before she could add anything else.

Nothing else weird happened during the rest of the workout, for which I was thankful. We continued to talk a bit in between sets, about nothing in particular, but I did try to keep it swimming related as best I could. I did have to admit, though, it was nice having someone to talk to throughout the workout. I'd gotten far too used to swimming alone over the last few months.

"Thanks for a good workout," I told her when I climbed out of the water.

"Well, I can't really take the credit. Coach Tanner wrote it, I just relayed it to you."

"You made it a little less lonely, and that was nice." I bent down to pick up my kickboard and fins. "It's been pretty boring swimming by myself these past few months."

"What happened?" she asked. "If you don't mind me asking, that is."

"It's a long story," I chuckled. "But basically, I got shot trying to protect Roman Howard from my crazy ex-girlfriend and Landon's father. Roman is one of our sponsors."

Her eyes widened ever so slightly, but otherwise her expression stayed emotionless. "Wow, that sounds pretty scary."

"It was, but something needed to be done."

She didn't respond, and instead continued to stare at me with wide eyes.

"Anyway," I said, feeling a little uncomfortable again. "Thanks again for the work out. I look forward to working with you, Ellie."

"Hey, do you have plans for lunch?" she asked. "Since we'll be spending more time together, I'd love to get to know you better."

She was definitely asking me on a date. I didn't want to be rude, but I also wasn't about to go with her alone. "Actually, why don't we all go out to lunch?" I suggested. "You'll be working with us all, so why not get to know us all, right?"

"Sure, that'd be fine." I could practically hear the disappointment in her voice.

"Landon has to go to school, but Charlie, Allison and I could take you out somewhere," I continued before turning my attention to Charlie, who had just gotten out of the pool and was walking towards us. Allison followed shortly behind her. "Charlie, you don't have any lunch plans, do you? I told Ellie we'd take her out somewhere. Allison, you're invited as well."

"I appreciate it, but I have to get to work right after the lifting session," Allison pouted. "Ellie, do you mind if I pick your brain for a minute about breaststroke techniques?"

"Oh, surely you don't want *my* advice," Ellie stammered. "You're already so good at it."

Allison chuckled. "Don't be silly! I'm always open to new ideas."

While the two of them walked off chatting about technique, I pulled Charlie to the side. "We don't have to go if you don't want to," I told her, secretly hoping she wouldn't so I'd have an excuse not to go. "But she wants to get to know us." I purposely left out the part where she was also trying to hit on me.

"No, that's totally fine." She nodded ferociously, her gaze wandering past me.

"Charlie, seriously, I'm not making you." I suddenly remembered her weird behavior towards Ellie this morning, and I started to feel bad for volunteering her to go to lunch with her. The last thing I wanted to do was make her uncomfortable. "Do you know her? Did she do something to you—"

"No, I thought she was Camila." The words fell out of her mouth and she immediately looked at her feet.

Her words shocked me and I didn't know what to say right away. Finally, I lifted her chin with my finger and looked into her eyes. "Charlie, you know that's impossible, right? Camila is dead."

"I know," she said, squeezing her eyes shut. "It was the blonde hair that freaked me out. It happened at the grocery store once, too."

"What did?"

She opened her eyes. "I saw a young woman coming towards me at the grocery store a few weeks ago. She had blonde hair and I didn't know who she was. I nearly had a panic attack until she got close enough for me to realize it wasn't Camila."

Frowning, I shook my head. "Why didn't you tell me that?"

"The same reason I didn't want to tell you why I freaked out before practice. It makes me sound like a crazy person. In my head, I know Camila is dead. So, why do I keep thinking I see her?" Her voice cracked a bit on the last word and I could see tears forming in her eyes.

"Hey," I cupped her cheeks with my palms. "You're not crazy. Okay? Crazy things have happened to you, but you are not crazy."

She pressed her lips into a thin line and nodded.

"I do think you should seriously consider calling Dr. Stevens though," I said. "Maybe she can explain why this is happening. I hate the idea of you being alone and scared. Especially if I'm not around to assure you everything is okay."

"I'll think about it," she said softly.

I pressed my lips to her forehead and took her into my arms, holding her tight. "I love you."

"Love you, too." Her face was pressed against my chest, and her words came out a little muffled. Finally, she stepped out of my embrace and picked up her bag. "We should get going before Coach comes after us." She tipped her head back and kissed me before she turned and made her way to the locker room.

******

After completing the lifting session and cleaning up, the three of us left the gym and took off for the Italian place that recently opened up. It was a short drive away, so Charlie piled into my truck, and we agreed to meet Ellie there.

When we arrived, Ellie had gotten there first, and waved us over to the booth she had been seated at. "Hope this spot works for both of you," she said as we took our seats across from her.

"This is perfect." I slipped my jacket off and set it next to Charlie against the wall.

The temperatures had been unusually cool for Florida in January, and having lived in Jacksonville all my life, I was not accustomed to the cold. Since Charlie came from the Midwest, and was used to *much* colder temps, she often made fun of me for wearing a big coat when it was still fifty degrees outside. She promised to bring me home with her to Minnesota sometime to experience what cold really felt like—I couldn't wait.

"What's good here?" Ellie asked, flipping through the menu.

"Not sure." Charlie shrugged. "This is our first time here, too."

"No worries, I'll ask the waiter." Her arm shot into the air a second later. "Waiter!" she called. "We need assistance."

I cleared my throat, "Ellie, we aren't in a hurry, we can wait until he comes back."

"Don't be silly." She waved off my comment and smiled sweetly at the young waiter who approached.

"How can I help you, ma'am?" he asked.

"We want to know what's good here. My friends and I have never been here before." She shot us a broad smile.

Charlie stared blankly, while I gave the waiter an apologetic grin.

He nodded. "Of course. Well, our special is the baked lasagna—"

"No, no, no." Ellie laughed. "We want to know what's *good*. Not what's on sale. Do you know who you're serving? This is professional swimmer, Brody Hayes—"

"Ellie," I warned.

Her face fell when she saw my stern look.

"I'm sorry, sir." I turned my attention back to the waiter. "I am curious as to what you would recommend, though."

"The eggplant parmesan is my personal favorite," he said. "But one can't go wrong with classic spaghetti either."

"That sounds great, I'll have the eggplant. Please, no oregano though. I'm allergic." I handed him my menu.

"Of course, sir." He took Charlie and Ellie's orders—they both got spaghetti—and turned to leave.

An awkward silence fell over the table once the waiter was out of sight.

"Ellie, I didn't mean to get upset with you," I finally said. "But you were being a little rude to that waiter, and I didn't want you to use me as an excuse. I don't need people to give me special treatment because I'm a professional athlete."

"I'm sorry, I guess I thought that's how rich, famous people acted." She looked at the floor. "I was just trying to fit in."

I couldn't help but laugh. "We do get a bit of a bad rep. But that's not me—anymore anyway."

"Brody has really turned his life around in the last year," Charlie said, coming to my defense. "And you can't believe everything you see in magazines anyway."

Placing my hand on Charlie's knee, I gave her a few pats to show her it was okay. "Just be yourself, Ellie. You don't need to try and be someone you're not." I felt Charlie's gaze on me, so I turned to give her a smile. "Right, Charlie?"

She returned my smile with a tight grin. "Right."

"Thanks," Ellie said. "So, you're allergic to oregano, huh?"

"Extremely," I chuckled, thankful for the change in subject.

We continued to chat throughout the meal, mostly just small talk and getting to know each other. Ellie told us more about the places she's lived, and about her college experiences so far. She said even though she wasn't born in Florida, some of her fondest childhood memories were from here, and she was excited to be back in the state for school.

The longer we chatted, the more relaxed Ellie appeared. In the short time I had known her, she had done a great job of creating uncomfortable situations, but I was starting to think it was because she was nervous. Halfway through our meal, she had calmed down greatly, and by the time we had finished eating, she was talking like we were old friends.

Charlie had understandably been a bit reserved when it came to Ellie, but even she had loosened up, laughing along with her, and adding stories of her own.

"I'm going to go to the restroom really quick," Charlie said when she was done eating. "Then can you drop me back off at the pool?"

"Yep, no problem." I stood up and allowed her to slide out of the booth past me and then returned to my seat.

"Thanks for paying for lunch," Ellie said after Charlie had walked away. "You didn't have to do that."

"It was no problem. It's something us 'rich' guys do," I joked.

She giggled and then leaned towards me with a big smile. "Listen, while Charlie is in the bathroom, I was wondering if I could ask you something?"

"Sure, what's up?"

"I know we just met, but I know about your reputation with the ladies." She rested her hands on the table in front of her and shot me a wink. "And I was kind of hoping you ignored my flirting earlier because you were working, so I'd thought I'd try again. Would you maybe want to go out with me sometime?"

Now, I was *really* uncomfortable.

"Uh, Ellie," I started, trying to sink further into my seat. "It wasn't because we were working. I ignored it because I'm dating Charlie. I thought that was obvious. How do you know about my reputation with women, but not the fact that I'm in a relationship? It was all over the tabloids a few months ago."

She cocked her head to one side and had a confused look on her face. "So, that's like, an exclusive relationship? Not just a friends with benefits type of thing?"

"Nope." I shook my head. "She's my girlfriend. We even live together."

Biting her lip, she slowly withdrew her hands from the table and slid them into her lap. Her gaze was everywhere but on me. "Well, that's slightly embarrassing."

Silence stretched between us for several moments. Ellie continued to stare at her hands in her lap, and I silently prayed Charlie would come back soon to save me.

"I shouldn't have said anything, I'm sorry." She finally looked up, and if I wasn't mistaken, she looked more *mad* than upset or embarrassed. "Look, I'm going to go."

Before she could slide out of the booth, I stuck my hand out to stop her. "Ellie, I'm sorry for the misunderstanding," I said, even though I wasn't sure I really had anything to apologize for. "I hope this doesn't affect our working relationship."

She sighed and gave me a tight smile. She looked like she was trying to think of something to say, but instead she shook her head and stood up from her seat. "I'll just talk to you in the morning, Brody." She left without looking back.

Sitting back in my seat, I felt the eggplant parmesan I had just eaten churning in my stomach.

What the hell just happened?

Hopefully she was just embarrassed and needed a chance to go lick her wounds. The last thing I needed was her blowing it out of proportion and Coach Tanner finding out I upset the new coaching assistant on the first day.

My next concern was what would Charlie say? It didn't seem to bother her when I had fans try to give me their number and flirt with me, but this was different.

As if she knew I was thinking about her, Charlie returned from the bathroom a moment later. "Where did Ellie go?" she asked, not even bothering to slide back into the booth.

"She left," I said, still trying to wrap my head around what just happened.

"She didn't want to wait?"

"No, I think I upset her." I stood from the booth. "Are you ready to go?"

She put a hand on my chest to stop me. "Hold on. You upset her? What happened?"

I shook my head. "Can we talk about this later?" I still wasn't sure how she'd respond, and I thought maybe it would be better if we were somewhere private.

Her brows furrowed. "No, just tell me what happened."

"Charlie, please. I promise to tell you at home." I attempted to move towards the door, but she put her hand up to stop me again. When her frown deepened, I sighed. "I guess she didn't know we were in an exclusive relationship. She wanted to go out with me."

If possible, she glared even harder. "Excuse me?"

"She said she knew about my 'reputation with the ladies.'" I shrugged, trying to play it off like it wasn't that big of a deal. "But I guess she missed the part where I was in a relationship now." I quickly explained the whole conversation to her and how Ellie had been trying to flirt with me even at practice this morning.

"That bothers me." She bit her lip and stared at the ceiling. "You're going to be spending a lot of time with her. What if she doesn't take a hint?"

I pulled her towards me and kissed her on the forehead. "You don't need to worry about that. You're the only one I want, and if she can't accept that, then Coach Tanner will have to find her somewhere else to work, because I won't put up with it."

"You sure?" she asked.

"Positive. Nothing is going to come between us." I took her hand in mine. "Now, let's get you back to the pool. I have some things to work on at home anyway."

"Like what?" she asked, following me out of the restaurant. "Do you have a secret project you're not telling me about?"

I smiled. "I had to find something to do with all this free time I now have."

"Are you remodeling?" she asked, hopeful. "We could definitely use some new kitchen appliances!"

"No, I'm not remodeling," I said, laughing at her response. "I'll let you know when I'm ready."

"Ah, come on," she whined. At this point, we had reached my truck. She walked around to the passenger side and climbed in before pressing for more. "Can you at least give me a hint?"

Starting the truck, I turned towards her and gave her a lopsided grin. "It's going to knock your socks off."

Chapter Three

Charlie

Once I was at the pool, changed, and ready for practice, I wandered onto the pool deck to see that Ellie was already there. She was sitting on one of the benches hunched over a notebook, furiously writing away. She was so focused, she didn't even look up when I came out of the locker room.

Not really wanting to address what happened at lunch, I quietly set my things down on the furthest bench from her and started stretching for practice. I hoped she would keep doing what she was doing as long as possible so I wouldn't have to speak to her until necessary, but that didn't happen. Only a minute or two after I started stretching, she looked up and realized I was there.

"Hey, I didn't even hear you come in," she said, standing and making her way to me.

"I wondered if you hadn't," I chuckled nervously. "You looked pretty focused, so I tried not to disturb you. Are you writing our swim workout?" I pointed to the notebook.

She looked down at the book in her hands and then back at me. "Oh, this?" She held it up. "Yeah, just brainstorming some exercises for all of you."

I nodded, but I couldn't manage to get any words out, so I stayed silent. *Why was she making me so nervous?*

"Anyway, Allison should be here soon, and we can get started," she continued. "Coach Tanner will be a little late. He has a doctor's appointment."

Again, I nodded, but said nothing.

She let out a heavy sigh. "Look, let's just get this over with. I take it Brody told you what happened while you were in the bathroom?"

"Yes, he did."

She brought one hand to her forehead and massaged her temple as if she had a headache. "I'm not trying to steal your boyfriend, okay?" She almost sounded annoyed. "I don't even want a relationship, I was just looking for a good time."

Somehow, that almost made me feel worse. I knew Brody made a bad boy reputation for himself, but it still bothered me that people only wanted to use him. Before I could argue, though, she continued.

"And I know that sounds bad. I don't have any excuses. But I won't judge your life decisions if you don't judge mine."

She was very forward and to the point, I'd give her that.

"Sounds fair," I managed to squeak out.

"Good." She gave me a tight grin. "So, we're cool?"

"Yeah." I nodded. "We're cool."

She went to Coach Tanner's whiteboard and started writing out the workout. I felt like I should change the subject and talk about something a bit lighter, but before I could say anything else, Allison came bounding out of the locker room and straight up to us.

"Hey ladies!" She beamed. "I chugged three cups of coffee at work, so I need to get in and start swimming STAT! Are we ready to go?"

"I'm ready if you are," Ellie said. "Coach will be late, but he wants you to do six 200s: swim, kick, pull, two times through as your warmup."

"Ready, girl?" Allison nudged me with her elbow.

"Yeah, let's do it." I couldn't help but laugh as she threw her cap on her head and skipped towards the water. Her good mood was infectious.

I stole a glance at Ellie, who was back to writing on the whiteboard. She looked up when she felt me staring and gave me another tight grin before looking away again.

Putting lunch behind me, I pulled on my swim cap and goggles and jumped in after Allison to start the warmup.

******

Later at Fit Happens—the gym where I worked as the manager—I was trying to focus on the financial statements, but my mind kept drifting off as it sometimes did when I was tired. Not only did I not sleep very well due to the Camila nightmare, but today's workouts had been particularly tough. We had done sprints during the morning workout, which were never my favorite to begin with, and Coach Tanner decided today was a good day to up all my weights during the strength workout. I was feeling fatigued before I had even made it to the afternoon practice.

That practice had gone well, though. Ellie worked us hard on each of our specialty strokes, so Allison had focused on breaststroke, and I had focused on backstroke. She had been helpful if we didn't understand a particular set, and she was encouraging when we were starting to fade at the end. I really did think she would make an excellent coach someday.

However, whenever my mind wandered back to our conversation about Brody, I couldn't help but feel a pang of anger. Not so much because she had tried to make a move on my boyfriend, but more because she wanted to use him and lose him. I felt protective over him, and didn't understand how someone would think that was a good idea. But, I promised not to judge her choices, so I'd do my best to do just that.

Shaking my head and letting out a long, slow breath, I attempted to redirect my focus back to the task at hand. I was now in charge of the place since Mr. Davis had been hauled off to jail, and part of my new duties was to keep careful track of all the financials at the gym. It wasn't the most exciting part of my job, but definitely one of the most important.

I had been scrolling through the statements for a few minutes before I found my mind starting to wander again. Realizing I didn't recall what I had just read, I let out a frustrated sigh and started over. It was a good thing I did, because halfway through the page, I noticed an account labeled *Freedom Fund*.

What the heck is that for?

Clicking on it, I noticed Mr. Davis had set up an automatic deposit of $500 each month to the account, but there were no further descriptions or attachments to shed light on what it was. All I knew was that the direct deposits started a little over a year ago, and the funds were still being deducted from the books each month. Someone here had to know what it was for. Maybe Allison would know?

Deciding I could use a little break anyway, I stood from my desk, stretched my arms above my head, and left my office to take a quick walk around the gym. Taking walks became a daily habit of mine since taking over so I could keep an eye on things. While I walked, I allowed the scene in front of me to distract me from what was going on in my head.

A petite blonde woman was running on the treadmill, laughing with an older woman—her mom?—who was walking on the treadmill beside her. A young dark-haired man was demonstrating to another, visibly less built red-headed man, how to do a proper squat. And by the free weights, Allison looked like she was finishing up with one of her clients, as she was walking through some stretches with him.

When she caught my eye, she smiled and held up a finger, signaling for me to wait a minute. I wandered over to a nearby chair and took a seat while I waited for her. A few minutes later, she waved goodbye to her client, and made her way over to me.

"Hey, how's it going?" she asked, taking a seat beside me. "I feel like I haven't gotten to talk to you all day. How was lunch with Ellie? She seems pretty nice."

I sighed. "Honestly, my head is still kind of spinning."

Allison frowned. "Why is that?"

"I guess Ellie had been trying to flirt with Brody during the morning workout, and then she asked him if he'd go out with her while we were at lunch this afternoon."

Allison's mouth nearly touched the floor. "You're kidding! In front of you?"

"No." I shook my head. "I was in the bathroom, but she was gone when I came out and Brody told me what happened."

She grimaced. "That had to have been awkward."

"The worst part was when I got back to the pool, she said she had only been looking for a good time from him. The girl didn't waste *any* time trying to shoot her shot on that one."

She made another face. "Yeah, I'll admit it was pretty bold of her."

"I don't know what to think." I shook my head and crossed my arms. "Other than I kind of feel angry for Brody. I know how he used to be around the ladies. I know he created a bad reputation for himself. But he's different now. Everything is different."

"Did Brody seem angry?" she asked.

I thought about it for a minute, then shook my head. "I don't think so. Uncomfortable, maybe. But not angry."

"Okay." She nodded. "And do you trust him?"

"Of course," I said, almost a little defensively.

"Then I think maybe you just need to let it go and forget it happened."

I felt another shot of anger run through me. "I'm sorry, but wouldn't *you* be upset if—"

She held up her hand to stop me. "Of course, I'd be upset. And you have every right to be a little frustrated right now. But Brody put her in her place, she confronted you about it, and you have absolutely no reason not to trust Brody. Yes, he's different now than he was before he met you, but just because he's famous doesn't mean everyone knows everything about him. It'll still take some time for the entire world to see the new Brody. If he's not angry about that, then I don't think you should be either."

I sat in silence as I absorbed her words. Maybe she had a point. It was a misunderstanding, and Brody did make it clear to her that he and I were dating, so did I really have anything to be mad about? Besides, Ellie apologized and she did ask me not to judge her. Getting angry about it meant I was doing exactly that.

"Besides," Allison continued, pulling me back out of my trance. "Brody is crazy in love with you. If she doesn't see that yet, it's not going to take her long to realize it. I don't think you have anything to worry about." She reached for my hand and gave it a squeeze.

Smiling, I squeezed it back. "You're right."

"One of these days you'll finally realize that I usually am!" She threw her hands up and laughed.

"Yeah, it's so crazy that I haven't gotten that yet," I joked back.

"You will." She winked. "So, changing the subject. How are things going now that you're in charge of this place?"

"It's a lot busier than I thought it would be," I said. "Going through the books, it was easy to tell Mr. Davis was trying to cut a lot of corners to save money. I'm guessing that's why he cut health insurance for everyone when I started."

"I guess it kind of makes sense now, doesn't it? With the whole Roman Enterprises thing."

I shrugged one shoulder. "I don't know. We still don't know *why* they were doing it. And with Camila dead, we may never know the whole story."

"I guess we just wait and see what happens at the trial," Allison said.

I nodded in agreement and then remembered the strange account. "Oh, I was going to ask you about something. When I was looking through the books, I came across an account I didn't recognize. You wouldn't happen to know what the *Freedom Fund* is for would you?" I quickly explained to her the details I had found on it.

She shook her head. "I've never heard of that account, and I'm not sure if anyone else here would know either. Mr. Davis didn't really share financial information with any of us."

"Do you think I should cancel the direct deposit?" I asked.

"I don't know." She shrugged. "Maybe keep it for now. The lawyers have to get back to us at some point about what's going to happen in Mr. Davis' absence, right? Maybe they'll let us know what to do."

"Good point," I agreed.

"Oh, there's my next client." Allison stood from her chair. "I'll see you later!"

I waved as she walked away. Letting out a deep sigh, I stood from my chair, too, and made my way back to my office. I felt a bit better after venting to Allison, and I hoped that meant I could actually focus on my work for the rest of the evening.

******

After work, I picked up Landon from practice before heading home. Brody was already at the house, and he had promised to have supper ready for us when we arrived.

"How was practice?" I asked Landon when he hopped in the front seat. "Did Coach Tanner have you do the ten 200s like we had to do this afternoon?"

"Ugh, yeah, that wasn't fun," he groaned. "Otherwise, it was good. Ellie was there, too. She helped the time go by quicker."

"Yeah?" I urged him to elaborate as I pulled out of the parking lot.

He nodded. "I like her, she's cool. Do you think she'd go out with me, sometime?"

My mouth dropped open.

"She's not that much older than I am," he added, as if that would affect my answer. "I mean, I know I'm still a minor, but I'll be eighteen in a few weeks. I don't think it would be that weird, would it?"

"Um, I don't know," I said, trying to hide the surprise in my voice.

Out of the corner of my eye, I felt his gaze fall on me. He watched me for a minute before speaking again. "I get the feeling that you think it's a bad idea."

I shook my head a little too quickly, and then stopped abruptly when I realized what I was doing. "That's not it, you've just never talked to me about girls before. I was caught off guard."

"You're practically a sister to me, Charlie, who else am I supposed to talk to about this kind of stuff?"

Warmth radiated throughout my body at his words, and I felt tears prick at the back of my eyes, but I quickly shook them off. I didn't need to embarrass him—he'd never want to come to me about this kind of stuff again.

Part of me wanted to be excited for him and tell him to go for it, but the other part knew it probably wasn't a good idea. Ellie had literally asked Brody out earlier today, and made it clear to me she wasn't looking for a relationship right now.

"Charlie?" he asked after I had been quiet for a few moments. "It is okay if I talk to you about that kind of stuff, right?"

"Of course, it is!" I breathed. "I'm sorry, I was thinking. Look, I'm very excited that you like her, but why not wait a little bit? You did make a good point earlier: you are still seventeen. Why not give it a few weeks, and if you still feel the same, ask her out after your birthday?" I purposely left out the part about Ellie asking Brody out. I figured I'd let him tell that to Landon. "Maybe ask Brody what he thinks, too."

"Yeah, you're probably right. You think he'll say the same thing?"

I shrugged. "Only one way to find out."

"True."

Wanting to change the subject, I remembered what Brody had mentioned when we left the restaurant earlier today. "By the way, has Brody told you anything about this special project he's been working on?"

"What special project?" Landon frowned in confusion. "He hasn't said anything about a project to me."

"Oh, I thought maybe he would," I said. "He said he was working on something, and it was going to knock my socks off, but he wouldn't tell me anything more than that."

"Maybe he's planning some romantic getaway for the two of you." He pulled out his phone and started scrolling.

"You think?" I asked, excitement bubbling in my stomach.

He shrugged and didn't look up from his scrolling. "Honestly, I have no idea."

It was clear Landon wasn't as interested as me in finding out what the project was, and silence fell over us for the rest of the trip home. When I finally pulled the car into the driveway, Landon jumped out of the car and immediately went inside. I followed close behind, carrying my purse and all my swim stuff.

"Smells good in here!" I called after I closed the door behind me.

Landon went upstairs to ditch his stuff while I made my way to the kitchen. There, Brody was bent over a steaming pot on the stove.

Wrapping my arms around his middle, I kissed him on the back of the neck. "What's cookin', good lookin'?"

He set the mixing spoon down and spun towards me, taking me in his arms. "I've got a pot roast in the oven and am making some gravy now." He kissed me tenderly. "How was work?"

"It was good." I kissed him again, not really wanting to talk about work. "I'm just happy to be home with you now."

"Is that so?" He smirked, pulling me closer to him.

"Mhm," I giggled before his mouth came crashing down on mine, longer and harder than before.

Wrapping my arms around his neck, I clung to him like my life depended on it. His tongue slipped inside my mouth, and a groan escaped from my lips. His hand slid down to my ass and he gave it a firm squeeze. I was ready to hop up on the counter and let him take me in the kitchen, when I heard Landon coming down the stairs.

"Y'all really need to do that in here?" he groaned. "You're going to make me lose my appetite." He went to the cupboard and started pulling out cups and plates to set the table.

I felt my face blush red as I unlatched my arms from around Brody and took a step back. "Sorry, Landon," I told him, turning to help him.

"Hell, I'm not sorry!" Brody smacked my ass so hard I squealed and jumped off the ground.

"Hey!" I teased, holding my hands over my butt so he couldn't do it again.

Brody laughed and turned his attention back to the stove. "Just you wait until you get yourself a girl, Landon. You'll be doing the same thing."

Landon made a face. "I doubt it."

"Speaking of girls," Brody said. "Anyone catching your eye lately?" He poured the gravy into a bowl and carried it to the table.

I looked up from setting out the silverware and met Landon's gaze. He also had stopped what he was doing, and he had an uncertain look in his eye, as if he was unsure how to tell Brody he had a crush on someone.

"Tell him what you told me in the car." I nodded encouragingly.

"So, there *is* someone?" Brody teased. "Well, who is it? Lay it on me!"

"What do you think about me asking out Ellie?" Landon said quietly.

Brody's smile didn't disappear as I initially thought it would. In fact, it was almost like he froze. He didn't move at all for several moments. In reality, it was probably only a couple of seconds, but it felt so long, I almost stepped in and said something.

Finally, he clapped his hands together, pursed his lips, and turned back to the oven. "Let me just take this out real quick." He took the pot roast out of the oven and set it on the table. There were sliced carrots and potatoes layered around the meat, and it smelled delicious. "Let's eat!"

Landon didn't move towards the table right away. Instead, he continued to stand where he was at with a confused look on his face. Brody and I sat at the table and started dishing up our plates, but my gaze never left Landon.

Eventually, he slowly turned towards his chair. "Did you hear my question?" he asked, finally taking a seat. "Am I missing something?"

Sighing, Brody stopped loading his plate and set down his silverware. "Landon, I have to be honest with you. I just want everything out in the open before you hear it from someone else."

"Okay." Landon nodded. "What is it?"

"Ellie actually tried asking *me* out earlier today."

"You're kidding." He frowned. "She didn't realize you were dating Charlie?"

Brody shrugged. "I guess not."

"Well, just because she asked you out, doesn't mean she'd say no to me, right?" he said.

Brody and I exchanged a look.

"Oh, come on," Landon said, noticing our hesitation. "I know I'm not as great as the famous Brody Hayes, but someone has to notice me eventually. You really don't think it would be worth me giving it a shot?"

My heart broke in two at his words. "It's not that we don't think she would like you, it's more that we think you want different things."

"Meaning what?" he asked, clearly confused.

"I talked to her a little bit before practice this afternoon. She made it clear that she wasn't looking for a relationship right now. She only asked Brody out because she knew about his reputation with the ladies. She was only looking for a good time."

"Wait, you knew this happened, and you didn't say anything in the car?" Landon said, frowning again. "Charlie, I confided in you, and you let me babble on like an idiot."

"Landon, I'm sorry, I really am." I reached for his hand across the table. "I wasn't sure if I was the person to tell you or not. I thought it would be better coming from Brody."

He let go of my hand and ran his fingers through his hair. "Well, that sucks. I thought we hit it off today."

"It doesn't mean it'll never happen, buddy," Brody told him. "It just means that for right now, I would focus on being her friend. If eventually she realizes you two make a good fit, she might change her mind. You never know."

He stared off into space for a few moments, lost in thought, then turned his gaze back to us. "Do you think she'd maybe come looking for a good time with me?"

My mouth almost hit the floor. I knew for a fact Landon was still a virgin—he told Brody once, who told me—and while his life choices were his own to make, the protective instincts in me didn't want him to start sleeping around just because he wanted someone to notice him.

Suddenly, he started laughing. "You should see the look on both of your faces. Relax. I'm kidding. I do have morals— no offense," he said to Brody.

Brody held up his hands in mock defeat. "None taken."

"I'll just focus on being her friend for now, like you said," he continued. "I'm just kind of frustrated, not going to lie."

"Frustrated how?" I asked. "Frustrated that she's not looking for a relationship?"

Landon shrugged. "I don't know. That's part of it, I guess." He fell silent for a moment while he loaded some potatoes onto his plate. Even after his plate was full, he didn't start eating. He picked up his fork and moved pieces of food around while avoiding our gazes. "I know I give you guys a lot of crap for making out and being overly affectionate around me, but in a way, I think I'm kind of jealous. I've never been in a relationship before. I see what you two have, and I want something like that for myself."

"Oh, Landon, you will. I promise." I placed a hand on his shoulder and gave it a squeeze. "You're still young, you have plenty of time to find the right lady."

"Plenty of time." Brody nodded in agreement. "I'll be your wingman whenever you need me."

Landon smiled so big, I couldn't help but smile myself. "Thank you. I don't know what I'd do without you guys."

"Well, you don't need to find out anytime soon." I smiled.

We continued to chat while we ate. I talked about work, Landon told us how school was going, and even though I tried to get Brody to tell us about his 'special project,' he wouldn't take the bait.

Eventually, the conversation turned back to girls and dating, and I sat in silence while I listened to Brody give Landon some advice. Watching the two of them made my heart swell with happiness. We really felt like a little family unit tonight, and even though nothing particularly monumental happened, I knew it was a night I wouldn't soon forget.

Chapter Four

Brody

"Did you sleep alright, dude?" I asked Landon on the way to practice the following morning. "You look awfully tired."

He yawned, not yet fully awake. "Once I fell asleep, I slept okay, but I was lying awake for a long time."

"Just a lot on your mind?"

He shrugged. "I was thinking about what we talked about last night. Kind of bummed over Ellie."

"Well, like I said, man, it doesn't mean it'll never happen."

"I know. It's just hard to be patient sometimes. Thinking about only being her friend kind of makes me a little sad."

I nodded but didn't say anything. I didn't realize how bad he had it for her already. In a way, it kind of reminded me of how I felt about Charlie when I first met her. Sure, I had initially tried to hit on Charlie the way I always used to hit on girls, but she hit me as different. Even when she tried to turn me down at first, I couldn't stop thinking about her. It made me hopeful that things would work out between Landon and Ellie.

After we had arrived at the pool and changed into our practice suits, we walked on deck to find Ellie sitting on a bench with her head buried in her notebook.

"Might as well go talk to her for a while," I told him. "You have to start somewhere, right?" I shot him a wink, and then turned to go set my things down on a different bench. Wanting to give them some privacy, I faced the other direction and started stretching out my sore shoulder.

By the time my shoulders were good and loosened up, Charlie and Allison came wandering out of the locker room, deep in conversation.

"Hey, give me just a second," Charlie told Allison when they had reached me. "I want to ask Brody something."

"No problem," Allison said in her usual chipper voice. "Good morning, Brody!"

I waved to her as she continued past, and then smiled at Charlie. "What's up?"

Charlie peered past me before she spoke. "What's Landon talking to Ellie about?"

"I don't know," I laughed. "I've been trying not to eavesdrop."

Still looking past me, she pursed her lips. "I feel bad. He sounded so sad last night. Do you think there's anything we can do to help him?"

I shook my head. "No, not really. Be there for him when he needs us, but we can't force a relationship on anyone."

"No, I know. It's just hard for me to sit back and do nothing—oh!" Her eyes got big, and her body stiffened. "He just got up and left the bench. She's still sitting there. Should we go talk to him? See how it went?" Her gaze went straight to mine as if waiting for permission.

I couldn't help but laugh again. "No, leave him alone. We don't need to ambush him."

"Ambush him?" She snorted. "I just want to know what they were talking about!"

"You're acting like an overprotective parent right now." I teased. "Just leave him be. If he wants to tell us later, great. Otherwise, it isn't any of our business."

She groaned. "Fine, fine. You're right."

We continued to stretch in silence for a few more minutes until Coach Tanner emerged from his office and told us which lanes he wanted us in.

"Ellie, you'll work with Brody again today," he said, handing her the workout he wrote. "How's the shoulder feeling?" he asked me as I walked by.

"It's feeling okay. I could probably be ready to compete at the home meet in a couple of weeks if I started doing the normal workouts," I told him.

Coach Tanner simply laughed. "Not until that physical therapist of yours gives you the all clear, but nice try."

I gave him a tight smile so I wouldn't open my mouth and argue with him. Once I was by my lane, I set my equipment down and looked to Ellie. "So, what's on the agenda?"

"You have one thousand yards, alternating swim, kick, drill by every 200," she read from the workout list. "And then we have some 100's after that for the rest of the warmup."

I sighed and pulled my goggles over my head. "You got it."

Looking across the pool, I watched as Allison and Charlie jumped into the water to start their warmup. Landon was still setting out his equipment and taking his sweet time doing so. He had a huge smile on his face though, so it looked as if he was caught in a daydream. When Coach asked him why he was taking so long, he jumped, shook his head rapidly, threw on his cap and goggles and jumped in. I chuckled to myself, and silently wondered if his conversation with Ellie had put him in a good mood.

"Hey Brody," Ellie said from beside me, as if she knew what I had been thinking about.

"I'm going," I said, thinking she was going to get after me like Coach Tanner had gotten after Landon. I slipped my goggles onto my eyes and was about to jump in when she stopped me.

"No, I want to ask you something."

I lifted my goggles back to my forehead and looked at her. "What?" After the thing she asked me yesterday, I was worried where this was going to go.

"Does Landon actually live with you?" she asked.

That was definitely not what I was expecting her to ask me. "Yeah, he does. Why?"

"He invited me to come hang out with all of you tonight. I wanted to make sure it wasn't going to just be the two of us. I don't want to give him any wrong ideas."

My heart sunk for Landon. It was a good thing we told him not to ask her out, I guess. "Yeah, we'll all be there. Charlie lives there too—but I told you that yesterday. Come over whenever."

She nodded. "Cool, sounds like fun." She looked down at the workout sheet for a brief moment before her head snapped back up to face me. "It's not going to be weird, is it? After what happened yesterday?"

I shook my head. "No idea what you're talking about."

She frowned, but it quickly faded as she realized what I was doing. "Right." She gave me a tight grin. "Thank you."

"No problem." I covered my eyes with my goggles and pressed them tight against my skin. "Alright, I'm going to get in the water now before Coach Tanner comes over here." I jumped in before she could respond.

The entire practice, Ellie felt distracted. She wasn't in the right headspace, and I had to snap her out of a daydream several times in between sets so she could tell me what to do next. She'd tell me good job, and that I looked good in the water, but I think it was more that she felt she had to say something because it was clear she wasn't paying attention. The whole time I wondered if it was because of me, but I wasn't sure what exactly I would have said to upset her. Unless she was still feeling embarrassed from yesterday?

When I had finished the main workout, she told me to do a long cool down on my own, and I figured I'd ask her if she was okay when I was done. However, by the time I finished my last lap, she was gone.

Coach Tanner approached my lane. "How was the workout? You look like you're gaining your strength back."

"It was good, and my shoulder felt good, too." I pulled myself out of the pool and picked up my kickboard and fins. "Where did Ellie go?"

"I guess she has a big test today she was stressing about. I told her to go home and study. She'll be back this evening."

"I was wondering if something was going on," I said. "She was out of it today."

He shrugged. "I guess I didn't notice. Go get changed for the lifting session. I want to get started soon."

Landon was already changed and tying his shoes when I walked into the locker room.

"How was your workout, man?" I asked him.

He looked up at the sound of my voice. "Really good, actually. It felt like it flew by, too."

"I couldn't help but notice your shift in mood after talking to Ellie," I pressed, hoping he'd feel comfortable enough to talk to me about it.

He smiled as he stood up and closed his locker door. "Yeah, I told her she could come over and hang out tonight if she wanted." He stopped in his tracks as if he just thought of something. "Wait, that's okay that I invited her, right? I should have checked with you first."

I waved my hand dismissively. "That's totally fine. She's part of the team, we might as well welcome her into our group and get to know her. Now, if you ever want to throw a party of some kind, you better be checking with me first," I teased.

"I don't think you need to worry about that," he laughed. "But thank you. If things keep going like this, maybe being her friend won't be so bad after all. And who knows? Maybe it won't take her very long to decide she wants to be more than friends. I have a really good feeling about her."

His good mood was so infectious, I couldn't bring myself to tell him what Ellie had told me before practice started. Besides, he could be right. Just because Ellie didn't want a relationship now, didn't mean she wouldn't change her mind.

"I like seeing you this happy, man," I told him as I sat down on a bench near my locker. I purposely avoided eye contact with him, and thankfully, he didn't seem to notice. "But remember to be patient. All good things take time."

"I know, I'll try." He swung his bag over his shoulder. "I better get going so I don't miss the bus. Have a good weight workout."

"Have a good day at school." I waved to him as he walked away.

I sat and watched him leave, and continued to sit there long after he'd gone, lost in thought. I know I had given Charlie shit for being so overprotective earlier, but now I felt the same way. I wished there was something I could do to make sure this worked out for him.

******

"Yes, I can go pick up Landon," I said into the phone. Charlie had called to let me know she was working late tonight and wouldn't be able to stop by the pool for a while. "What time do you think you'll be home? Don't forget, Ellie is supposedly coming over tonight."

"Yeah, I remember," she said. "I'm hoping to be out of here soon. I have a lot of invoices I need to finalize so they can be mailed off tomorrow. Don't wait for me to eat."

"Okay, try not to stay too late. I think Ellie would be more comfortable if you were here." I had told Charlie at lunch today what Ellie had said about not wanting to be alone with Landon, and she had the same reaction that I did. She might have even been a little more upset than I was.

"Well, like I said earlier, if she's going to be like that, she doesn't have to come at all." I could hear the anger in Charlie's voice.

"Charlie, we can't be mad at her for not feeling the same way. She doesn't even know that's how Landon feels. Try to understand where she's coming from. At least she isn't trying to lead him on."

"I know, I'm sorry," she huffed. "I'll be better. But I have a ton of paperwork to do, so I'm going to let you go. Thanks for picking up Landon, I'll let you know when I'm going to head home."

"One of these days, we should teach the kid how to drive," I joked.

"Maybe that's another thing you can do with all this free time you have now," she shot back.

I laughed. "Okay, fair enough. I'll talk to you soon."

After ending the call, I grabbed my keys and went to head out the door, but before I reached it, Landon came walking in with Ellie right behind him.

"Oh—hey," I said in surprise. "I was just coming to get you."

"Sorry, I meant to text Charlie that I didn't need a ride, but I forgot," Landon said. "Ellie offered to drive."

I shook my head. "No, that's okay. I should have thought of asking you when Charlie said she was working late."

"Will she be home soon?" Ellie asked.

"Yes," I assured her. "Just has to finish up a few things at the office. How did your test go?"

"My test?" She looked confused.

"Yeah, Coach Tanner said you were worried about a test, and that's why you left early."

"Oh, yes!" She slapped her palm on her head as if she just remembered. "Sorry, I was confused. I didn't think I had told you about it, so I didn't think you knew, but that makes sense. I think it went okay." She shrugged. "I guess I'll find out soon enough."

"So, is dinner ready?" Landon changed the subject. "I'm starving."

"Yes, there's baked chicken in the kitchen. Help yourselves," I told them. They followed me to the kitchen, and I rounded up some plates for them.

"Actually, can I use your bathroom first?" Ellie asked before she took her plate.

"Sure." I nodded. "You can use ours. We haven't had time to clean the downstairs one in a while. It's up the stairs, second door on the left."

"Thank you." She grabbed her purse and disappeared up the stairs.

"Would it be okay if Ellie and I ate by ourselves in the living room?" Landon asked as he loaded up his plate with chicken and some veggies. "I want to put on a movie."

Not wanting to burst his bubble, while at the same time not wanting to make Ellie uncomfortable, I shook my head. "What if I want to watch a movie, too?" I joked.

"Come on, man, be serious." He sounded annoyed.

"I am being serious. This is the first time you guys have hung out outside of practice. If you go watch a movie and eat dinner with her—just the two of you—that's going to feel like a date. Did you ask her on a date, or did you ask her to come hang out with all of us?"

"Well, no, technically I didn't ask her on a date, but—"

"But nothing!" I cut him off. "How are you supposed to be friends with her if you try to skip straight to a first date? Especially when you don't even know if she would consider this to be a date."

"How am I supposed to know if I don't try?" he whined.

"That's the point of being friends first, remember? You're not even going to worry about dating her right now. Just be her friend."

"This sucks." He pouted like a small child. "How long do I have to wait?"

I shook my head and bit back a laugh. "We just talked about this this morning, Landon. You need to be patient. It's going to take some time."

"Fine." He took his plate to the living room and plopped down on the couch. Reaching for the remote, he started looking for the movie he wanted.

Once I had loaded up my own plate, I sat down on the chair opposite the couch. I figured I'd at least give Ellie the option to sit next to Landon. I started eating in silence as I watched him scroll through the channels. After several minutes of sitting in silence, Ellie still hadn't come back downstairs.

"Do you think Ellie is doing okay?" I finally asked. "She's been up there for a while."

Landon shrugged but stood from the couch and went to the stairs. "Ellie?" he called. "Are you okay?"

Suddenly, we heard her hurried footsteps before she came scurrying down the steps. "Yes! All good. Sorry, I was fixing my hair. I saw some of Charlie's dry shampoo and couldn't help myself. I'll get her a new bottle."

"Oh, yeah … okay. No problem," I stammered. Apparently, she had no problem making herself at home in a stranger's house. "Landon, why don't you help her get some food." I changed the subject. "Then we can start this movie."

A few minutes later, we all had our food and Landon turned the movie on. Ellie did end up sitting on the couch with him but sat on the opposite side. She tucked her feet up underneath her and leaned against the arm rest. She couldn't have put more distance between them without moving to an entirely different spot, and I silently wondered if she did that on purpose.

Throughout the first part of the movie, I spent more time stealing glances at the two of them than I did actually watching the movie itself. Every couple of minutes, Landon would steal a glance over at Ellie. He laid his right hand on the cushion beside him, palm facing up, clearly trying to say she could hold it if she wanted to. Whether Ellie noticed or not, she made no effort to hold his hand or even sit closer to him. I knew she wasn't looking to date anyone, but part of me wanted her to take it anyway.

Roughly halfway through the movie, Charlie finally got home. She turned on the living room light when she set down her things, not realizing we were all sitting in there.

"Oh, I'm sorry!" she said, immediately turning the light off again. "I didn't see you." When no one said anything, she quietly made her way to the kitchen. I got up and followed her, taking the dirty dishes with me.

"How are things going?" she asked me.

"Kind of hard to tell," I said as I loaded the dishwasher. "How was work?"

"Busy." She sighed. "But I got all the invoices done. What's for dinner?"

I pulled a plate full of food that I had prepared for her earlier from the fridge. "Chicken and veggies. Might want to throw it in the microwave for a bit."

"Thank you, I'm starving." She took the plate and carried it to the microwave. "Go ahead and go back in there. I'll be out in a few."

"Sounds good."

I went back to the living room where Ellie and Landon were exactly the same as I had left them. Landon almost appeared to be leaning closer towards Ellie, but she remained in place. I sat back down in my chair, and a few minutes later, Charlie sat in my lap with her plate of food. I didn't want to rub our relationship in Landon's face, especially after what he had told us last night, but I also missed my girl and I wanted to hold her.

Wrapping my arms around her middle, I pulled her close to me while she ate her food, and once she was done eating, she snuggled in even closer. I continued to steal glances at Landon, who by now had crossed both of his arms over his chest and slouched in his seat. He appeared to have admitted defeat in trying to get Ellie to hold his hand, and my heart broke for him all over again. I remembered the days when I crushed on girls who didn't crush on me back. I knew exactly how he was feeling, and I wished there was something I could do about it.

Finally, the movie ended, and Landon grabbed the remote to turn off the TV.

"What a great movie!" Ellie said when the screen had gone dark. "I'm a sucker for a happy ending."

"Me too," Charlie chimed in.

"What did you think, Landon?" I asked him.

He stretched his arms above his head. "It was alright. Wasn't what I expected it to be."

I nodded, not sure if he was referring to the movie or the evening in general.

"I should probably get going." Ellie looked at her smart watch. "We've got an early morning tomorrow. I'll let you all get to bed."

"Can I walk you out?" Landon asked her.

She nodded. "Sure, let's go. Good night you two." She waved to us before the two of them disappeared outside.

"That was almost painful to watch," I said.

Charlie nodded. "I'm glad I wasn't the only one who noticed. Do you think she could've sat any farther away from him? I felt so bad."

"She was probably nervous," I said, trying to defend her. "I guess I can understand if she doesn't want to give him the wrong idea."

"I wonder if she'll even want to come hang out again."

Before I could respond, Landon walked back inside. Instead of sitting back down, he went straight for the stairs. It was hard to read his expression in the dark room.

"Hey, everything okay?" I called to him before he hit the stairs.

"I'm fine," he mumbled. "Just tired."

"Did she say anything outside?" Charlie asked.

He sighed. "She said she saw me reaching for her hand and basically told me what she told you: that she's not looking for a relationship and didn't think I was the kind of guy to give her what she wanted right now."

I didn't know if I should feel angry or relieved that she was so brutally honest with him.

"But she also said she wants to be friends," he continued before I could respond. "And that she would be more than happy to continue hanging out in group settings like this."

"And how does that make you feel?" I asked.

"I don't know." He shrugged. "I kind of feel like I got kicked in the nuts a little bit."

"But she wants to be friends," I reminded him. "And remember, that was the goal for right now anyway."

"Yeah, I know." He rolled his eyes. "I was just hoping she felt it too."

"Well, now that you know exactly how she feels—"

"Brody," he interrupted, noticeably frustrated. "I get you're trying to help, but I don't want to talk about it anymore. Is it okay if I go to bed?"

"Sure." I nodded. "Goodnight Landon."

Charlie and I sat in silence while we watched Landon ascend the stairs and disappear around the corner. A moment later, we heard his bedroom door close.

"I suppose we should probably head to bed too." Charlie slid off my lap and stretched her arms above her head before she picked up her dinner plate and brought it to the kitchen.

I stayed seated, still staring at the staircase. I worried about Landon. His life hadn't been easy, and I wanted something to finally go right for him. Ever since I first met him, I'd felt a little protective over him, and I don't know if I could really explain why. Maybe he reminded me of myself, and I wanted to make sure he didn't have the same struggles I had. And while our situations were different—at least I knew my parents loved me before they died—I felt like we were similar in the fact that we both had to figure out how to do life without parents to help us, especially at such a crucial time in starting our adult lives.

And even though I tried to look out for Landon the best I could before his father went to jail, now that he was behind bars, I had to find that happy medium between friend and guardian. If there was anything at all I could do to make his life easier, I wanted to do it. It was just times like this where I didn't know how or what to do.

"What are you thinking about?" Charlie asked. She was leaning against the wall by the kitchen, and it was clear she had been watching me.

"Landon." I stood up from the chair and went to her, slipping my arms around her waist. "Trying to figure out how I can help him."

She wrapped her arms around my neck and held my gaze. "Like you told me earlier today: I don't think there's much you can do besides what you're already doing. We've all crushed on someone that doesn't like us back. It's part of growing up. I know you want to take away his pain, but this is something that unfortunately just happens. You can't take away all his heartbreak."

"I can try though, can't I?"

She shook her head and smiled. "You can't save him from everything. I know you worry about him—I do, too. But this is normal, and he'll be fine. He might be bummed for a few days, but it'll get better with time."

"But if there's anything I can do—"

She placed her fingers over my mouth. "In this case, there isn't. You can't *make* anyone have feelings for someone, rember? Just be there for him. Be that person he can go to. That's all you can do."

I chewed on my lip, wanting to argue that I'd figure out something to do, but I knew she was right. I needed to accept that. I kissed her gently on her lips. "You're right."

She smiled and kissed me again. "I know."

"Don't get cocky," I laughed, pulling her closer to me.

"Me? Never." She winked. "Come on, let's go to bed, it's late."

She took my hand in hers and I followed her up the stairs to our room. When we walked by Landon's door, I paused for a moment, saying a silent prayer that life would get easier for him soon.

Chapter Five

Charlie

"Hey, Charlie, have you seen my new Speedo tech suit?" Brody called from upstairs. "I need it for my photo shoot this afternoon."

A couple of days had passed since the first night Ellie had hung out with us, and I hadn't slept very well since then. Not so much that I was worried about Landon's feelings towards Ellie, but because work had been exceptionally busy, and I was getting home later and later each night. Now, it was early, I was sleep deprived, and not in the mood to be keeping track of Brody's stuff.

I sighed, set my bowl of cereal on the counter, and went to the bottom of the stairs. "Is it in the bathroom?" I called up to him.

"No, I already looked," he said.

"Landon, have you seen his new suit?" I turned back towards the kitchen where Landon was making some toast.

He shrugged and shook his head but didn't say anything.

"Will they give you another one?" I asked Brody as he descended the stairs.

"Charlie, that thing was almost $700. If they give me another, it'll get taken out of my paycheck."

"Okay, well then you should have kept better track of it," I mumbled.

Brody wrapped his arms around my middle and held on tight, picking me up off the floor. "Oh, did someone wake up on the wrong side of the bed?" he teased.

"Stop," I whined, trying really hard not to smile. "I have no idea where you put your suit, and I don't need any attitude this early in the morning."

He kissed my cheek. "I'm sorry, just frustrated is all. If they have to give me another it's not the end of the world. It's not like we're struggling financially." He let go and walked into the kitchen. "I could have sworn I left it on top of my dresser, though."

"I have no idea," I said as I leaned against the counter to finish my cereal.

"Anyway, Landon, how are you this morning?" Brody asked. I assumed he was asking because Ellie and Allison had come over last night for a group hang out. "Things seemed to go pretty well last night."

Landon shrugged. "I think it went okay. Ellie didn't really talk to me much." He shoved a bite of toast into his mouth.

"Yeah, but to be fair, she didn't say a lot to anyone," Brody said. "She's pretty quiet."

"It just makes it hard to try and become friends if she doesn't talk to me."

Landon was clearly still pretty bummed about Ellie, although he did seem better since that first night. Now, he just seemed more frustrated than heartbroken.

"Gotta be patient, man." Brody slapped a hand on Landon's shoulder. "All good things take time. If you want, I can hook you up with one of my female friends from another American Swimming team. We'll all be together at the home meet in a couple weeks."

"No, I'm good."

"Come on," Brody pressed. "Maybe it'll make Ellie jealous."

"Brody!" I scolded, throwing a stern look at him.

"What?" He threw his palms up in defense. "It was just an idea."

I rolled my eyes and turned back to my cereal, drinking the last of the milk from the bowl.

"Damn, you really did wake up on the wrong side of the bed, didn't you?" Brody laughed as he stood up and crept towards me like he was going to grab me again. "Do I need to show you what happens to grumpy girls?"

I held an arm out in front of me to block him, but he pushed right past and grabbed me around the middle again, this time tickling me.

"Stop it!" I giggled, trying to fight him off me. "Brody, stop!"

"You two disgust me," Landon said. He put his plate in the sink and walked out of the kitchen. "Are you ready to go?" he called as he went.

Brody stopped tickling me, but still held me close. "Are you going to put a smile on your face and have a good day?" he said in a mocking voice. "It's Friday. You don't have to work this weekend, and you can sleep after practice tomorrow. There's no reason to be in a mood."

I pouted anyway. "Yeah, yeah."

He kissed me and then released his grip. "Maybe you just need to take it out on the water."

"Maybe I do."

And I definitely did. Coach Tanner had us do a combination of 50 and 100-yard sprints this morning. We would start with the 100's on an easier interval, subtracting five seconds off each one until we could no longer make the time, then take thirty seconds rest and do the same with the 50's—and then he made us do it all over again. I don't know how many of each I ended up doing, just that each one got harder than the last, and by the time we were done, I was breathing a lot harder than usual, but I felt a million times better. It was the perfect workout to get out some frustration.

"Nice job, everyone," Coach Tanner said when practice was over. "Let's hurry up and get changed so we can get to the weight room."

As soon as Landon was done cooling down, he popped right out of the water and wandered over to Ellie. She had taken a seat on one of the benches after giving Brody his cool down and was scribbling in her notebook as usual. She looked up when Landon had reached her and smiled and nodded at whatever he had said to her.

"Charlie, can I talk to you a second?" Coach Tanner asked, snapping my attention away from them.

"Sure." I nodded. "What's up?"

"I have a new weight circuit I want you to try. It's supposed to be great for backstrokers as it really works your core. I gave the workout to Ellie, and she'll run through it with you this morning."

"Is everyone else doing something different?" I asked him.

"Just for today, and then you'll all be back to the same workout," he said. "Does that sound okay?"

"Yeah, sure, I'll give it a try."

"Awesome. Thanks for being flexible."

Elli still wasn't there by the time I had changed and gotten to the workout room, so I stretched my muscles while I waited. Coach Tanner got Brody and Allison started, and after several more minutes, I began to wonder if Ellie had left. Before I could go ask Coach about it though, she came sauntering out of the locker room.

"Hey, sorry, let's get started," she said. She set her purse down on a bench and pulled out the piece of paper with my workout on it.

"No problem," I said. "Were you still talking to Landon?" I didn't want to pry, but part of me was curious what her thoughts were.

"Yeah, I waited for the bus with him." She didn't look up from the piece of paper as she spoke.

"That was sweet of you," I said, my heart skipping a beat with excitement. She wouldn't have waited for the bus with him if she didn't *kind of* like him, right?

She finally looked up and shrugged. "Well, I had some technique questions for him, and I didn't want him to be late to school. Nothing crazy."

"Ohhh." My stomach dropped. "That makes sense."

She chuckled. "Sorry to disappoint. I know he's got a crush on me—he doesn't hide it very well. But I was serious when I said I'm not looking for anything."

"No, I totally understand." I shook my head quickly.

"Cool." She nodded, giving me a lopsided grin. "Should we get going so we can get this done? It looks like it's going to be a doozy." She glanced down at the workout sheet again.

"Goody," I said sarcastically, which got a chuckle out of her.

She started reading off the workout list. "First thing you're going to do is lay on your back and do sixty seconds of flutter kicking with your arms in streamline."

I nodded and did as she said. We made our way through the workout painfully slowly. She hadn't been kidding when she said it was going to be a tough one—my abs were on fire by the time we were only halfway through.

The further we got into the circuit, the more my bad mood from earlier began to make its presence known again. I had wanted a good workout to take out my frustrations on, but now I was so exhausted, I couldn't even do some of the exercises properly, and that was frustrating me more.

Especially when Ellie didn't seem to realize I was running out of gas, and *that* was why I wasn't performing as well as I should have been. I think she thought I actually didn't know how to do it and she made me repeat a lot of the moves. She would demonstrate it for me and encourage me—so I had to give her props for her coaching skills—but her awareness skills needed some work.

After a while, Coach Tanner made his way over to us. "Are you still doing the workout? I thought you two would have been done around the same time as us. We've been done for almost fifteen minutes."

"I think you're both determined to make sure I can't move tomorrow," I huffed. I was on the ground again, as I just finished holding a five-minute plank—for the second time.

Ellie let out a nervous laugh. "Sorry Charlie, I wasn't trying to make you do more than you could handle. I just wanted to help you."

"You did great, Ellie." I rested my cheek against the rough surface of the mat. "I'm just spent. Is it alright if I be done?"

"Yeah, I think so," she said, looking to Coach Tanner. "I'll get you a towel."

"She's a bit of a slave driver, isn't she?" Coach joked when Ellie had walked away. "Here, let me help you up."

I pushed myself up to a kneeling position, took Coach Tanner's hand, and he pulled me up the rest of the way. Ellie returned a moment later and handed me a towel.

"Thanks," I said, taking it and wiping my face.

"Alright, go rest up," Coach Tanner said. "You still need to be able to swim this afternoon!"

I waved goodbye to him and walked over to where I had set my bag down against the wall. As I started packing things into my bag, I heard Ellie come up behind me.

"Hey, sorry about that," she said. "I couldn't tell if you were getting tired, or if you just weren't familiar with some of the moves. I should have asked."

"It's okay," I told her. "I could have said something, too."

She nodded slowly and seemed to think about her next words. "Sometimes, I wonder if I'd make a good coach."

"Why would you say that?" I asked, genuinely surprised by her comment.

"I don't know." She shrugged. "A good coach should be able to tell when their athletes are literally about to drop dead from exhaustion."

I laughed. "You're new to this, and we don't know each other that well yet. When we get to know each other better, you'll be able to tell when I'm tired before I will. I think you were very encouraging and helpful. You'll be fine."

"Thanks." She bit her lip and fidgeted nervously as if there was something else she wanted to say. I waited patiently for her to continue. "I also hope we're able to get to know each other better as friends, too?" she finally said. Although, she said it more like a question than a statement. "I'm not always the best at putting myself out there, but you probably already knew that." She chuckled nervously. "I'm sorry again for that trainwreck I caused on the first day we met."

I shook my head. "It's in the past."

She nodded. "Anyway, because I'm not very outgoing, I've had a hard time making friends at school. I do really enjoy hanging out with all of you and I hope we can do that more often."

"Of course. You're welcome to hang out with us whenever you want," I said with a smile. "Do you want to have dinner with us tonight?"

"I'd love to, but I have a thing at school this afternoon. I don't know how long it's going to last, and I don't want to say I'll come and then not be able to."

"Are you not going to be at practice this afternoon then?"

"No, that's why I had to work you so hard this morning before I left." She winked.

I couldn't help but laugh. "Alright, well if it finishes early, feel free to stop by."

"Thanks, I will."

Walking away, I smiled to myself. I was actually starting to like Ellie. Sure, a part of me would always feel bad for Landon that she didn't reciprocate his feelings, but she was a nice girl. She was shy, and maybe a little awkward, but there was nothing wrong with that. She was like the rest of us in the fact that she just wanted to feel like she belonged somewhere, and I was more than happy to welcome her into our group with open arms.

Chapter Six

Brody

Later that same evening, I was at my Speedo photo shoot. They had been forgiving and offered me another suit to use since I couldn't find mine—I tried looking again this afternoon after practice, but still couldn't find it.

However, the missing suit was only the first of many problems we'd been having at the shoot. It was one thing after another: the camera's memory card was full, so they had to track down another one; the green screen had a tear in it, and we had to wait for it to be repaired, etc. The shoot should have ended over an hour ago, and I was starting to get antsy.

"Sorry, Brody, we're having some more issues with the lighting," the producer of the shoot said. He was a short man, with balding hair and a large tummy, but still young. I'd peg him at thirty-five at the oldest. "We'll see if we can get it fixed quickly, otherwise we may need to call it a night."

"No worries, take all the time you need." I stepped off the set and my manager, Mike, handed me a robe and a bottle of water. I threw the robe around my shoulders and took a seat in one of the oversized armchairs.

"What a day this has been," Mike chuckled.

"No kidding." I took a swig from the water. "I should have known today would have been a nightmare when I couldn't find my suit this morning."

"Yeah, what happened with that?" Mike asked, taking a seat across from me. "That's not like you."

I shrugged. "Honestly, I don't know. I tore my house apart looking for it. It's like it just disappeared."

He frowned. "Weird."

"Tell me about it."

"So, how's Charlie?" he changed the subject. "I haven't seen her in a couple of weeks."

"She's been alright. Work is keeping her busy now that she's taken over for Mr. Davis. There's been a lot of damage control to keep the place running smoothly."

"I suppose we shouldn't be that surprised now, huh?" He shook his head. "How's Landon doing with the whole situation?"

"As good as I think you'd expect," I said. "I have noticed a change in his attitude since he's moved in with me. It seems like he's getting more comfortable loosening up and breaking out of his shell a little bit. He's even interested in dating now, which I honestly don't think he really ever let himself think about before. He just had too many other things on his mind."

"You're doing a really good thing for him, Brody." He nodded approvingly. "I don't know many twenty-five-year-olds who would take someone in like that, but you didn't even think twice. You're changing that kid's life."

I smiled and nodded, contemplating if I should tell him what I had up my sleeve. Eventually, I decided I wanted to tell someone—and I knew there wasn't a chance Mike would tell Landon. "Can you keep a secret?" I asked, leaning forward in my chair. When he nodded, I continued. "I don't want to give away too much right now, but I'm working on a fundraiser for kids like Landon. It's been my special project now that I have a bit more free time. I'm hoping to have most of the details finalized by his birthday so I can tell him then."

His eyebrows shot to the top of his head. "Wow, that's awesome, Brody. I can't think of a better birthday present. Let me know when it's ready. I'd love to help if I can."

"Thanks, I appreciate that."

We continued to chat while the crew tried to figure out what was going on with the lighting. We chatted about his family and their upcoming ski trip to Colorado, went over a couple of upcoming marketing events, and commented on the most recent swim meet and the athletes who had competed until Mike's assistant, Angela, came bursting into the room.

"Brody!" she shrieked, a look of panic on her face. "You need to see this."

She handed me her phone, where a breaking news story was playing. The headline read: ***Prison Break—Inmate Ben Davis Missing.***

I jolted upright in my chair. "Holy shit, Landon's dad broke out of prison?"

"What?" Mike asked, the smile that was on his face moments ago instantly gone.

"It's all over the news," Angela said, breathing hard. "He's the only prisoner who got out. Earlier, the story said surveillance tapes had been tampered with, and guards had potentially been bribed. They think someone helped him."

Combing my fingers through my hair, I started to panic. I needed to warn Landon. Looking at the clock, it was after seven already—he'd be at practice. "I need to go." Bolting out of the chair, I handed Angela her phone back and went for the changing room. "Mike, please explain the situation to the cameramen and reschedule."

"Be careful, Brody!" Mike called after me.

Changing in record time, I drove as fast as I could to the pool. A million different thoughts swirled in my head the whole drive.

How did Mr. Davis get out of prison?

Who helped him?

Where is he now?

Does he want revenge, or does he just want to disappear?

Are any of us safe?

When I pulled into the parking lot to the pool, I recognized Roman Howard's black Audi parked near the front. Roman hadn't been around nearly as much since the incident last summer, which made me wonder if he had also heard the news.

Running inside, I found Roman and Coach Tanner deep in conversation on the pool deck. Landon was nowhere to be seen.

"Where's Landon?" I asked, running right up to them. "His dad is out of prison. Where is he?"

Coach Tanner held up his hands to calm me down. "Brody, we heard the news. I ended practice early. Allison heard about it, too and beat you here. She took Landon home."

I started pacing in front of them. "What do we do? What does this mean? Do you think he wants revenge because of what we did? What's going to happen—?"

"Brody." Coach Tanner grabbed me by the shoulders and held them tight. "Take a deep breath. Roman and I were just discussing this as well."

"I'm going to leave town for a while, and stay low," Roman said. "I don't think he'd be stupid enough to come after me and my company again, but I'm not going to give him the chance to. Who knows what his motives are?"

"Maybe we should all go with you?" I suggested. "We can swim from anywhere, really. We can go somewhere he wouldn't expect us."

Coach Tanner shook his head. "No, we can't uproot everyone's life like that. And we can't expect Roman to do that either. I strongly believe the chances of him wanting to draw attention to himself at this point are pretty slim, and he'll more than likely just go into hiding."

"Tanner, I have a flight to catch," Roman said, checking his watch. "I need to go over some financials with you before I go."

"Of course. Please go wait for me in my office." He gestured toward the tiny room off to the side of the pool. "I'll be there shortly."

"Coach, what if he doesn't, though?" I repeated. "We are the reason he ended up in jail. His own son shot him in the foot, and I killed Camila." My voice cracked on the last word, and I tried to clear my throat. "What if he wants to get back at us?"

"I honestly don't know what's going to happen." He shook his head. "And I don't know why he was trying to get all that money, but a part of me has to believe that another party is in play here."

"What do you mean?"

"I mean, if he wanted all that money for himself, he should have been satisfied after the first breach at Howard Enterprises. The fact that he tried to go back for more tells me he owes someone a lot of money. Someone who knows he's not going to get it while he's sitting in jail."

"You think that's why someone broke him out?" I asked, trying to wrap my head around what he was saying.

"I can't say for sure. It's just a theory." He turned towards his office where Roman was waiting for him. "Look, Brody, we'll figure something out. Maybe tomorrow morning when we're all together for practice, we'll take some time and talk about it further. For now, I need you to go home and make sure Landon's doing okay. He was pretty shaken up when he left."

I nodded, not sure what else to say.

Coach patted me on the shoulder before he turned towards his office. "I better not keep Roman waiting any longer. I'll see you in the morning."

******

After I had left the pool, I called Charlie and told her what happened. Her reaction was similar to mine, and she immediately started asking a million questions. Trying to calm her down, I told her to meet me at home, and that I'd pick up some pizza for all of us on the way. When I hung up with her, I called Allison to let her know I was bringing food, and she said that she was still at the house with Landon, and Ellie was there as well.

Now, all five of us sat in the living room, picking at pieces of pizza, since none of us seemed to have much of an appetite.

"What's going on in your head right now, Landon?" I asked him. He was sitting on one end of the couch, Ellie sitting close, but still far enough away that they weren't touching.

He shrugged but didn't speak. He'd been awfully quiet since we got home, the shock from the news still fresh.

"Landon, we don't know that he's even going to stay in this area," Allison said. "He'll probably take off so he can hide. I'm sure he's more concerned with staying discrete than coming after any of us."

Nobody said anything. We knew Allison was attempting to ease his mind, but she hadn't been with us that night in Atlanta. She didn't know what depths he'd be willing to go to, and quite frankly, neither did any of us.

"Did they ever release his statement of why they were stealing all that money last year?" Allison continued. "Maybe that could give us a clue of what his next move would be."

I shook my head. "We don't know. We were waiting to find out when he went on trial. Charlie, do you remember the date of when that was supposed to be? I thought it was coming up soon."

"February 10th," Ellie piped in.

All heads in the room turned to her at the same time.

"What?" she asked defensively. "I read the news."

"It's awfully convenient he disappeared before he went on trial," Charlie huffed. "I've been dying to know what the motive for all of it was."

"Coach Tanner had a theory." I told them what he had mentioned at the pool tonight. "I have to admit it makes a lot of sense."

"But who would he owe that much money to?" Landon asked. "I'll be the first to admit my dad didn't make the best decisions, but I have a hard time believing he found himself in that much debt."

"Him and Camila both," I reminded him. "They both were trying to get the money. Obviously, whatever happened, they were in on it together."

"So, you're saying that someone broke him out of prison so he could find a way to get the rest of the money he owes?" Allison asked. She looked from me, to Landon, to Charlie and back as if gauging our reactions. "If what you're saying is true, then he's not going to just disappear. He's out to make more trouble. Who's going to be his next target?"

"I don't know." I shrugged.

"Maybe we need to investigate ourselves," Landon said. "We should try to find him."

"Absolutely not," I said, shaking my head. "The police are on it. Let them do their jobs."

"Well, why not?" Landon sat forward in his chair, clearly upset. "We got involved last time, how is this any different?"

"Last time, we almost got killed," I reminded him. "We were lucky to escape with our lives, and there's no way in hell I'm putting any of us through that again."

Landon stood up and started pacing in front of the couch. "This is so stupid!" he screamed. "I guarantee he's going to hurt *someone* trying to get what he wants, and I can't just sit here and wait for that to happen."

"Calm down." I stood up and grabbed him by the shoulders. "What are we supposed to do? We have no idea where he's going, and even if we did find him, he wouldn't tell us what he's planning. If we go after him, we'll just be in his way, and I don't see that ending well for us."

"Brody's right, Landon." Allison stood and put a hand on his shoulder next to mine. "Just because he's family doesn't mean you're responsible for what he does."

"It's not fair." Landon looked at his feet and I couldn't see his face, but I could tell by the way his voice cracked that he was holding back tears. "He's the only family I have left. Why does he have to be such a monster?"

"We're your family, too," Allison said. "We care about you like you're our own blood. I know you want to find him, but we're not going to let you put yourself in harm's way. And if that means we have to strap you down kicking and screaming, then so be it, but we're not going to let you go after him."

Landon was silent, still staring at his feet.

Finally, Charlie joined us standing as well. "I'd believe her, Landon. You know she's stronger than most of us."

That got a little chuckle out of him. "That's true."

"We love you, man." I gave his shoulders a final squeeze and dropped my arms to my side.

"Love you, too," he mumbled.

"Let's go to bed, it's getting kind of late," Charlie said. "Allison, you're welcome to stay the night if you'd like."

"You can, too, Ellie," I added, not wanting her to feel left out.

"Thanks, but I'm going to get going," Allison said.

"I probably will too," Ellie said, stealing a glance at Landon. "I have a bit of homework I need to do anyway."

We said goodnight to Allison and Ellie, and the rest of us disappeared up the stairs and into our rooms.

"What a crazy day," Charlie said when we crawled into bed. "I feel so horrible for Landon. This has to be scary for him."

"*I'm* scared for him." I pulled the covers up to my chin and then rolled over to hold Charlie.

"I mean, what else can we do to help him?"

She continued to ramble on, but I stopped listening. I ran my hands along her thighs, up over the smoothness of her stomach and cupped one of her breasts in my palm.

"Brody, are you listening to me?" She rolled over to face me.

"Charlie, I'm stressed. You're stressed. We need to take our minds off it." I pulled her to me and kissed her.

It didn't take her long to open her lips for me, and soon our tongues swirled against one another's.

"Okay, you're right," she breathed in between kisses. "We're not going to solve it tonight."

"Shhh." I kissed her again, this time only stopping when I needed to breathe.

I rolled over on top of her, and took both of her breasts in my hands, tugging at her nipples. Her hands clung to my back, raking her fingers over the muscles. It didn't take long for her hands to reach the waistline of my boxers, and she tugged at them greedily.

Quickly wiggling them off, I slipped my hands under her loose t-shirt and pulled it over her head. She was laying there in nothing but her panties and I wanted to take my sweet time loving every inch of her, but my body had other plans.

Leaning over to the nightstand, I grabbed a condom out of the drawer, ripped it open with my teeth and rolled it onto my erection. Then I slipped my thumbs into her underwear, made quick work of them, and plunged myself deep inside of her.

"Oh, my God, Charlie," I breathed. It hadn't been that long since the last time we made love, but it felt like an eternity at the same time. I'd have her every minute of every day if I could.

She started to moan, and I smashed my lips to hers once more. We moved together in rhythm and before long, we were both screaming out in pleasure. When we had finished, we stayed laying naked together, listening to the sounds of our breathing.

It didn't take long for Charlie's breaths to turn into soft snores, and I knew she had fallen asleep. Pulling her even closer to me, I kissed her shoulder and was about to fall asleep myself, when a car alarm started going off.

It jolted me awake, and after several moments of listening to the shrilling call, I was about to get up and see if someone had set off *my* car alarm. But before I could get up to investigate, it was turned off. Relaxing back into my pillow, it only took me a few minutes to forget about the alarm and drift off to sleep.

Chapter Seven

Charlie

The ringing of my cell phone woke me with a start. Checking the time, it was only 4:30 in the morning.

Who in their right mind is calling me at this hour?

"Hello?" I answered, rubbing my eyes so I wouldn't fall right back asleep.

"Is this Charlie Price?" a female asked.

"Yes, who's calling?" I whispered.

"This is April. I'm a member at Fit Happens Gym. I'm trying to get into the member door and it's not taking my key fob. Your information was on the door to call in case of an emergency. I'm sorry if I'm waking you."

I tried not to groan. "Is this the emergency you're calling about?"

"Yes. Again, I'm sorry," she said. "But there's a group of people out here waiting, and none of us can get in. We were hoping you could come down and unlock the door."

"Of course. I can be there in twenty minutes." I hung up the phone and rolled over to Brody. Nudging him awake, I gave him a kiss on the cheek. "I have to run into work."

"What time is it?" he asked, sitting up. "Did I sleep through my alarm?"

"No, you can go back to sleep for a little bit," I told him. "I'm going to go open the doors at the gym and just hang out there until practice starts."

He nodded and laid his head back on the pillow. "I parked behind you when I got home last night. My keys are on the kitchen counter. Go ahead and take the truck."

"Thanks." I kissed him on the cheek one more time and got up to get dressed. Throwing my things together as quickly as possible, I ran downstairs and tiptoed to the front door, trying not to make noise and wake up Landon, too. Soon, I was out the door and backing out of the driveway.

Knowing there wouldn't be as many drivers out on the road at this hour, I pushed the speed limit so as not to make my customers wait any longer. After a couple of minutes of cruising down the main street, I started hearing a weird noise coming from the vehicle.

"What is that?" I said out loud, turning the radio down to hear better.

A clunk came from somewhere under the hood, and the truck jerked forward. I tried to hit the brakes, thinking I should pull over, but it wouldn't slow down. I started to panic when pushing the brake pedal all the way to the floor still didn't slow the truck.

"Shit, what's going on?" I cried.

I was rushing down the road, going over sixty miles an hour, and my brakes weren't working. Getting closer to a red light, I prayed it would turn green by the time I got there. When it was evident it wasn't going to, I gripped the steering wheel so hard with one hand my knuckles turned white and laid on the horn with the other. There were only a couple of vehicles in the intersection, but they all slammed on their brakes as I plowed through, honking their own horns at me in anger.

"I can't stop!" I screamed, knowing no one could hear me anyway.

The truck wasn't slowing down fast enough. I pumped the brakes, praying they would start working, but the truck kept speeding on.

There was another intersection coming up in about a mile, this one busier than the last. I would need to stop this truck before I got there.

Suddenly, I came to the realization that the only way I was going to stop this truck was to run it into something. I didn't have a lot of time, so I started scanning my surroundings, looking for anything that would help me stop this vehicle. About a block ahead, I saw a group of larger bushes lining the road.

Those would have to do.

Gripping the steering wheel tighter yet, I aimed for the bushes. In a matter of seconds, I was coming up on them, and I screamed as the truck went off the road and into the shrubbery. It didn't stop the vehicle right away, but it allowed the truck to slow down enough so I could yank on the emergency brake and bring it to a halting stop—but not before smashing my forehead onto the steering wheel.

Breathing hard, I still gripped the steering wheel tight. In a daze, I stared straight ahead for several moments while I processed what had just happened.

Finally snapping back to attention, I dug around for my phone, finding it on the floor on the passenger side. I dialed 911 and told the dispatcher everything that happened. The woman on the line told me unless it was not safe for me to stay in the truck that I shouldn't try to get out or move around a lot, and that an ambulance would be here soon. She asked a lot of questions trying to determine how hurt I was, but I still felt like I was in a daze. My entire body felt numb. It didn't take long for the medics to reach the scene, and a few minutes later, a couple of them were helping me out of the truck.

"Ma'am, you have a huge gash on your forehead," the taller of the two said. "You're going to need stitches."

Still in shock, I touched my forehead with my fingertips and when I took them away, they were covered in blood. "Oh, I guess I do," I said. "I think I hit my head on the steering wheel." Now that the adrenaline was starting to pump its way out of my body, my mind went fuzzy, and I suddenly felt woozy.

"She's not looking so good," the shorter medic said to the other. "Do you think she has a concussion?"

"You don't need to talk about me as if I'm not standing right here," I grumbled. My legs suddenly felt like jelly, and they gave out from underneath me.

The medics caught me before I hit the ground and assisted me to the ambulance. "She'll need to be checked for a concussion," someone said.

My vision was going blurry, and I couldn't even tell who was speaking anymore. Once they had me lying down in the ambulance, I allowed my body to relax and promptly passed out on the stretcher.

******

When I came to, I was in a room I didn't recognize. I tried to lift my head to get a better look, but my vision became blurry again, and a sharp pain shot down my neck. I dropped my head back to the pillow, not feeling strong enough to hold it up any longer.

"Charlie?"

I turned towards the voice to find Brody sitting in the chair next to my bed. It was hard to tell, but he looked like he was frowning.

"How are you feeling?" he asked, reaching for my hand.

"Where am I?" I groaned.

"You're in the hospital. You hit your head pretty hard. They gave you six stitches and said you have a concussion. Do you remember what happened?"

I frowned, trying to remember. Suddenly, my mind was filled with images of the truck roaring down the road and not being able to stop. "Brody, your truck!" I tried to sit up, but Brody held me in place.

"Woah, take it easy," he soothed. "If you sit up too fast, you'll get dizzy again."

"Brody, I have no idea what happened," I said, searching my brain for a cause. "I was driving just fine, then I heard a clunk, and the brakes just stopped working."

"Charlie, I'm not worried about the truck," he assured me. "It can be replaced. You can't. I'm just glad nothing worse happened."

My eyes shot open further when another thought crossed my mind. "What if that had been you? Oh my God, Brody. What if you had been on the highway?"

He shook his head. "Let's not think about that."

"Have you been having issues with it?" I asked.

"No, she's been working fine. They're going to take it to the shop to find out what happened though. We'll know soon enough."

"Oh, the gym!" I tried to sit up again, but Brody still held me down.

"Allison is there now taking care of it," he said. "You need to rest."

There was a knock at the door and when I glanced over, I saw Coach Tanner, Landon, and Ellie standing in the doorway.

"Is it okay if we come in?" Coach Tanner said.

I nodded and they filed into the small space. "What time is it?" I asked. "Is practice over?"

Coach Tanner shook his head. "No, I ended up canceling it. Landon was the only one able to be there, and Ellie wanted to see how you were doing."

"That was nice of you," I said to her.

"You had us all worried sick," Ellie said, her voice a touch softer than usual. "When I heard about the accident, I assumed the worst. You're lucky you knew how to stop the truck safely."

"I think it was just the adrenaline reacting," I said.

"Well, either way, you're very lucky." She gave me a small smile.

"I'm going to go check in with the nurse and see when you can get out of here, Charlie," Coach Tanner said, turning to walk back out the door he had just come in.

"I'll go with you," Brody offered. "Can you two keep an eye on her while we're out?" he asked Ellie and Landon.

"Yeah, sure thing." Landon nodded and took a seat in the chair Brody had just been sitting in.

"What exactly happened?" Ellie asked when they had left the room.

"The brakes stopped working." I replayed the morning drive to her in detail. "And I hit my head on something when I finally got the truck to stop."

"How fast were you going?" she asked, her eyes wide.

"I don't remember. Over the speed limit, I'm sure."

"Well, I bet you won't ever speed again," she chuckled nervously.

I gave her a sideways glance. "Yes, because *that's* what caused the truck to breakdown."

Her face went white and the smile on her face vanished. "Charlie, I was just trying to lighten the mood. I'm not trying to suggest it was your fault."

"I know," I sighed. "I'm not feeling well. Forgive me for not being in a joking mood."

Ellie fell silent and glanced over at Landon. He hadn't said a word since Brody and Coach Tanner left, but his gaze shifted between Ellie and myself, a look of concern etched on his face.

Finally, after the silence had stretched on for several minutes, he leaned forward in his chair. "Ellie, we should let Charlie rest."

"We can at least stay until Brody gets back if you want?" Ellie asked me.

I shook my head. "I'll be fine. Go ahead and go."

Ellie turned and waited by the door while Landon pushed his chair back to the far wall. Before they could leave, I held a hand towards him to stop him.

"Hey Landon, can I talk to you for a sec?" I asked.

"Sure." He nodded and then turned his attention to Ellie. "I'll be out in a minute. If you don't want to wait, I'll grab a ride with Coach Tanner."

She nodded and left the room.

"What's up?" Landon asked, taking a seat on the edge of the bed beside me.

"How are you doing?"

"How am *I* doing?" he repeated, chuckling ever so slightly. "I wasn't the one in the accident."

"But how are you after finding out the news from last night? Were you able to get any sleep?"

He shrugged. "I'm doing okay. Didn't get a lot of sleep last night, but I'm sure it'll get better."

His words didn't sound that convincing, but I didn't push. "You know you can come to any of us for anything, right?"

Chewing his lip, his gaze met mine. "I know."

I took his hand in mine and gave it a squeeze.

A moment later Brody came strolling back into the room, Coach Tanner shortly behind him. "Everything okay?" he asked when he saw us. "Ellie's out in the hallway."

"Everything's fine." Landon stood up from the bed. "We're going to take off and let Charlie get some rest."

"I'll probably head out too, then," Coach Tanner said. "Charlie, feel better. The nurse said you'll probably get to go home later today. We'll talk later about when you can get back in the pool. You'll have to take a few days to rest."

I waved goodbye and they both filed out of the room. Brody wandered to the side of my bed and placed the back of his hand on the side of my cheek.

"Are you feeling okay?" he asked tenderly.

I nodded. "As good as to be expected right now, I guess."

He gave me a tight grin, leaned over and planted a kiss on my cheek, and then pulled his chair back out to sit next to me. He reached for the TV remote and started flipping through the channels.

"Brody?" I whispered after a beat.

"What's up?" He turned his attention away from the TV, back to me.

"I'm sorry I broke your truck."

He shook his head. "It wasn't your fault, Charlie. Okay?" He leaned over and took my hand in his. "I'm not worried about the truck. Like I said earlier, it can be replaced. I'm just thankful *you're* going to be okay."

I gave his hand a squeeze and let my body relax into the hospital bed. Brody turned his attention back to flipping through the channels until he finally landed on something with sports. We watched in silence for a while, and soon, my eyelids started to feel heavy. I was about to let sleep take over when Brody spoke up again.

"By the way," he said, as if it was an afterthought. "Was the truck locked when you left this morning?"

I lifted my head off my pillow to look at him. "Yeah, I think it was."

"Hmm." He stared off into space and his mouth twisted at the corner as though he were lost in thought.

"What?" I asked, turning my head to face him. "Was it not supposed to be locked?"

He shook his head. "No, it should have been locked. It's just that right before we fell asleep, I heard a car alarm go off and I wondered if it was the truck."

"A car alarm went off?" I racked my brain trying to remember if I had heard it, but I couldn't.

"Yeah, but it was turned off before I could look, so I assumed it wasn't mine. But now I don't know."

"Are you suggesting that someone did this on purpose?" I asked, dread sinking into my gut. "Like someone was trying to hurt you?"

"It just seems a little suspicious that it happens right after Landon's dad breaks out of prison."

"Do we say something?" My head started throbbing and I grasped my forehead. The bandages where they had covered my stitches felt thick. "I can't even think straight right now. What do we do?"

He placed a reassuring hand on my arm. "We'll wait and see what the shop says about the truck. Right now, I need you to rest."

"What about Landon?" I asked, closing my eyes.

"I think it's best if we don't mention this to him right now. He's worried enough as it is."

"Do you think we're safe?"

"I don't know."

Chapter Eight

Mr. Davis

It had now been twenty-four hours since I'd been broken out of prison. And while I hated every second of being in that God forsaken place, I also knew I was a hell of a lot safer in there. Not completely safe, but my chances were better with guards available twenty-four seven.

Unfortunately, when you owed millions of dollars to the Codicia cartel—one of the deadliest drug cartels in the world—nowhere was exactly safe.

Sighing, I tried shifting my weight on the old couch I was laying on. It was only about three in the afternoon, but since I was stuck hiding in this tiny apartment while I waited for Jellybean to get back, I figured I might as well try to get some rest.

Jellybean was the one who had arranged the whole "break me out of prison" operation. Her father, Grimaldo, was one of the district leaders of the Codicia cartel, based out of Sacramento. He was the one I owed the money to. And while Grimaldo didn't typically send his own kid after those who owed him money, Jellybean offered her services in exchange for a favor of her own.

She had been awfully close to my latest partner, Camila Hale, and was mad as hell that my son and his friends had killed her. She told me she'd help me get out of prison, get the money I owed her dad, and then ensure my safety afterwards if I helped her get revenge. And since my other option was most likely death—whether Grimaldo had someone kill me from inside the prison, or he broke me out just to kill me right away—this seemed like my best bet.

I jerked upright on the couch when the apartment door suddenly opened, and Jellybean walked in carrying several plastic bags.

"Jeezus, Jellybean, where have you been? I expected you back hours ago." I sat up and rubbed the sleep out of my eyes. "I haven't eaten since breakfast—yesterday."

"I got caught up with something." She took a pair of blue jeans and a dark t-shirt from one of the bags and threw them at me. "Put these on, they should fit. You'll be more comfortable in those than that lovely jumpsuit." She set the other bags on the coffee table in front of me. They were filled with various food items including a sandwich, a box of crackers, and a stick of salami.

"Thanks." I stood and began stripping out of my inmate uniform. "So, what exactly is the plan? You got me out of jail. Now what?" Once dressed, I tore into the bags of food, barely tasting it as I shoved each piece into my mouth.

"Now, we have to get the money," she said, pacing in front of me. "He's not thrilled that I'm helping you, by the way. He wanted me to remind you that if you try anything, there's nowhere you can hide where he won't find you."

"Yeah, I'm aware. But thanks," I said with a mouthful of food. "Do you have any ideas on how to get the money?"

She shrugged. "I thought I did, but it's too slow. What little money I've given him already isn't going to hold him over for very long. He's going to get impatient."

"How did you get that money?"

"Don't worry about it," she snapped. "Like I said, it's not going to get us very far. We need to come up with another plan to get the rest of the money as quickly as possible."

"Such as?"

"I don't know yet." She continued to pace in silence for a long moment, then stopped and faced me, putting her hands on her hips. "Maybe we should rob a bank? Kidnap the president?"

I rolled my eyes. "This isn't a movie, Jellybean. This is real life."

"Quit calling me Jellybean, I'm not a little kid anymore," she whined, taking a seat on the chair opposite me. "I'd like to see what kind of plan *you've* thought of."

"I'll call you whatever I damn well please," I shot back. I sat back and thought about it for a moment. "We could go after Roman Howard again?" I suggested. "Maybe he's let his guard down since I've been locked up. I bet I could get into his system this time."

She shot me a glance. "That idea is worse than mine. The man isn't stupid. Besides, he skipped town once he heard you were out of prison. He knew he'd be a target, I'm sure he's tripled down on security."

"Well, fuck. I got nothing then."

Suddenly, her phone started ringing. "It's my dad," she said, looking at the caller ID. She stared at it instead of answering.

"Don't ignore him, that'll just piss him off. Answer it already."

"What do I tell him?"

"Answer it, we'll think of something," I urged. "We can't risk making him upset."

"Hi, Dad," she said into the phone. "Yeah, it worked. He's sitting right here ... you want to talk to him?" She glanced at me. "Okay, here he is." She handed me the phone and I gulped before I answered.

"Hello, sir, long time no talk. How have you been?"

"I don't have time for small talk, Davis," he barked into the phone. "Now, we got you out of prison, I need to know how you plan on paying me back."

"We're working on that right now, sir," I told him.

"You mean, you don't know how you're going to get my money?"

"Well, we've—we've started brainstorming," I stammered. "We don't have all the details locked down just yet, but don't worry. We'll know what to do the next time we talk."

"You better," he warned. "This deal rides on you getting my money. You know what will happen if you don't."

The line went dead before I could respond. I took a deep breath as I handed Jellybean her phone back.

"I hope you didn't just promise him something we can't deliver," she said. "What if he calls tomorrow? That doesn't give us a lot of time."

I shook my head. "I'll think of something. I always do. How's your side project going?"

She stood from her chair. "It's taking longer than I hoped it would, but with any luck, Camila's killers will meet the same sticky end soon." She went back for the door. "I need to go. Remember, do not leave this apartment under any circumstances. I'll try to find us a better hideout, but this will do for now."

"You just got here. Shouldn't we be using this time to brainstorm ideas?" I asked.

"Looks like you've got some time on your hands, why don't you get to it?" She smirked. "Besides, I've got my side project to work on." She placed a hand on the doorknob, paused, and turned back towards me. "Oh, there's a burner phone in one of those bags. Only call me if it's important. We need to lay low. I'll be back tomorrow." She turned and slipped out of the apartment just as quickly as she had come.

Chapter Nine

Brody

Charlie was released from the hospital a few hours after she had woken up, and the doctor told her she needed to rest for at least a week before she'd be allowed back in the water. She also had to limit her screen time so the bright light wouldn't increase her headaches.

"I'm going to be so bored," she whined from the couch when we'd returned home.

I had drawn the shades and turned out the lights so she could relax and hopefully take a nap. "You have doctor's orders to basically do nothing but sleep. Isn't that everyone's dream?" I joked, trying to lighten the mood.

"Not mine." She threw the blanket over her head. "I want to swim." Her voice came out a little muffled from the blanket.

Taking a seat next to her on the couch, I drew the blanket back so I could see her face. "I'm going to tell you the same thing you told me after my shoulder surgery: it's temporary. It's not the end. You'll be back in before you know it."

She grimaced. "It's a lot easier said than done."

"Are you saying you can't take your own advice?" I cracked a smile and poked her in the shoulder. "That's not the Charlie I know."

She tried to hide a smile and threw the blanket over her head once more. "Yeah, yeah."

"Well, I suggest you take a nap," I said, standing from the couch. "Landon is in his room if you need anything. I have a PT appointment, but I won't be gone long." I went to the kitchen, filled a glass of water, and grabbed the pain meds she'd left on the counter. Bringing them into the living room, I set them on the coffee table next to the couch. "Here's your meds and some water if you need it."

She pulled the blanket down to her chin so I could see her face. "You take such good care of me, Brody," she said dreamily. "Imagine how you're going to be with our kids someday."

I froze, and the gears inside my mind started working overtime. *Kids?* Where was this coming from all of a sudden?

I chuckled nervously. "I think maybe those are your pain meds talking. It's time for you to sleep."

She propped herself up on her elbows so she could face me, the blanket falling to her waist. "I'm perfectly aware of what I'm talking about. Does that weird you out that I mentioned kids?"

"Well, I—uh, we've never talked about it before," I stammered. My heart felt like it was beating faster than usual. I ran a hand through my hair and tugged on the ends of it. "We've only been dating for a few months. You're thinking about kids already?"

"Obviously I don't want kids this very second." She swung her legs to the side so that she was sitting straight up with her feet on the floor. "But if we stay together—which I fully expect to—then yeah, the thought has occurred to me."

"Oh, man, I think we're getting ahead of ourselves," I said, panicking a little. "How do we even know that's going to happen?" Her face fell, and I knew immediately I had said the wrong thing. "I mean, Charlie—that's not what I meant."

"You don't think we're going to stay together?" she asked, standing from the couch and gathering up her blanket. "You said you loved me. You told me I was different and that you wanted to spend your life with me. Were all of those just empty words to you? I thought we were on the same page." She started for the stairs, but I sidestepped in front of her to stop her.

"Charlie, I didn't mean—"

"Then what did you mean?" She crossed her arms, hugging the blanket close to her.

"I definitely see us together long term. I do love you. More than anything. I … I guess I just haven't ever pictured myself having kids."

"Are you saying you don't want kids? Because if not, then we need to decide if we're wasting our time here." Her voice cracked on the last few words, and I could tell she was holding back tears.

I put my hands on her shoulders. "Charlie, please I'm not trying to upset you. Can we talk about this later?" I glanced at the clock on the wall behind her. "I really need to get to my appointment, and you need to rest."

Tears welled in her eyes, and she fought to keep them at bay. "Fine." She shrugged out of my hold and stepped around me to go to the stairs.

"Charlie, I promise we'll talk about this when I get home," I called after her. She didn't respond, and I stayed rooted to my spot until I heard the bedroom door close upstairs.

Frustrated, I ran my fingers through my hair some more and debated if I should skip my appointment and go after her. Ultimately, I decided to let her cool down and talk to her when I got back from physical therapy. Grabbing my keys and my wallet, I headed out the door, leaving Charlie alone to rest.

******

"Brody, your shoulder is improving greatly," my physical therapist, Amy, said as I went through my stretches with her. She was a middle-aged woman with a slender figure and long, blonde hair. "How does it feel?"

"A lot better than it did before." I held onto a resistance band and slowly moved my shoulder from in front of me to the side and back again. Two months ago, this same exercise still hurt like hell. Now, I hardly felt any pain at all.

"Good, I'm glad." She smiled. "You can stop now. I want to test your rotation. Hold your arm out in front of you and point your thumb to the floor."

I did as I was instructed and she took hold of my arm, moving it gently from side to side and up and down.

"Any pain there?" she asked.

I shook my head. "Nope, none."

"Perfect." She picked up her clipboard and jotted down a few notes. "Well, Brody," she said after she finished writing. "I think you are ready to be cleared."

"Seriously?" I asked, making sure I heard her right.

She smiled again. "Yes, seriously. You've shown great improvement. I think your shoulder is in good shape and you can get back to normal swim workouts. Don't go all in on the first day, though. You're going to want to build up to it again."

"So, I can compete again as well? Our home meet is only two weeks away."

She nodded. "Yes, you can."

I got so excited, I jumped up and hugged her, but then quickly released my hold. "Sorry, I don't know why I did that. It's just the best news I've heard all day."

"It's okay," she laughed. "I'll write you a note to take to your coach before you go. I don't think we need to schedule anymore appointments, but if it starts hurting again or giving you any kind of trouble, I want you to promise me you'll come right back."

"Yes, ma'am, I will."

******

While I was driving home in Charlie's car, I was so excited about the news Amy had given me I had almost forgotten about the conversation Charlie and I had earlier. My stomach sunk a little.

Did I want kids? I honestly didn't know. That was clearly a conversation we needed to have.

I decided to stop and get her some ice cream on the way home. I wasn't sure how upset she was still going to be when I got home, and even if she wasn't that upset anymore, she had a rough day and deserved a sweet treat.

When I finally arrived back at the house, Charlie wasn't downstairs, so I wandered up to our room to check if she was still there. She was passed out on our bed, so I quietly closed the door and went back downstairs. I heard a voice at the door just as I was putting Charlie's ice cream in the freezer.

"Hello?" Allison called in a soft voice.

I went to the entryway and waved her in.

"Hey, I just came to see how Charlie's doing," she said, closing the door behind her.

"She's sleeping right now, but I think she's doing okay. Do you want anything to drink?"

"Sure, I'll have some water." She plopped down on the couch and kicked her shoes off.

After grabbing a water from the kitchen, I came back to the living room and handed her the bottle. "Everything at the gym taken care of?" I asked.

She nodded. "Yep. The fob scanner kicked the bucket and needed to be replaced. The guy who replaced it said the thing should have been replaced years ago. He was surprised it made it as long as it did."

"I guess you're lucky that it was locking people out instead of letting anyone and everyone in," I said.

"Yeah, I guess. But just another example of how Mr. Davis was being a cheap ass. I've lost track of how many things we've had to replace or fix since he's been locked up. No wonder the guy was trying to rob Roman clean. He obviously didn't have any money."

"What's going to happen to the gym in the long run?" I asked her. "Is there going to be a different owner?"

She shrugged. "I don't know. Some lawyers dropped by a few days after they arrested Mr. Davis and told us to take over for now, and just keep running things the way we have been. They said they'd be back with updates but haven't been back since. And now that Mr. Davis is on the loose, I'm really not expecting them to come by anytime soon."

"Well, hopefully everything works out."

"It will," she agreed. "All in good time."

"Oh, I have some good news," I said, suddenly remembering what Amy had told me. "I've been cleared to practice full-time again! And I can compete. I'm hoping I can still get registered for the home meet."

"Brody, that's great news!" Her face lit up. "We're ready to have you back in our lanes. And I have no doubt Coach Tanner will find a way to get you into the meet."

"I sure hope so. I don't think I could take another meet where I have to sit back and watch."

"I hear ya." She nodded. "So, what do you think he's going to have Ellie be doing now that you'll be back practicing with us?"

I shrugged. "I don't know, probably have us take turns doing some one-on-one work with her or something."

She made a face. "Well, I hope she knows more about the other strokes than she does about breaststroke. The other day when I asked her about breaststroke drills? She didn't know any. She told me to just keep doing what I was doing."

"Was that the first day she was with us?" I laughed. "I think she was pretty nervous that day. She probably didn't know what to say to a record-breaking breaststroker."

"Yeah, maybe," she agreed. "I guess I just expect a professional swim coach to have a pretty good idea of what she's doing. How has she been working with you?"

"She's been fine." I nodded. "I can tell she's more comfortable now that she's been with us for a few weeks. It just took her a while to warm up to a new position."

"Well, good. That makes me feel a bit better about potentially working with her if that's the route Coach wants to take."

"Yeah, it'll work out." My gaze lowered to my lap, where I played with the zipper on my jacket. Silence stretched between us for I don't know how long as I started thinking about Charlie again.

"Hey," Allison finally said. I looked up and she was leaning forward in her seat. "Everything okay? You seem distracted."

I sighed. "Sorry, I've got a lot on my mind. I think Charlie might be upset with me."

"About what?"

"It's kind of a long story," I said. I replayed the conversation to her, telling her how I had been caught off guard when she brought up wanting kids, and panicked. "I think I stuck my foot in my mouth. My mind was spinning, and I didn't know what to say. But she said we need to figure out if we actually want the same things. She doesn't want to feel like she's wasting her time if our end goals aren't the same."

"You *don't* want kids?" she asked with a hint of surprise in her voice. "Brody, you've always been so good with them. All the kids we have at swim camps? They worship you! I always admired how it seemed to come so naturally to you. I would have never guessed you didn't want some of your own."

"I don't know." I shrugged. "Maybe it is what I want. I've just never really thought about it."

"I guess that makes sense," she said. "You've been on your own for so long, and you're so focused on swimming. It's hard to think about anything past today."

I licked my lower lip and nodded, processing her words.

"Well, what happens when you think about it now?" she asked after a beat.

"What do you mean?"

"I mean, can you picture yourself marrying Charlie? Or do you think the relationship will eventually fizzle out?"

I shook my head. "I don't want to live without her. I think I'd die if I saw her in someone else's arms."

"Okay." She nodded. "And can you honestly tell me you don't want kids? You're amazing with them, and they love you. You'd be an awesome father."

"I'm not so sure." I looked down at my fingers again. "What if they end up like me? Up until last year, I was kind of a mess."

"That's mostly because of the people you chose to surround yourself with," she reminded me. I knew she was referring to my old friend, Chase, who I hadn't talked to since last summer. "Besides, everyone makes stupid mistakes at some point in their lives. Even as a parent you will make mistakes."

"I've never really been responsible for someone before," I rolled off another excuse. "I don't have any siblings, and it's not like I did any babysitting. I don't know what I'm doing."

"To a degree, I understand, but also, you've been taking care of yourself since your parents died. Look at you now.

You're thriving, Brody. And look at Landon! You've taken him under your wing. You're literally his legal guardian right now. You can't tell me you've never been responsible for someone before."

"Okay, okay," I laughed. "I get your point."

She laughed with me. "I just don't want you to ruin what you have with Charlie. I've never seen you happier. It is scary, but the two of you will know what to do when the time comes. Just talk to her."

I gave her a tight smile. "Thanks, Allison."

"Hey, that's what I'm here for." She smiled, then slipped her shoes on and went to the door. "I've got to get going. Have Charlie call me when she's awake."

******

Later that evening, I was eating leftover pizza in the kitchen. Ellie had stopped by to check on Charlie and was now in the living room with Landon. She was sprawled out on one side of the couch, and he was sitting in the recliner. I was about to take my pizza in and sit with them when Charlie finally came downstairs. She came into the kitchen and opened the fridge to scan its contents, paying no attention to me.

"Hey, are you feeling any better?" I asked.

"A little." She didn't look away from the fridge when she answered. After another moment of scanning, she closed the door and turned around to face me. "Is that all the pizza that's left?" She pointed to the pizza box sitting in front of me, only two pieces remained.

"Yeah, you can have them." I pushed the box closer to her.

"I'll just make a sandwich," she grumbled.

"There's two pieces left, Charlie," I told her. "I can always order another one if you want more."

"It's fine." She opened the fridge back up and began pulling out bread, meat, and condiments. Once she had everything she wanted, she placed them all on the counter and started making her sandwich in silence.

I got up from my chair and stood behind her, wrapping my arms around her middle. "Are you mad at me?"

No answer.

"I'm sorry about what I said," I said, nuzzling my nose into her hair.

She stopped what she was doing and rested her palms on the counter, but still didn't say anything.

"I was being stupid, Charlie," I continued. "Can we go upstairs and talk?"

"Why can't we talk here?" she finally said.

"Because I don't want the two in the other room to overhear."

She sighed but agreed to go upstairs. I took her hand and led her back to our bedroom where we took a seat on the edge of the bed.

"I'm really sorry, Charlie," I said again. "I don't want you to think I don't want to be with you, because that couldn't be further from the truth."

"But you don't think we'll have a family someday?" she asked. "I've always wanted to be a mother, Brody. And if that's not what you want, I can't force it onto you. But that also means if we want different things, we should end this now before it gets even harder."

I shook my head and fought back the tears that threatened at the thought of her leaving me. "No, I don't want you to leave me, and if having kids is what you want, then that's what we'll do."

"But is that what *you* want?"

"Honestly? The thought scares the living shit out of me."

She choked out a laugh and reached towards me to wipe away a tear that had managed to escape.

"But the thought of losing you scares me more," I said. "I will do anything to make you happy, and if you want kids someday, then let's do it. I'm all in."

"Really?" She smiled so wide, I was sure her cheeks would split.

"Yes, really." Placing my hand on her jaw, I pulled her into me and kissed her. When I broke the kiss, I looked into her eyes and massaged her cheek with my thumb. "I just hope they get their looks from you."

She burst out laughing and gave me a playful swat on the arm. "I wouldn't be too upset if they looked a little like you." She winked.

I gave her another quick kiss. "Whatever you say." Standing up, I propped up her pillows against the headboard. "Here, make yourself comfortable. I'll go finish making your sandwich."

"You don't have to do that."

"Yes, I do. You're supposed to be resting." In one motion, I had leaned over and scooped her up in my arms.

"Hey!" she squealed as she broke into another fit of giggles.

I set her down against the pillows and pulled a blanket over her. "Make yourself comfortable my dear. I'll be back with one sandwich with ham, turkey, mayo, and extra pickles—and some ice cream. I picked some up for you earlier, but you were asleep."

"Well, I can never say no to ice cream." She beamed. "What kind did you get me?"

"Cookie dough, of course."

She held her hand to her head in a mock swoon. "You know the way to a girl's heart."

I leaned in and kissed her again. "I'll be back in a few minutes."

Quickly descending the stairs, I made my way back into the kitchen to finish making Charlie's sandwich. I knew exactly how she liked it, and even made two in case she was really hungry. When I was finished, I opened up the freezer to grab her ice cream, but it wasn't where I had left it. After scanning the whole drawer, and even moving some things around, I started to wonder if someone had taken it.

"Hey, Landon," I called as I closed the freezer door. I took a few steps toward the living room. "Have you seen the ice cream I got for—" I stopped talking as soon as I entered the living room, for I had found Charlie's missing ice cream. Ellie was scooping the remaining pieces of cookie dough from the bottom of the cup.

"Oh, was this for someone?" she asked, looking to Landon. "Landon said I could have it."

"Sorry, dude, I didn't know," Landon said. "I can get another if you want."

I waved it off. "No, that's okay. They're probably closed by now anyway." Walking back to the kitchen for Charlie's sandwiches, I prepared to tell her she wouldn't be getting the ice cream I had promised her.

"Tell her I'm sorry!" Ellie called from the living room.

Instead of responding, I went for the stairs. I guess I should have mentioned to them that the ice cream had been for Charlie. I hoped she wouldn't be too upset.

When I returned to the bedroom, I poked my head inside before entering. Charlie was leaning against the pillows with her hands folded across her chest, resting her eyes.

"Hey, I got your food," I said, stepping into the room and taking a seat beside her on the bed.

She sat up and took the plate. "Thank you. I haven't eaten much all day." She looked at me expectedly. "Where's the ice cream?"

Pursing my lips, I broke it to her easy. "There might have been a little confusion on whose ice cream it was—"

"Someone ate it, didn't they?"

I sighed. "I'm sorry. I'll get you some more tomorrow."

She shook her head. "It's fine."

"How does this feel?" I asked, brushing my fingers across her bandaged forehead.

She shrugged. "Doesn't hurt as much as it did earlier. I'm hoping I can get the stitches out in a few days."

I nodded but didn't say anything. After she had taken a few bites of her sandwich, I got up and picked up a book off the dresser. "Is this the book you've been reading?"

"Yeah, why?" she said in between bites.

"I want to read to you." I propped up a few more pillows on my side of the bed and sat down beside her.

She stared at me with wide eyes. "You're going to *read* to me?"

"Well, we can't watch TV in your situation, so yes, I'm going to read to you." I opened it up to the page she had bookmarked.

"It's Nicholas Sparks," she giggled. "It might be a little 'lovey-dovey' for you."

"I don't care. I just want to spend some alone time with you."

Her expression softened and she leaned in to kiss my cheek. "You are too sweet." She rested her head on my shoulder and continued to take small bites of her food while I read to her.

We stayed like that until she fell asleep on my arm, and I couldn't have asked for a better way to spend my evening.

Chapter Ten

Charlie

By Thursday morning—Landon's birthday—I was ready to get back in the pool. I had my stitches removed the night prior, and my doctor had cleared me to exercise again.

It had been a long week of sitting at home doing nothing. During the day it had been okay. I was home alone, and I could hang out and read downstairs—I finished three more books since the day of the accident—but as soon as evening came, everyone and their dog would be over at our house. Ellie would come over to hang out with Landon and Brody, and Allison would come to catch me up about work and hang out with everyone.

Literally every single day.

While I appreciated the check-ins, it got to be a little overwhelming with everyone there all the time. Usually, I'd stay downstairs until after supper, and then I would retreat to my room for some peace and quiet. Especially in the early days of recovery, my head would really start to hurt if I stayed where the noise was for too long.

Brody would split his time between hanging out with them downstairs and coming upstairs to hang out with me. He didn't give me any grief for leaving my friends hanging, for which I was thankful.

Now that I was cleared to get back to the pool and get back to work, I was eager to get going. I even left earlier than I usually would so I could have plenty of time to stretch. Walking out of the locker room, I was the first one on deck, but Coach Tanner's office light was on, so I knew he was around.

I worked on stretching all the kinks out of my muscles in silence. The doctors ended up letting me come back before the whole week was up, so really, it hadn't been *that* long since my last practice. But even that short amount of time can make a swimmer sore. It's definitely not a sport you can hop back into right away and not feel a little sluggish. I was sitting on the floor reaching for my toes when Coach Tanner emerged from his office.

"Charlie, it's good to see you!" he beamed. "How are you feeling?"

"Antsy," I laughed. "I'm so ready to get back in the water."

"Well, we're going to take it easy today to play it safe, but I'm glad you're feeling better."

I attempted to stifle a groan. "Does that mean Ellie is going to be giving me my workout?"

"At least for today, yes." He nodded. "We'll see how it goes before I decide what to do with you for the next few practices."

Since I knew complaining wasn't going to change anything, I decided to keep quiet. Putting my swim bag down on one of the benches, I began to pull out the gear I would need for the practice. Once I had everything where I wanted it, I continued to loosen up my muscles so I would be ready to go when we got started.

After a few minutes, Ellie entered through the side door, her nose buried in her phone.

"Morning, Ellie," I said when she was near me.

She looked up from her phone and gave a small smile to acknowledge me but didn't say anything as she kept typing away.

"Coach Tanner said you'd be giving me my workout today," I said, attempting to make conversation.

She looked up at me again. "Oh, he didn't tell me that. It makes sense though since it's your first day back. How's your head feeling?"

"Better." I nodded. "I'm ready to get back in."

"Good, I'm glad." She looked back to her phone, and I assumed that meant our conversation was over. She seemed a little distracted by whatever she was looking at.

Instead of pushing for more I let her be and continued to stretch. I wasn't sure how much more stretching I really needed at this point, but at least I'd be good and loosened up for the warmup.

A few minutes later, Brody and Landon came meandering out of the locker room, deep in conversation. When they reached us, I gave Landon a big hug.

"Hey, happy birthday, Landon!" I told him. "I didn't get a chance to tell you before I left this morning."

He beamed. "Thanks, Charlie."

"I didn't know it was your birthday," Ellie said from her seat.

"It sure is! We've got another *adult* in the house now!" Brody grasped Landon's shoulders in both hands and gave him a quick shake. "We should go register to vote, or buy some lottery tickets to celebrate later," he laughed.

"Happy birthday, Landon." Ellie stood up and gave him an awkward hug.

His face turned a deep shade of red and he couldn't hide the smile on his face if he tried. "Thank you."

"Is there anything you want to do for your birthday?" I asked. "We can take you out to eat if you want? We can get the whole team to go."

Landon nodded. "That sounds great."

"What about Matthew's?" Brody suggested.

"Who's Matthew?" Ellie asked, confused.

"Matthew's restaurant," Brody laughed. "It's a pretty fancy place. It's expensive, but the food is good. Charlie and I went there before Christmas for a special dinner."

"It's worth the money, if you ask me," I said.

Just then, Allison came bounding out of the locker room and ran right up to Landon and scooped him up in a big hug. "Happy birthday, Landon!" She picked him up off the floor and spun him around a few times.

"Thank you, Allison," he laughed. His face turned a million more shades of red, but you could tell he liked the attention.

"Do you already have plans?" she asked when she had set him down.

"We were just suggesting we go to Matthew's tonight," I repeated.

"Oh, that would be perfect!" Allison beamed. "It's not every day you turn eighteen. Matthew's would be the perfect place to celebrate. Has someone already made a reservation? I can do that after practice."

"What are we making reservations for?" Coach Tanner asked as he re-approached the group.

"Landon's birthday dinner," I told him. "We're going to Matthew's. You should come along."

"I'd love to." He nodded. "Happy birthday, Landon."

"Thanks, Coach." He smiled.

"Alright, let's get this celebration started, shall we?" He slapped his hands together. "I've got a special practice for the birthday boy today."

We all groaned collectively, knowing if Coach said he had a "special" or "fun" practice, it was probably going to be a killer.

He threw his head back and laughed. "Ah, I love the sound of excited swimmers in the morning." He rattled off a short warmup for Allison, Landon, and Brody, and then turned to me and Ellie. "Here you go," he said, handing Ellie my workout. "Keep track of her splits during those 50s. Charlie, I do want you to work them, but please don't push yourself if you start feeling ill."

I nodded. "Got it."

Grabbing my bag and hauling it to my lane, I pulled my things out and set them on the pool deck. Ellie wandered over with me and told me my warmup. She avoided eye contact as she spoke, and once she had finished, she walked back to the bench before I could say anything.

She was usually pretty quiet, but she felt more distant this morning. She still seemed distracted, and I silently wondered if it had anything to do with what she had been doing on her phone earlier. Then again, maybe she was just tired and needed a little more time to wake up. Either way, I didn't feel the need to bother her about it.

However, when Ellie stayed quiet during the entire workout, I started to worry that something really was bothering her. I guess I had never worked with her one on one in the pool before, but she was acting different than she had when we went through the weight circuit last week.

She simply sat cross-legged on the pool deck next to my lane and rolled off the next set as I worked my way through them. She didn't offer any advice or words of encouragement like she had before. Instead, she just kept track of my splits as Coach Tanner had asked, and made no other effort at conversation.

When things hadn't improved by the time the workout was over, I decided I had to say something and make sure she was okay.

Once I had exited the pool, I made my way over to her. "Ellie?" I said to get her attention. When she looked up, I continued. "Everything okay? You've been awfully quiet this morning."

"Oh." She glanced at the floor again. "I guess I just have a lot on my mind."

"Do you want to talk about it?" I offered.

"No." She shook her head and looked back down at the workout sheet in her hands and continued to scribble a few notes on it.

"I know I always feel better when I talk about it. I won't judge remember?" I gave her a small smile.

She finally looked back up and gave me a tight grin. "Fine. I, uh … didn't do well on a test. Algebra. My last algebra test."

"Well, that would probably put me in a bad mood as well."

"Yeah," she agreed. "So, just thinking about how I could do better is all."

"I could help you if you want?" I offered. I wasn't the best person at math, but I had to take college algebra as well, and I did okay. I figured I could offer my services if she wanted it.

She hesitated for a moment, but then smiled at me. "Okay. Can I come over this weekend? I think I remember Landon saying he had a math test coming up as well. We could all work on it together."

"Yeah, sure." I nodded. "That sounds like a plan." I picked up all my equipment and started loading it back into my bag as Ellie took a seat on the bench beside me. She went back to looking through her phone, but I couldn't deny her mood had definitely shifted. There was a hint of a smile playing on her lips and she seemed more perky than she had only a few minutes earlier.

When I had my bag put back together, I threw it over my shoulder and turned towards the locker room. "Shall we get ready for the lifting session?"

"Right behind you." She finished typing something on her phone and stuck it back in her purse before joining me on the walk to the locker room.

"So, Ellie, I couldn't help but notice that you've been spending a lot more time talking to Landon," I said, a hint of hope in my voice. "And you've been coming over an awful lot. Is there anything—"

"We're just friends, Charlie." She smiled, but she didn't meet my gaze.

"No, I know," I said quickly. "I just thought maybe since you were spending a lot of time with him, and he just turned eighteen, maybe …"

"I'm not changing my mind," she said abruptly, finally meeting my gaze. "Landon and I talked about what our professional relationship is going to be as well as our friendship. I made it clear to him that we would not be dating, and he seems cool with it."

"Oh—okay," I said. "He didn't tell me that."

She shrugged. "Which is why I'm telling you now. Landon and I can be friends without the expectation that we are going to start dating."

"You're right," I agreed, feeling bad for having suggested it again. "I'm sorry. I know how much he likes you, and all I want is for him to be happy."

"Which is great, and I'm flattered that he likes me, but I don't feel the same way. He might be upset about that for now, but he'll find someone else. I still look forward to being his friend."

I nodded, knowing she was right. At least she was honest with him, I would give her credit for that.

"Anyway, I better hurry up and get changed for the lifting session," I said, wanting to change the subject. "I hear the coaching assistant can be a real slave driver."

She burst out laughing. "She might be willing to cut you a break this time!"

******

"Hey, guys," I said to Ellie and Landon as I walked into the house after work. "Are you ready to go? I've got to change quick, and we can take off."

Landon stood from the couch, wearing black dress pants and a green button-down shirt. "I think we're ready. Brody had a meeting with his manager but should be home soon. We can take off when he gets here."

"Okay, sounds good." I looked over to Ellie, who was wearing a simple black dress that went down to her knees. Her blonde hair was tied up on top of her head, and she had large hoops dangling from her ears. "You look lovely, Ellie."

She gave me a small smile. "Thank you."

"Would you want to come upstairs and help me decide what I should wear?" I asked.

She nodded. "Okay, sure."

When we entered the bedroom, I set my purse down on the dresser and went for my jewelry box. "I know I want to wear this pendant." I dug around inside the box looking for the necklace Brody had given me for Christmas, but I couldn't find it. "What the heck?" I mumbled to myself when I had taken every piece out of the box, but still didn't see the pendant.

"Which one?" Ellie asked, apparently not noticing my confusion. "Is it one of these?" She pointed to the fistful of jewelry I had taken from the box.

"No, it's not in here." Frowning, I scanned the top of my dresser and opened other drawers in case it had been moved. "Brody got it for me. It's a big two-carat diamond solitaire necklace. I haven't had a chance to even wear it yet."

"It has to be around here somewhere," she said. "I can help you look."

I waved it off. "No, I'll look for it later. We don't have a lot of time. I'll just wear this one." I picked the pear-shaped sterling silver pendant my mom had given me instead. "Alright, now a dress." Entering my closet, I took out an olive-green flowy dress with thin straps, and a skin-tight navy-blue cocktail dress. "Which do you like better?"

"Definitely the green one," she said, pointing to it. "I think green is your color."

I smiled. "I was kind of leaning towards that one, too."

Ellie took a seat on the edge of the bed and looked around the room. "You guys have a really nice house, and this bedroom is huge."

"Thank you," I said. "It's a lot cleaner now that Landon and I live here. Brody is kind of messy. Love the guy, but his cleaning skills need some work."

She laughed. "Yeah, that's what Landon told me."

I went back inside the closet to hang up the blue dress. "So, I've never really asked you," I called to her from in my closet. "Are you liking the coaching position?" I wandered back out to the bedroom. "Can you see yourself doing something like that as a career?"

"Yeah, I think so." She smiled. "I still have a lot to learn, though. I'm not sure how Coach Tanner comes up with such rigorous and effective workouts."

"I think that's a mystery to all of us," I laughed.

A moment later, I heard Brody's footsteps on the stairs.

"Hey, I'll be ready in five, I promise," he said when he had entered the room. He did a double take when he noticed Ellie was also in our room. "Oh, hey Ellie. I didn't expect you to be in here."

"She helped me pick out a dress for tonight." I held up the green dress for him to see.

Ellie stood from the bed. "I'll step out and let you two get ready." She closed the door behind her when she left the room.

Brody pointed to the door with a huge grin on his face. "So, y'all are getting pretty close, huh?"

I nodded. "She's a very nice girl. Although she did tell me this afternoon that she told Landon there was no future for the two of them. Has Landon said anything to you?"

He shook his head. "No, he hasn't. He seems okay though. Maybe he's gotten over it."

Although I doubted he had gotten over it that quickly, maybe Brody was right. But unless Landon came to me about it, I was going to mind my own business. I didn't want to overstep my boundaries any more than I already had. I turned to go back into the closet to change into my dress when a pair of muscular arms wrapped around my middle and spun me around.

"I never asked you how your first day back was," he said tenderly, kissing me on the forehead where my stitches had been. "How do you feel?"

"Good." I nodded, wrapping my arms around his neck. "I was starting to get a bit of a headache at work this afternoon, but I think it was probably because I was on the computer so long."

"Don't be afraid to ease back into work. I'm sure Allison wouldn't mind covering for you."

"I'm sure she wouldn't either, but I'm fine. I promise." I pulled him closer to me, knowing I needed to get ready, but also just wanting to stay in his arms as long as possible. "How was your meeting? Was it about your side project?"

"Side project?" He tried to hide a smile. "I don't know what you're talking about."

"Oh, come on!" I pressed. "I've tried not to bother you too much about it, but I'm dying to know what it is. Landon thinks you're planning a big romantic gesture."

Brody laughed. "Does he now?"

"What is it? Tell me!"

He kissed me on my lips. "Well, I hate to tell you, but Landon is wrong." He kissed me again. "I don't want to burst your bubble, but I also don't want you to get your hopes up on that. I'll tell you soon enough."

I stuck my lip out and pouted. "Fine, if you have to be that way," I teased. "I was just getting really excited about the thought of making out with you on a fancy beach somewhere."

"Oh, were you now?" he growled, wrapping his arms even tighter around my waist. "We don't need the beach for that." He gave me a sly grin before crashing his lips onto mine once more.

I opened my mouth for him as his tongue swirled with mine. His fingers started working at the hem of my blouse when I suddenly remembered we had somewhere to be, and I reluctantly pulled away.

"We are going to be late for Landon's birthday dinner if we don't get moving," I breathed.

"Hang on, I'm not done kissing you yet." He wrapped his arms around me again, and practically tackled me onto the bed where we fell into a fit of giggles as he attempted to kiss every inch of my face.

"Brody!" I protested, despite my laughter.

"Okay, okay." He finally rolled off me and allowed me to stand. "Gosh, Charlie, quit messing around. We have a birthday dinner to get to."

I gave him a playful smack on the shoulder, then went into the closet to pull on my dress. I decided to wear some strappy black heels with the olive dress and pulled my hair into a high pony.

"Is this dress new?" Brody asked when he saw me. He came up behind me as I applied the finishing touches to my hair and ran his hands over my curves. "Damn, I like it."

"Well, you clean up pretty nice yourself," I said, turning around to face him. He was wearing a pair of slim fitting black dress pants and a white button down. I watched as his eyes did a full sweep of my body.

He took a step closer to me and placed his hands on my lower back, pulling me in tight. "You think Landon will believe us if we suddenly fell sick and couldn't go?"

Laughing, I shook my head. "No, he won't believe us."

"Well then, I can't wait until we get back home," he whispered.

I gave him a quick kiss but didn't allow anything more than that. If I did, then we really would be late. "Oh, did you put my necklace somewhere?" I asked, remembering it was gone. "The one you got me for Christmas. It's not in my box where I left it."

"Are you sure that's where you had put it?" he asked.

"Yes, I'm certain."

"It probably just got lost in the clutter," Brody suggested. "Your dresser is pretty messy."

"Oh, *I'm* the messy one, am I?"

"You know I tease." He smiled. "We can look for it when we get home." He turned for the door, but then stopped in his tracks as if he had remembered something. "Oh, I almost forgot to tell you." He turned to face me, the smile that was on his face a moment ago was now gone. Instead, he looked serious and maybe even a little worried. "The shop called me this afternoon. They found out what happened to my truck."

"What's that?" I asked, trying to read his expression.

"It wasn't a freak thing, the brakes not working. They found evidence that the brake lines had been cut."

I felt like I was going to be sick. "What?"

"The truck had been tampered with. Someone was trying to hurt us."

"But my brake lines hadn't been cut. Is someone after you, specifically? Who would do that?"

He shrugged. "I don't know. Chase, maybe?" Chase used to be Brody's best friend growing up, and was the reason he found himself in so much trouble in the past. They had a falling out last summer after Brody met me and they didn't leave things on the best of terms.

I shook my head. "It's been months since you've last seen or talked to him. Why would he try to do something now?"

"I don't know." He chewed on his lip and stared into space as if he was deep in thought. Finally, he met my gaze again. "You don't think it could have been Mr. Davis, do you?"

My stomach dropped. Brody had been worried about Mr. Davis wanting to seek revenge now that he was out of prison. And while it could be possible it had been him, there were some things that didn't add up.

"But if it was Mr. Davis wanting revenge, why wouldn't he have cut my brakes, too? Wouldn't he want to get revenge on all of us?"

He shook his head. "I don't know." He took his hand in mine. "But let's go, we don't need to keep the others waiting any longer. We'll talk about it later tonight."

"How am I supposed to enjoy the evening now, knowing someone might be after you?"

He leaned in and kissed me softly. "I'm sorry. I should have waited to say something."

"No, I'm glad you told me. I just wish it wasn't something we had to deal with."

"Are you going to be okay to go to dinner?"

"Yeah, I think so." I took a deep breath. "Let's go."

******

By the time we arrived at the restaurant, Allison and Coach Tanner had already been seated and were waiting for us. Coach Tanner waved to us as we approached.

"I was starting to wonder if you had forgotten!" Allison joked when she saw us. She was dressed in a flowy yellow cocktail dress with sleeves that fell to her elbows.

"Sorry, it was a hectic day at work." I plastered a smile on my face, pushing the thought of Brody's truck to the back of my mind so I could enjoy the evening. "I love your dress, by the way."

"Thanks! Got it at that new little boutique on Main Street."

Coach Tanner was dressed in a sports jacket and khakis, which was a total 180 from his usual t-shirts and jeans.

"Coach, you clean up nice," Brody said when he sat down.

"Well, this is a special occasion, I need to dress appropriately. Happy birthday again, Landon." He raised his water glass in the air before taking a sip.

"Thank you," Landon said with a smile. "And thank you everybody else for celebrating with me. You guys are the closest thing to family I have, and I wouldn't want to spend my birthday with anyone else."

"Aw, Landon, you're going to make me cry," Allison pouted. She raised her water glass in the air as well. "To Landon!"

We all followed suit and then fell silent as we all began perusing the menu. After a couple of minutes, our server came to take our orders and then we fell into casual conversation.

"So, Brody, do you think it's time to share your exciting news?" Coach Tanner asked after we had been talking for a while.

We all turned to face Brody at the same time.

I perked up in my seat. "Your special project?"

"It hasn't been officially announced yet," Brody said to Coach Tanner. "Shouldn't I wait?"

Coach waved his hand through the air. "It'll be announced on the news tonight. I think your friends can keep a secret until then."

"Alright." Brody placed his hands together and set them on the table in front of him. He took a deep breath before he continued. "Well, I've had something in the works for a while, and I'm excited to announce that I'll be partnering with the non-profit Children Without a Voice USA, by putting on an annual fundraiser here in Florida."

I put my hand to my chest as warmth filled my heart. "Brody, that's even more amazing than I imagined! I can see now why you wanted to keep it a secret."

He smiled. "I'm sorry I didn't tell you sooner, but I didn't want to say anything until I knew for sure it was going to happen."

I leaned over and gave him a peck on the cheek. "It's okay. I totally understand. I'm so proud of you."

"What do they do?" Ellie asked. "And what's the fundraiser?"

"They advocate for children in the US that are victims of child abuse." Brody looked to Landon. "I wanted the news story to break today specifically so I could tell you on your birthday. You were the inspiration behind it. I hope you like it."

Landon's eyes had filled with tears, and he quickly tried to wipe them away when everyone looked at him. "Thank you," he managed to choke out. "I do."

Ellie gave him a pat on the shoulder to comfort him, and Allison offered him a tissue which he accepted.

"Anyway, the fundraiser will be a gala held at the Omni Amelia Island Resort in Fernandina Beach. It'll be next month, and the plan is to invite as many professional athletes as I can. Obviously, they won't be the only ones invited. Tickets will be available for $250 apiece for anyone who would like to give to a great cause and have a wonderful evening. There will be music, dancing, a silent and live auction, and tons of good food and drinks."

"Brody, that's truly amazing," Allison said. "Think of the difference you can make."

"Exactly what I told him, too," Coach Tanner said. "I think we need some champagne to celebrate." He raised his hand in the air to get a server's attention. "Can we get a round of champagne for the table please? And two sparkling ciders for those two." He pointed to Landon and Ellie.

The waiter nodded and left to fetch us our drinks.

"I think I'm going to run to the bathroom quick," Allison said, standing up from her seat. "Don't toast without me!" She darted off to the lady's room and was soon out of view.

"I think I'm going to go as well," Ellie chimed in a moment after Allison had left. "I'll make it quick, I promise!"

While we waited for the two of them to return, Brody continued with a few more details on what the fundraiser would all entail. There'd be a band and dancing, top chefs would be cooking a lineup of gourmet meals, and there would be tons of opportunities to bid on some pretty cool donations.

Sometime while he was speaking, the server returned with a champagne flute for each of us. Allison had also returned, and we were now waiting on Ellie before we started our toasts.

Several more minutes passed by before we finally saw Ellie making her way back to the table.

"Sorry!" she said, taking her seat. "There was a line."

"I must have hit it at the right time," Allison said. "There was no line when I was in there."

"Shall we raise our glasses?" Coach Tanner raised his glass high into the air, followed by everyone else. "Here's to Brody, for helping to make a difference in the world."

"And here's to Landon!" Brody added. "For being one of the coolest people I know. Happy birthday!"

"To Brody and Landon!" We all clinked our glasses and sipped on champagne.

Soon after, our food was brought to the table, and we were eager to dig in.

"That looks really good," I said, leaning over to Brody. "What kind of pasta did you get?"

"Pasta Radiatori." He shrugged, swallowing a forkful. "I don't know, it had beef in it."

I laughed. "Well, it looks good."

Brody continued to talk more about the fundraiser while we ate. "I'm definitely not going to limit it to just professional swimmers. I'm opening up the invite to all realms of sports. The owner of the Jacksonville Jaguars has already expressed interest." He wiped his brow with his napkin.

"Do you need any help?" Landon offered. "This sounds so cool. I'd love to be involved if I can."

Brody coughed. "I'll have to see where I can use you, but I'm sure we can come up with something." Sweat beads were forming on his forehead and he coughed a few more times.

Starting to get concerned, I set down my fork and placed a hand on Brody's shoulder. "Are you okay? You're sweating an awful lot."

"Your face is as red as a tomato," Coach Tanner added, a worried look on his face as well.

Brody shook his head. "It's just a little spicy. I'm fine."

"Didn't we get the same thing?" Allison asked. "Mine isn't spicy."

I leaned over to inspect his plate. "Did they put oregano in it? Did you tell them you're allergic?" He was always good about mentioning it to the servers when we went out to eat, and I was almost certain he had said something tonight, too.

He nodded and covered his mouth to cough again. "Yes, I always tell them."

I flagged down our server, and he rushed to the table. "Is there oregano in the pasta?" I asked him. "He had asked for no oregano. He's very allergic."

The young server's eyes went wide in panic. "I'm almost certain I put a note on the ticket to not add oregano. Did I mix up your plates?" He pointed to Allison.

Brody started coughing more violently, scooting his chair back from the table so he wouldn't cough all over the food. "Charlie, I think my tongue is swelling."

"Oh my, God." I rubbed his back and tried like crazy to stay calm. "Call 911!" I told the server. "Allison, check the plate to see if there's oregano in there."

"Does he have an EpiPen or something?" Landon asked, getting up and standing on the other side of Brody.

I shook my head, no. "Brody, it'll be okay, just focus on breathing."

"There's definitely oregano in here," Allison said. "We need to get him to a hospital, now."

"The ambulance is on the way!" The server reappeared at our table. "I'm so sorry."

"Come on, Brody, let's lie down." Coach Tanner got up and helped me lower him to the ground. "Roll him on his side in case he throws up."

Brody's eyes were now closed, and his breathing was so heavy, you could see his chest rising and falling with each ragged breath. I held on to his hand tightly and tears pricked at the back of my eyes.

"It'll be okay, Brody. Help is coming."

A couple of servers went about moving other diners who had been seated near us so we would have some space. Obviously, everyone knew it was Brody Hayes who was lying on the ground, so Landon and Allison stood guard to drive off anyone who was trying to take a picture or crowd us. Ellie sat still at the table, her eyes wide and her face white.

A few painstakingly slow minutes later, a couple of medics came running up to us with a stretcher. They quickly assessed the situation, and with record speed, had Brody loaded up on the gurney.

"His pulse is very low," the female medic with short, blonde hair said. "Let's get him in the ambulance and monitor him. Be ready to start CPR." They started to push him away and I yelled after them.

"Can I please come with? I'm his girlfriend, I need to be with him," I pleaded.

They may have agreed just to avoid an argument, but they agreed nonetheless, and I jumped into the back of the ambulance with them, leaving the others behind. As soon as we were in the vehicle, they started hooking Brody up to several machines. The female medic thrust an EpiPen into his thigh, the sight of which made me cringe.

When Brody had told me he was allergic to oregano, I asked him why he didn't carry an EpiPen with him. He told me it had been so long since his last reaction that he didn't feel like he needed to. Well, today changed that. I'd be going to get some myself if I had to.

"He's not breathing, start CPR!" A male medic yelled.

The female jumped onto the stretcher and ripped Brody's shirt open to start chest compressions. I immediately started sobbing and buried my face in my hands. I couldn't stand to watch. I listened and prayed that the love of my life would make it through.

Chapter Eleven

Mr. Davis

A week after I left the prison, I was still stuck in the tiny apartment with nowhere to go and still no idea how I was going to get Grimaldo's money. Jellybean stopped by every couple of days to drop off food and give me an update on things, but even she hadn't come up with a good plan yet. Luckily, Grimaldo hadn't called us yet for an update, but we both knew it was only a matter of time.

Sighing, I flipped through the television channels, hoping something would inspire me and give me an idea of how I could get out of this mess.

While I was flipping, I thought about my son, Landon. Today was his eighteenth birthday. I knew he'd been looking forward to this day for a long time, and truth be told, so was I. It's not that I hated the kid, it was just that every time I looked at him, I was reminded of his mother, and how it had been my fault she died.

I loved that woman more than life itself, and all I wanted was to give our family a good life. But growing up in the Codicia cartel gave me little chance to do so. My father—the corrupt bastard that he was—joined the drug operation when I was only twelve years old. He worked closely with Grimaldo when he first came into power, and that's how I eventually met Jellybean. By the time I had turned eighteen, I had little choice but to join the cartel as well. I was too involved and knew too much for them to let me go free.

Jellybean was born shortly before I officially became a member. I followed my dad's footsteps and worked closely with her father as well, and as cold and heartless as Grimaldo was, he had a soft spot for his children. She was always around whenever I met with him, and she almost always offered me a handful of jellybeans as a welcome gift—hence her nickname.

Anyway, I met my wife a few years into officially joining the cartel. She didn't realize I was a part of that life until quite some time after we had married, and when she finally found out, she threatened to leave me unless I found a way out of it. Landon was only five at the time. I started sniffing for ways to get out without putting my family in danger, and about a year later, nearly had a fool-proof plan together when I failed one of my assignments.

We were supposed to have been meeting with another cartel group to make peace and join efforts, but I had seriously misread the situation. It was a set up, and two dozen of our people were killed, nearly a dozen more arrested.

Grimaldo was furious, and as punishment, he had my wife executed. He told me Landon would be next if I messed up again. Obviously, I didn't want them to hurt Landon, but at the same time, I couldn't bear to be around him anymore. The guilt tore me apart, and every time I looked at him, I was reminded of what I had done.

Things got pretty messy the older Landon got. I drank to forget the pain, but it didn't help. And if I was going to be in pain, I made damn sure Landon would be, too.

It wasn't until I had started working with Camila—over a decade after my wife died—where things got *really* messy.

My burner phone rang at my side, jerking me back to the present. "What?" I barked into the phone.

"I'm sorry, is this a bad time?" Jellybean spat back. "Turn on the Channel 4 news. I think I know how to get us out of this."

I did what she said and saw a breaking news segment with the headline: *Brody Hayes, professional swimmer, hospitalized after severe allergic reaction.*

"Is this why you're calling?" I asked. "I know you want them gone, but I'd prefer that you focus on how we're going to get the money first."

"Shut up and keep watching," she snapped.

I listened as the female news caster continued:

"We hope to have more info on Brody's condition later this evening. Back to you, Brian."

"Thanks, Emily." A man—I assumed he was Brian—appeared back on the screen. "As we were saying before the breaking news, Brody Hayes has partnered with Children Without a Voice USA to host a gala later next month to raise funds for children affected by child abuse and neglect."

"That right there," Jellybean said. "That's how we're going to get the money. I believe your master computer hacking skills are going to come in handy once more. There's going to be an auction, and the place will be crawling with rich people who have money to burn."

It was as if a lightbulb went off in my head.

"We can make that work."

Chapter Twelve

Charlie

My body shook with sobs as I knelt on the ground a few yards away from Brody. I called his name and reached out for him, but he didn't move. His eyes stared unblinking at the dark sky above him, his lips were tinted blue, and his skin was ghost white.

"Revenge is so sweet!" A hooded figure cackled, standing over Brody's lifeless body. "You thought you could get away with murder? Think again."

"Brody!" I screamed his name once more. "Please don't leave me!"

The figure turned to face me as if it just realized I was there. I squinted in an attempt to see who it was, but in the dark, I couldn't see a face.

"Oh, Charlie," it said. The voice sounded female and eerily familiar. "You didn't really think you'd get away with killing me, now did you?"

What did she mean, get away with *killing* her?

She took a few slow steps in my direction as she continued, "This is what happens when you meddle in other people's business. You had to have known this was going to happen sooner or later."

Panic settled in my gut as she got closer and closer, now only an arm's reach in front of me. "Brody!" I continued to scream, even though it was useless.

The figure finally lifted her arms to her head and threw back her hood.

Camila.

Raising her right hand, she held a gun in front of her, the barrel aimed right between my eyes. "Any last words, Charlie?"

I screamed louder. I kept screaming until I realized someone was shaking me and my eyes shot open.

"Charlie, wake up!" Landon was standing over me, his hands on my shoulders, a look of concern etched on his face.

"Where am I?" I asked, my breaths coming hard and fast. I ran a hand through my hair and realized I was drenched in sweat.

"You're at home," Landon said. "It's almost noon. I only had half a day of school today and took the bus home. I came inside and heard you screaming."

"Shit, it was just a dream?" I asked. "It felt so real."

"Everything's fine. You're okay now," he said in a calming voice. He waited until my breathing had slowed before he continued. "Coach said we should all go visit Brody over the lunch hour. Are you going to swim this afternoon?"

"Yeah, I'll be there. What about you? I'm not sure you should be home alone this afternoon." There was still no news on the whereabouts of his father, and I didn't like the idea of him being unsupervised.

"I talked to Coach already, so I'll be swimming this afternoon as well."

"Oh, good," I breathed. "I'll get ready, and you can ride with me. Thanks for checking on me."

"No problem. Holler if you need anything. I'll be downstairs." He closed the door a crack on his way out.

Suddenly, the events from the night before came flooding back to me. Brody had been taken to the hospital, and they had to perform CPR on the way over. They didn't have to do it for long before the EpiPen they had stabbed him with kicked in, and he was able to breathe again. His breathing was still shaky, but his eyes were open by the time the ambulance had arrived at the hospital.

They took him back to a room, gave him some more medication, and before long, he was looking much better. The doctor said he was extremely lucky that we all acted as fast as we did. Any longer, and he might not have been able to pull through. They decided to keep him over night to monitor him, and even though I insisted on staying with him, he urged me to go home and get some rest.

Finally caving in, I got home a little after two in the morning. When I arrived, I saw Landon had fallen asleep on the couch with the TV on. Deciding not to wake him, I turned the TV off, placed a blanket over the top of him, and quietly made my way upstairs to get ready for bed.

I had texted everyone several times throughout the evening with updates on Brody's condition, and decided to send one more to everyone letting them know I was home and would be going back to the hospital tomorrow. Not expecting a response at that hour, I was surprised when Coach Tanner pinged back right away. He thanked me for being there with Brody and told me to skip the morning practice so I could get some rest. Even though part of me wanted to argue, another part of me was completely drained and just wanted to sleep, so I turned off all my alarms and slept through the morning workouts.

Even though Brody was going to be okay, I was certain the events from last night had prompted the Camila nightmare. Dr. Stevens had warned me that certain events could trigger more nightmares, but even so, the dream still left me feeling uneasy. I made a mental note to check in with her soon to discuss it.

Feeling sweaty and disgusting, I decided I needed to take a shower before going to see Brody. Taking a long, hot shower to help me relax, I felt much better afterwards. I threw a bag together for practice, and then Landon and I made our way to the hospital.

Allison was already there when we arrived, and she was having a light-hearted conversation with Brody, who was sitting up in his bed.

"Hey guys!" Allison chirped when she saw us. "Brody and I were just talking about the gala. I think we could nail down a few more invites at the swim meet next weekend."

I nodded in agreement. "I think you're right. They'll be plenty of people there who I'm sure would love to come." I approached Brody's bed and took his hand in mine. "How are you feeling?"

"Better." He gave my hand a squeeze. "My chest hurts like a bitch though."

I winced. "I'm sure it's going to for a while."

Unfortunately, the medics had cracked one of Brody's ribs last night when performing CPR. His doctor said it was pretty common, since they have to apply so much pressure, but what's one cracked rib if you can live to see another day?

"You think you'll get to go home today?" Landon asked. He took a seat in a chair next to Allison.

Brody shrugged. "I think so, but who knows?"

A knock came from the door and all of us turned to look at the same time. Brody's doctor, Dr. Ray, stood in the doorway with a smile. "Hope I'm not interrupting anything. Mind if I come in?"

Brody nodded and waved him in. Dr. Ray was an older gentleman, with graying hair and round wire-rimmed glasses. He had the build of an avid runner and was in pretty decent shape for someone in his mid-sixties.

"I have good news and bad news," he said when he had reached Brody's bed. "Good news is that we are going to release you from the hospital this afternoon. Everything is looking good, and I'm confident we won't have any reoccurring symptoms."

"So, what's the bad news?" Brody asked.

"The bad news is that I must insist you stay out of the water and limit your physical activity for at least two weeks to let that bone heal." He pointed to Brody's chest.

"Dammit, Doc," he cursed. "I literally just got cleared from the last injury. I'm going to start losing sponsors if I'm out of competition much longer. They were counting on me competing in our home meet next weekend."

Dr. Ray shrugged one shoulder. "I'm sorry, Brody. But unless you don't want that bone to heal properly, you need to take it easy. We'll bring you back in a couple of weeks and re-assess." He went over a couple of other details with Brody, and then quietly left the room.

Not long after he was gone, Coach Tanner came strolling in. "Just talked to your doctor, Brody. He told me what he told you."

Brody still sat up in bed, but his arms were now crossed over his chest and his head rolled back as he stared at the ceiling in frustration. "You couldn't have told him how much I need to keep swimming? Especially after all the time off I've had. I'm going to have sponsors pulling out left and right."

"No, you're not," Coach Tanner said, shaking his head. "And if they do, do you really want them sponsoring you anyway? It's not like you're purposefully getting yourself into trouble anymore. It was an unfortunate accident. They need to understand that."

"Even if they don't, my times are going to go to shit because I can't swim," he rolled off another excuse. "My career will be over."

Coach Tanner shook his head again. "Brody, you need to relax. It's two weeks. We'll get you whipped back into shape in no time."

"But—"

"No buts!" Coach Tanner held his palms up. "I'm sorry, Brody, but your doctor is right. You need to let your body heal. I also wish you didn't have to take more time off. And I *really* wish my swimmers would quit finding their way into the hospital every other week." He sighed and then patted my shoulder. "Charlie, how are you feeling?"

"Just tired." I nodded. "I'll be at the pool this afternoon."

"Excellent, I've got a pretty good workout planned for you."

"Was Ellie going to stop by?" I asked.

"No, she had a study session over lunch today that she had already agreed to," Coach Tanner said. "I told her it was fine if she wasn't able to stop over here."

We continued to chat for a while before Brody said he was tired and was going to get some rest before they released him. All the others filed out of the room, but I stayed back for a moment.

"I had another Camila nightmare," I told Brody when we were alone.

He sat up partially so he could look me in the eye. "Last night?"

"Well, this morning, but yeah." I rested my hand on his shoulder, urging him to lie back down. "Do you think it means anything? It just seems crazy that it happened the same night you almost … died."

He shook his head and took my hand in his. "No, I don't think it means anything. Camila is dead. She had absolutely nothing to do with what happened last night. It was an unfortunate mistake, and the dream is just a coincidence. You said yourself that certain events can trigger the nightmares."

I lowered my gaze and ran my tongue over my bottom lip. "Yeah, you're probably right. I think maybe I need to reach out to Dr. Stevens though."

"If that's what you think you need, then I will support you," he said. "If for no other reason than to tell her you're having the dreams again. Maybe she has some more ideas on how to combat them."

I nodded and leaned down to give him a kiss on the forehead before turning to leave the room. "Call me when you're released. I'm going to go into work after practice, but I can give you a ride home if you need."

He gave me a thumbs up. "I'll let you know."

Leaving the hospital room, I saw Landon waiting for me a few feet down the hall. We walked to the car in silence and were soon on our way to the pool for practice.

The workout went by slowly. I tried to focus all my energy on the set of 200s Coach had us doing, but the events from last night and this morning kept creeping back into my mind. I knew it sounded crazy, but for the life of me, I could not shake the feeling that the dream and Brody's allergic reaction was more than just a crazy coincidence.

There was *no way* Brody had forgotten to tell the server last night about his allergy. He always mentioned it. A part of me was worried it hadn't been an accident. Especially when I remembered what Brody had told me about his truck before we left for the restaurant.

Was it possible someone had added it on purpose? This was the second time in less than a week that Brody had escaped death. Even though I had taken the fall last time, it was clear Brody had been the intended target. These couldn't be mere coincidences.

The thought of Mr. Davis wanting revenge came to mind again. I suppose it could have been possible he had made his way to our neighborhood to tamper with the truck, but he wouldn't have risked being seen in a public restaurant. Would he? It didn't make sense.

Not wanting to give the idea any more consideration, I kicked my pace up a few notches. Maybe if I wore myself out enough, I wouldn't be able to focus on anything else.

I blew the rest of the practice out of the water. Coach was giving us some pretty quick intervals to begin with, and I was consistently beating them by more than ten seconds each. I was so tired between each 200, that I spent the whole rest period sucking in huge gulps of air before diving into the next one. By the time practice was over, I was thoroughly exhausted. The only thing I could do was crawl out of the water and lie on the ground.

"Now that's a sign of working hard!" Coach Tanner chuckled when he saw me sprawled on the pool deck. "I was starting to wonder if those intervals were too easy for you."

I shook my head and closed my eyes. "No, it wasn't too easy. I just have some frustration to work out."

"I totally understand." His voice changed from playful to serious. "Sounds like Brody is going to be okay though. He texted me a few minutes ago, he's officially been released from the hospital."

"Did he say if he needs a ride?" I asked, opening my eyes.

"I told him I'd go get him and take him home. I know you have to go to work this afternoon."

"Are you sure? I don't mind."

He nodded. "I'm sure. Take it easy, Charlie. I'll see you in the morning."

I gave him a tight smile as he turned and made his way to the exit. Before I had the chance to stand up, Ellie appeared next to me.

"Hey, Charlie, how's it going?" she asked.

"It's going. Where have you been?" I hadn't noticed her on deck during practice, and it just occurred to me that she hadn't been there.

"I was in Coach Tanner's office." She pointed to his now closed door. "He had me filing some paperwork this afternoon."

I nodded, but I didn't say anything further. I didn't want to be rude, but I wasn't really in the mood for chit chat right now.

"Coach said Brody is doing better," she continued, clearly not reading my mood.

Letting out a deep sigh, I slowly sat up. "Yeah, he just left to pick him up. He won't be able to swim for a while though."

"That's probably okay, considering the alternative. Everyone was saying he should have died."

"He *could* have died," I corrected her.

Her eyes went large. "Yes, sorry! I didn't mean—"

I held up my hand. "I know you didn't mean it." Working my way to my feet, I picked up my swim gear and slowly started towards the locker room. My legs felt heavy with fatigue, and I already knew I'd be sleeping well tonight. "Hate to rush off, but I need to get ready for work."

"Of course," she said. "See you tonight?"

"Are you coming over again?" As soon as I said it, I regretted it. Even I could tell it came out a little rude, so I tried to play it off. "I mean, you're welcome over anytime. Did Landon invite you to hang out?"

"Yeah." She nodded. "I figured it would be a pretty lowkey evening with Brody coming home. If there's anything I can bring, just let me know."

"I appreciate that. I'll keep you posted." I turned towards the locker room again. "Anyway, I have to go. I'll see you tonight, then." I waved to her as I walked away.

"See you later." She turned and took a seat on a bench nearby. Pulling her notebook out of her purse, she started scribbling away, lost in her own world.

******

The gym was surprisingly quiet—even for a Friday afternoon—and I took the time to catch up on some paperwork. I tried anything and everything to keep myself busy, but a few hours into my shift, my mind started wandering back to my nightmare and Brody's accident. When I couldn't take it anymore, I finally cracked and decided to call Dr. Stevens.

"Hi, Charlie. How are you?" she asked when I had gotten through to her.

"I've been better." I let out a nervous laugh. "That's actually why I'm calling. I've been having nightmares again. I was wondering if I could make an appointment to come see you?"

"Of course. Let me check my availability." She was silent for a moment while she checked her calendar. "The earliest I can do is next Friday afternoon. Does that work for you?" she asked.

"That should work. I can get someone to cover me here at the office."

"Perfect, I'll pencil you in. If you have any more nightmares before our appointment, just remember the exercises we talked about."

I thanked her and hung up the phone. Determined to keep myself busy until quitting time, I opened up our payroll account to review any time off requests I had received. When there were no new requests, I was about to log out when something caught my eye. Under the recent activity, a withdrawal of fifteen hundred dollars had been made this morning around three o'clock.

Frowning, I clicked on the activity to see more info. *I certainly hadn't made a withdrawal that big, and I would have remembered approving someone else to take out that much money.* Scanning over the screen, I saw it was made out as a personal check to a Taylor Smith.

"Who the hell is Taylor Smith?" I said out loud as I continued to scan the screen. *Who approved this?* When I reached the bottom of the page, my hand flew to my mouth to stifle a gasp.

Mr. Davis had approved the transfer.

What the hell!

That means he would have been in the office and logged into his account. He was *here*. I stared wide-eyed at the screen as if that would make it go away.

It didn't.

Snapping myself out of it, I immediately picked up my phone and called the police. I quickly explained the situation to them, and they said a few officers would be there as soon as possible. When I had hung up the phone, I leaned my forehead against my desk to think.

Would Mr. Davis really risk getting caught to come into the gym? He knows we have cameras.

"Holy shit—the cameras." I bolted upright in my seat and pulled up our security camera software, but quickly realized our cameras had been disabled. After checking when they were last turned on, I wanted to scream.

Cameras disabled at 2:48 AM.

How convenient.

But how would he have even gotten in? The fob readers had been changed, and as far as I knew, Allison and I were the only ones who had a physical key. Had there been any signs of a break-in? No one had told me if there was.

I got up from my chair and marched out to the lobby where I found Allison leaning up against the counter talking to our front desk guy, Brandon.

"Hey, question for you two," I said, interrupting their conversation. "Was there any sign of a break-in when you got here today? Doors unlocked? Windows open?"

Allison stood a little straighter and frowned. "Not that I noticed. Why? Did something get taken?"

I nodded but didn't elaborate. "Did you see anything?" I asked Brandon.

"The back entrance was open," he said. "But there was also a delivery scheduled for this morning. I assumed someone had just left the door open for the protein bar guy."

"What time was the delivery?"

He shrugged. "I don't know. I got here at eleven, so sometime before then."

"Crap," I mumbled under my breath before turning back to them. "Okay, thanks." I turned on my heel and stormed back to my office.

"Charlie, hold up," Allison said, following me. "What's going on? What was taken?"

Ushering her into my office, I closed the door behind her. "I was checking the financial statements, and the log shows that Mr. Davis approved a withdrawal from our account at three o'clock this morning."

Her mouth dropped open. "Is that something he can do remotely, or does that mean he was *here*?"

"I would assume that meant he was here. We can't access the server off-site. But the cameras were disabled, so I can't be certain if it was him or someone who logged in as him."

"How much did he take?"

"Fifteen hundred dollars." I shook my head. "That's over a quarter of our monthly profit."

"Shit." She frowned, focusing on something on the far wall. Then her gaze darted back to mine. "So, why do you think he didn't clean house?" she asked. "I mean, if you're going to steal from your own business, why would you only take fifteen hundred?"

She did have a good point. Maybe I should be considering myself lucky he only took a portion of it.

"The only reason I can think of," she continued. "Is that maybe he thought if he only took some, it would take longer for us to notice. And then he could just come back in later and take more if he needed to."

"Maybe." I leaned against my desk and contemplated what she had said. Honestly, if I hadn't checked the time-off requests this afternoon, I probably wouldn't have noticed the money was gone until later.

A knock came at my office door, interrupting my thoughts. I signaled for Allison to open it, and Brandon stood there with two police officers behind him.

"Charlie," he said, leaning inside the doorway. "These officers are here to speak with you."

"Great, send them in."

"Good evening, ladies," the bigger of the two men said. "I'm Officer Johnson, and this is my partner, Officer Carter. We received a call about a burglary. We'll try to figure out what happened, but we need to ask each of you some questions first."

******

"Thank you, Ms. Price, that should be everything we need." Officer Johnson stood from his chair. "Right now, we can't say for certain that he was here in the building. We'll contact the patrons that signed in during the potential time frame, but since it was so early in the morning, I'm not positive we'll have many—if any—eyewitnesses. We'll also be in touch with the surrounding businesses to see if any of their cameras caught a glimpse of those coming and going at that time."

"Thank you for coming in, officers." I stood and shook their hands.

Officer Carter handed me a couple of business cards. "We have your info, and here are our cards if you need to get a hold of us sooner."

I thanked them again and walked them out of the building. Once they were out of sight, I turned around to go back to my office. Allison was leaning against the doorframe with her arms crossed and lips pursed.

"Now we just wait?" she asked.

I nodded. "Now we wait."

Chapter Thirteen

Brody

The week following my trip to the hospital dragged on terribly slow. I admit it was nice to sleep past five o'clock each morning, but I'd still rather be swimming.

If it wasn't for the upcoming fundraiser, I think I would have been terribly bored during this healing process. Luckily, there was still a lot of work to be done, and at least I had plenty of free time to focus on that. Especially with the upcoming home meet this weekend. I planned on meeting with a lot of potential donors to see if they were going to attend or not and needed to get all of my ducks in a row.

In the evenings, when Charlie and Landon—and usually Ellie and Allison, too—came home, I'd have plenty of time to spend with them before turning in for the night. We'd usually eat dinner together, watch a movie or talk about that day's practices, and sometimes we'd have to take turns helping Landon or Ellie with their homework. It truly felt like a little family unit, and I loved every second of it.

This evening, I was sitting on the couch fine-tuning some details for the gala while I was waiting for everyone to get home. The swim meet would kick off Saturday morning, which meant I only had a little over a day to finish preparing my pitch for potential attendees. For the most part, I wasn't too worried about it though. Word had traveled fast, and I already had several of my swim colleagues reach out and express interest. However, I knew there would be a few I'd have to convince, and I wanted my speech to be solid.

I was in the middle of scratching out a sentence when the front door opened, and Charlie came walking in. "Ugh, what a day," she huffed. "I think I'm ready for bed already."

"Tough practice, or did something happen at the gym?" I patted the couch cushion next to me and wrapped an arm around her when she sat down.

"Both." She leaned her head on my shoulder. "Practice was brutal. Eight 400 IMs. Then way too many 200s after that."

"Wow, that does sound rough." I chuckled, but was actually pretty disappointed I had missed it. That would have been a good workout.

"And then we had two more cardio machines take a shit at work today," she continued. "I'm basically rebuilding this place from the ground up. Mr. Davis clearly wasn't taking care of the place like I thought he was."

"Does that surprise you?" I asked.

"Not anymore, but if you had asked me a few months ago, then maybe." She fell silent while she fiddled with a loose thread on her work skirt. After a moment she adjusted her head on my shoulder so she could look me in the eye. "Have you heard anything new about Mr. Davis?"

"No, have you?"

She shook her head. "No. The police haven't even gotten back to me yet about the break in at Fit Happens. It's like he just vanished."

"I know. I have no idea what his plans are, but if he's been quiet this long, it worries me that he has something big planned."

"Do you think he's actually been quiet though?" she asked. She continued to play with the thread, avoiding my gaze. "What if he's behind these near-death experiences? We already have proof the truck was tampered with. What if he was somehow behind the incident at the restaurant as well?"

"Trust me, the thought has crossed my mind." I sighed. I took her hand in mine so she'd stop playing with her skirt. "I have no idea how he would have gotten in the restaurant without being seen though."

She made a face. "That's what's stumping me, too."

"Unless someone is helping him?"

"Who?" she asked, finally looking at me. Worry shined in her eyes. "Someone we know?"

I shrugged. "I honestly don't know, but someone obviously helped him escape. That same person could be helping him get revenge."

"What are we supposed to do? They're still out there. If they really are seeking revenge, it's only a matter of time before something happens again." The color had drained from her face, and she almost looked like she was going to be sick.

Shifting in my seat so I could face her better, I gave her hand a squeeze. "The police are looking for him. I can't say there's anything we can do that they aren't already trying. He can't hide forever, right? I'm confident they will find him soon."

"I get that, but what if they *do* try something again? When and where is it going to be? That's what's scaring me: the not knowing."

"It scares me, too." I admitted. "But life is too short to live in fear. For now, we need to keep living our lives normally, and try to prove to him that we aren't afraid of whatever he has planned."

"Easier said than done." She rested her head on my shoulder and let out a long, heavy sigh. She absentmindedly started playing with the string on her skirt with her other hand. Placing my other hand on top of it, I closed my fingers around hers to bring attention to the nervous habit she had started.

Sitting up and shaking her head, she let out another frustrated sigh before standing from the couch. "Anyway, what should we do for dinner? Landon won't be home from practice for at least another hour, but I don't think I can wait. I'm starving." She wandered into the kitchen, and I could hear her opening cupboards as she searched their contents.

"Why don't we go out?" I suggested. Gathering my gala notes into a single pile, I stood and followed her into the kitchen. "We haven't had a proper date night in a long time."

She made a sour face. "The last time we went out, you ended up in the hospital."

"So, are we going to let that stop us from ever going out to eat again?"

"I guess not." She shrugged. "Where do you want to go?"

A smile crept across my lips as an idea came to mind. "Let me make a few calls. I think I know the perfect place."

******

A short while later, I pulled the car into an empty parking spot at the Ortega River Marina. Charlie leaned forward in her seat to get a better look.

"Why are we stopping here?" she asked, clearly confused.

"I thought maybe we'd go for a sunset cruise." I smiled.

"A sunset cruise?" She laughed out loud. "Brody, it's February! The sun has already set and it's like fifty degrees."

"I told you to dress warm, didn't I?" I joked.

She looked down at the jeans and oversized green cardigan she wore. "Yeah, I guess you did."

"Besides, we'll be in the boat most of the time." I opened the car door and turned to get out. "It'll be fun."

Once we were both out of the car, I took her hand in mine and we walked down to the boat landing together. The docks were mostly empty this time of year, but at least a dozen boats still remained. Once I saw the boat we'd be boarding, I pointed it out to her.

"That's our boat?" she asked, her eyes wide in amazement.

"Well, it is for the evening." I gave her hand a squeeze.

The boat was even more beautiful than I had imagined. It was about forty feet long, and at least that tall. The main cabin was white, with wooden flooring stained a dark brown. My manager had a connection to the guy who owned the boat—he's the reason we were able to do this tonight—and he said there were three full-sized suites on board, each big enough to hold a queen-sized bed. The thing was massive, and tonight, it was all ours.

"You must be Brody!" A large man with a red beard stepped off the boat and extended his hand towards me. "My name's Greg, and I'll be your captain for this evening."

"Nice to meet you." I shook his hand and directed his attention to Charlie. "This is my girlfriend, Charlie."

She extended her hand and he brought it to his mouth to give it a kiss. "Pleasure to meet you, Charlie."

She blushed. "You as well, Greg."

"Now then!" He clapped his hands together. "Let me show you around and we can get on our way. Once we leave the dock, I'll be out of your hair."

Greg gave us a brief rundown of what to expect on our journey, and what to do in case of any emergencies. We glanced inside each of the suites, mostly out of curiosity since we would only be on board for a couple of hours. However, the rooms were lovely. Each was a pretty good size for being on a boat, and the beds looked very comfortable.

Finally, Greg led us to the main cabin where a dining table was fixed up with our dinner. Two chairs were placed on either side of the round table, both facing the front window, giving us a gorgeous view of the lights on the river.

"Tonight's meal is chicken piccata—with no oregano— and angel hair pasta, some steamed asparagus, and a side salad. There's champagne in the ice bucket, and over here—" he pointed to a table to the left of the table, "—is the dessert table. Please help yourself. I'll be up top if you need anything."

We thanked him and took a seat at the table. I opened the bottle of champagne and filled our glasses to the top. After I had returned the bottle to the ice bucket, I raised my glass to hers and we clinked glasses before taking a sip of the sweet liquid.

"Brody, this is wonderful," she said. Her eyes then darted to the window. "Oh, we're taking off!"

We watched as the boat slowly backed away from the dock and the light outside dimmed the further we pulled from shore. We both loaded our plates with food and dug in right away.

"So, do you know what you're going to be saying to the athletes this weekend about the gala?" she asked after taking a few bites.

I nodded and swallowed a piece of chicken before I spoke. "I think so. I've been going over my notes every day this week. I've nearly got the stuff memorized by now."

"That's good! See? There's at least one plus side to being out of the water all week."

"I guess." I shrugged. "I swear if I get hurt again though, I'm going to scream. I can't stand being out of the water this much. Especially since I've only got a few good years of swimming like this left."

"Oh, please, Brody, you're not even twenty-six yet," she said. "You've got at least five or six more years before you even need to *think* about retiring."

"Maybe. It's just hard to think about doing anything other than swimming, you know? It's been my entire life. I have no idea what I'm going to do when it's over."

"Well, what about coaching? Or are there any other jobs that interest you? You never went to college. You could get a degree in whatever you want. Expand your options."

I took a few more bites of chicken and thought about it. Honestly, I really didn't think there was anything else that interested me. I've always wanted to swim, and I was confident enough I would make it that I never had a backup option in mind. I suppose coaching wouldn't be a terrible option, but was there something better for me out there?

Our conversation from the other day suddenly popped into my head. Ever since we had talked about getting married and having kids someday, I thought about it a lot more frequently. I'd see engagement ring advertisements around every corner, and whenever I saw a couple with small kids, I pictured Charlie and me with our kids. The thought didn't scare me as much as it used to, and I truly did believe it was something I wanted.

"I've been thinking a lot lately about what it would be like to be a dad," I whispered, stealing a glance at Charlie to see her reaction.

She set her fork down and a smile danced on her lips. She reached across the table and took my hand in hers. "Brody, I wasn't lying when I said you'd make a wonderful father. I really meant that."

"I don't really think I ever thought about it growing up. And then when my parents died, I really didn't want to have a family and leave them open to that kind of heartbreak." I paused for a moment, trying to put the feelings I was having into words. Taking a deep breath, I continued. "I don't think I'm afraid of that anymore, though. When I look at you, Charlie, I know what I want: I want you in my life. I want to grow old together, have a family, and make memories that I've had to miss out on since my parents died."

"I want that, too." Her lips began to quiver.

"Are you going to cry?" I asked, suddenly worried I had overwhelmed her.

She wiped at her eyes before any tears could escape. "I'm sorry, they're happy tears," she chuckled. "It just makes me so happy to hear you say those words. A part of me was worried you were just giving in to what I wanted. But after hearing you say that I know you mean it. You want it, too."

"Trust me, on something that big, I would tell you if I didn't want it," I chuckled. "It's just that the more I think about it, the more I can see it. And I can't see it happening with anyone other than you."

Overcome with emotion, she stood from her chair, pulling me up with her and kissed me. Her arms circled my neck, drawing me closer to her. I combed my fingers through her hair as my lips ravaged hers, and desire shot straight to my groin. God, I wanted her.

I wonder if Greg would mind us using one of those suites …

Before I could voice my thoughts, Charlie pulled away from the kiss. "Do you hear that?" she asked.

"I don't hear anything." I tried to lean in and kiss her again, but she held her hand to my lips.

"I think there's music playing outside." She smiled and took my hand in hers once more. "Come on, let's go see!"

I reluctantly followed her, trying to calm my raging hard-on as we left the cabin. Once we were outside, we realized one of the restaurants that lined the shore had a live band playing Frank Sinatra covers.

"I love this song!" she squealed, clasping her hands together.

Smiling, I watched as her eyes closed and she let the music take over. She swayed back and forth and hummed along to the beat. Her excitement was infectious.

"Do you want to dance with me?" I asked, extending my hand to her.

She opened her eyes and smiled so wide I could see all of her teeth. "I would love to."

She accepted my hand, and I pulled her close, wrapping one arm around her waist. I wasn't much of a dancer, so I let her take the lead. Soon, we were both lost in the music, unable to take our eyes off each other. I briefly released my hold on her waist to smooth some of her hair behind her ear, and then I planted a soft kiss on her lips.

"This has been the most perfect evening," she said when our mouths had parted. "Thank you."

"Anything for you."

She smiled and then rested her head on my shoulder as we continued to dance along to the music. We danced until we could no longer hear the band playing, and even for a while after it had fallen silent. Eventually, hunger won us over and we ventured back inside to finish eating.

We polished off the champagne and cracked open another bottle. The food was delicious, and we practically licked our plates clean, even doing a fair amount of damage to the dessert table. Feeling full and slightly buzzed, we grabbed a bunch of blankets and pillows from one of the suites and lined them up in front of the window.

Cuddling in nice and close, we continued to talk about life, and made plans for our future family. She said she wanted three or four kids, and strangely, that didn't seem as scary to me as I would have thought. The idea of having a big family actually sounded exciting. Eventually, the conversation shifted to swimming and work, but I was listening to Charlie more than I was talking at that point. My mind kept going back to the idea of having a family again someday.

And honestly? All the stress from not being able to swim faded to the back of my mind. It still bothered me, sure, but not nearly as much as it did before.

For the first time—maybe ever—I wasn't so worried about what would happen when my swimming career was over. There was a life after swimming. It just took the right person to make me finally realize that.

Chapter Fourteen

Charlie

It felt like it had been a long wait, but it was finally Friday. I had my appointment with Dr. Stevens today, so I took the first part of the afternoon off work and left Allison in charge. The appointment probably wouldn't last longer than an hour, and Friday afternoons at the gym were usually slower anyway, so I wasn't too concerned that anything major would happen in my absence.

Things had been quieter in general since the police had stopped by. I *still* hadn't heard anything back from Officer Carter about the stolen funds, despite three phone calls asking for updates. Either there wasn't any news to share, or other cases took precedence. Regardless, I was watching the statements like a hawk. If anything else went missing, I'd know about it and alert the police straight away. The more evidence they had, the higher priority it would be—at least, that's what I hoped.

Shortly before two o'clock, I sat in the waiting room, scrolling through my email on my phone when Dr. Stevens stepped out of her office.

"Charlie, good to see you," she said with a smile.

Standing, I shook her hand. "Good to see you, too, Dr. Stevens."

"Come on in and we can get started." She turned and I followed her back into her office.

Dr. Stevens was a middle-aged African American woman with long, brown hair that was nearly as voluptuous as her figure. She was beautiful and smart, and I had a feeling she would sit down and listen to you pour your soul out even if she wasn't being paid to do so. She was simply an amazing woman.

"So, tell me what brings you in today." She took a seat at her usual chair and picked up a notepad and pencil. "You said you were having the nightmares again?"

I took a seat on the couch across from her and nodded. "Yes, I've had two more since I called you."

"Hmm, okay." She put on a pair of reading glasses and made a quick note on her pad. "What do you think is causing you to have these dreams again?"

"Well, I think I've been having more lately because Brody was hospitalized last week. I think it's the PTSD that has me freaking out again."

She nodded. "Yes, I do remember seeing that on the news. Is he doing okay now?"

"Yes, he's doing much better. Just waiting on a cracked rib to heal."

She grimaced. "That probably didn't feel very good, but I'm sure he's also very fortunate nothing worse happened."

I nodded in agreement but didn't say anything.

"Did you have any recent nightmares before last week?" she asked.

I ransacked my brain as I thought about it. "Yes," I remembered. "The day that Ellie started working for our team."

"And who's Ellie?"

I took a few minutes to explain to Dr. Stevens Ellie's role on our team, how she had asked Brody out, and then Landon had a crush on her but things didn't work out, and now we were all just good friends. I also mentioned the part where I initially thought she was Camila because of her blonde hair.

"But you said that was normal, right?" I asked when I had finished explaining. "I know in my heart Camila is gone, but sometimes I still panic when I see someone with blonde hair. Especially if I can't make out their facial features right away."

"Yes, unfortunately that is normal in PTSD cases," she said, jotting down some notes. "Every PTSD patient has triggers. Yours happens to be blonde hair."

"But that seems so silly. You know how many people out there have blonde hair?"

"The brain works in weird ways, Charlie," she chuckled. "Is it safe to assume that you calm down considerably once you see their face? And what about people you already know who have blonde hair? Do they trigger anything?"

"Yeah, once I see their face, I calm down since I know it isn't her." I paused and thought about her second question. "Allison has never made me nervous before. She has blonde hair. And Ellie hasn't made me nervous since that initial reaction."

"Good, good." She jotted down some more notes. "And neither of these ladies have done anything that would easily trigger the nightmares, correct?"

"Of course not," I said, almost defensively. "Allison is my best friend. She'd never do anything to cause me harm. And Ellie is a sweetheart. I don't know her as well as Allison, but I really don't think she'd do anything like that either."

She waved a hand at me. "Oh, no Charlie, I'm not trying to accuse your friends of anything. I'm just trying to get a good reading on what's going on in your life." She paused to cross her legs and take her glasses off. "From what you've told me, some of the nightmares were obviously caused from the events that happened to Brody. Since you had a reoccurrence before anything happened, I'm trying to figure out if there was anything else that could have triggered it, or if it was simply random."

Chewing on my lower lip, I thought hard about whether Allison or Ellie had indeed done anything that could trigger a nightmare.

"Have you had any similar situations at work?" Dr. Stevens continued the questions before I could respond. "Or have you noticed any other circumstances where you've nearly had a panic attack, maybe something that didn't involve blonde hair?"

Over the next several minutes, she continued to ask me questions about my day-to-day activities, the people I saw daily, and any conversations I may have had that would have triggered the nightmares. She asked if I remembered if I had talked about Camila or the situation in the warehouse before that first dream came back, but I couldn't remember.

Apparently, just talking about the incident—even if only for a minute—could cause the nightmares to come back.

She was in the middle of explaining this when my phone started ringing in my purse. "I'm so sorry, I must have forgotten to silence it." I reached for my phone and saw Allison's name flash across the screen. I quickly silenced it and stuffed it back into my bag. She probably just had a question about the gym, I'd call her back as soon as I was finished here.

"No worries at all," Dr. Stevens said. "Anyway, let's focus on how we can combat these dreams."

For the rest of the hour, Dr. Stevens ran through several exercises that were supposed to help me relax my mind, and hopefully taper down on the number of nightmares. Some of them I had attempted before and others were totally new.

"How are you feeling about these exercises, Charlie?" she asked when we were about finished.

"Good." I nodded. "I think these could help."

"They should, yes," she agreed. "Now, I want you to spend the next couple of weeks working on them. If they don't seem to work, I'll have you come back in, and we may have to prescribe something. I want you to be able to get some good sleep."

"Sounds good. Thank you, Dr. Stevens."

"Of course." She smiled briefly before it disappeared. "And Charlie, it might not hurt just to pay extra attention to what your friends say and do around you. If they are doing something that triggers the nightmares, it may need to be addressed."

"I sincerely believe they are not doing anything that would, but if you think it will help, I'll pay closer attention." I stood from my chair and shook her hand.

"I'm sure you're right, but I want to make sure we tackle this from every angle." She stood and walked me out of her office where we said our goodbyes.

On the way out of the building, I pulled my phone out to call Allison and saw she had tried to call me three more times.

Shit, what's going on?

I dialed her number immediately and she answered on the first ring.

"Charlie, I need you to get down here right now," she said in a panic. "The police are here."

"What?" I almost screamed into the phone. "What happened? Is everyone okay?"

"Yes, we're fine. I'll explain when you get here, just hurry."

Hanging up the phone, I ran the rest of the way to my car and sped off to the gym. I was a little hesitant to speed ever since what happened in Brody's truck, but I was also anxious to find out what had happened, so I pushed the speed limit just a little in order to get there quicker.

Had there been another break-in? Did someone get hurt? Did they find Mr. Davis?

Questions continued to swirl around in my head the entire drive. I had no idea what had happened, and even though Allison had said everyone was fine, my mind still immediately went to worst case scenario. I should have answered the phone the first time she called.

When I arrived, I ran to the door and was out of breath when I had entered the building. I saw Allison across the room talking to Officer Carter and another female officer I didn't recognize.

"Charlie!" Allison called when she saw me. She waved me over to them.

"I'm sorry, I got here as fast as I could," I breathed. "What happened?" Looking around, I didn't see any signs of someone being hurt. There wasn't an ambulance outside or any paramedics either. In fact, it looked like the gym was completely empty besides the four of us. "Where is everyone?" I asked.

"We closed the gym early," Allison said. "In fact, it sounds like we'll have to stay closed for a while."

"What?" I spun to face Officer Carter. "Why? What's going on?"

"Ms. Price," he said calmly. "While we were investigating the stolen funds you reported, we found something else that gives us reasons to believe Mr. Davis has been smuggling funds out of this gym for well over a year."

"That's impossible. I've been watching the books religiously since I took over last summer. I hadn't seen anything out of the ordinary until I saw the statements from last week."

"Are you familiar with the account called *Freedom Fund*?" The female officer next to Officer Carter handed me a piece of paper. She was short, stocky, and built like a weightlifter. She had the meanest resting bitch face I'd ever seen, and I made a mental note to never cross her.

"I've heard of it, yes, but I wasn't sure what it was for exactly." I exchanged a look with Allison. It was the same account we had talked about a few weeks ago.

"We didn't know what it was either, so we took a deeper look at it." She pointed to the piece of paper she had handed me. "It took some time and a lot of digging, but we discovered the account was located in Mexico City, under the name Grimaldo Pérez. Have you heard of him?"

I shook my head.

"He's been a person of interest for years. He's believed to be running his own branch of the Codicia cartel."

My mouth nearly dropped to the floor. *Mr. Davis was working with a drug cartel?*

Allison voiced the question out loud before I could. "You're saying Mr. Davis was smuggling money out of his own business to give to a drug cartel in Mexico?"

"Yes, that's exactly what we're saying." Officer Carter nodded. "We'll need to do further investigation to find out exactly how much he's involved in the drug operation, and that's why we're insisting on closing down the gym. We need to search all the hard drives, and we cannot allow any more financial activity until we have some more answers. It's also possible that he'll try to break in again if he finds out the account has been deactivated. He'll want to know what happened."

"What are we supposed to do in the meantime?" I asked. Not only was I shocked by the news, but that also meant we'd be out of work for an undetermined amount of time.

"Our employees will be out of work. Our customers won't be happy."

"You can file for unemployment in the meantime," the female officer said. "As for your customers, they're just going to have to understand. It's a police matter now."

"We'll be in touch if we have any more information," Officer Carter said. "And please watch out for any calls we may send your way. We may need you to answer some more questions as they arise. I do apologize for the inconvenience. We'll hopefully have this under wraps in no time."

******

"You're home early," Brody said when I walked through the door. He did a double take when he saw Allison walk in behind me. "Allison, I wasn't expecting you. Did something happen at the gym?"

We sat down and explained to him what the officers had told us. Even as we retold the story, I had a hard time believing it. After everything we'd been through with Mr. Davis, I knew he was a bad person, but a drug cartel? I wondered if Landon knew anything about it.

"Holy shit, are you serious?" Brody said when we finished.

"I wish we were kidding," Allison grumbled. "Just when you think it couldn't get any crazier, it does."

"Brody, that also means we're out of work for the foreseeable future," I said. "I'm going to have to get another job. I don't make enough from swimming yet, and I'm not going to make you pay all the bills."

He leaned towards me and took my hands in his. "Charlie, I know you're worried, but that is the least of my concerns right now. We have plenty of money to get us by, you don't need to worry."

"Do you think Landon knows?" Allison voiced the question we were all wondering.

Brody shrugged. "I don't know. He's never said anything about it before."

"We need to talk to him tonight," I said. "He deserves to know. And if he already does, maybe he could help the police answer some questions."

"It's not going to be an easy discussion," Brody sighed.

"No, it's not," I agreed. "But it needs to happen. We can get dinner ready in the meantime and figure out what we're going to say."

The other two agreed and we all went into the kitchen to prepare some food. Although I'd admit I was hungry, I mostly wanted something to keep me busy while we waited for Landon to get home.

Brody was right: it was going to be a very hard discussion. Landon had already been through so much. It was bad enough he had an abusive relationship with his father, not to mention that he had broken out of prison—and we had no idea where he was or what he was doing—but now it was possible he was part of one of the deadliest drug cartels in the world. Where did it end?

I tried to focus on the task at hand instead of what Landon's reaction would be. We decided to grill up some burgers for dinner and make homemade fries. Brody was outside working on the grill, and Allison was helping me in the kitchen. We were in the middle of talking about our events for the swim meet this weekend when Brody walked inside with a plate of burgers, Landon and Ellie shortly behind him.

"Here goes nothing," Allison whispered as she carried a plate of buns to the table.

Taking a deep breath, I dished up the fries onto a platter and put them on the table with everything else. "Dinner's ready, so I hope everyone's hungry."

"Smells nice and greasy in here," Landon said, taking a seat at the table. "I love it."

We all gathered around the table and started dishing up our plates. I kept stealing glances over at Brody wondering when he wanted to start talking about Mr. Davis, but they were now deep into a conversation about some hockey game they had watched the other day.

I chewed my food in silence. I tried like hell to enjoy it, but I was so worked up and worried about the situation that it tasted bland, and I could only eat half of my plate before I gave up. When the hockey conversation was over, a brief period of silence stretched over the table, and I couldn't take it anymore.

"Landon, we have something we need to talk to you about," I said as calmly as I could. I stole a glance at Allison and then Brody, and both of them stared at me expectedly.

"Is it something about my dad?" he asked after swallowing a big bite.

"Do you already know what I'm going to tell you?" I asked.

He shook his head. "I doubt it. I haven't heard anything new about him."

"Well, it is about your dad." I took another deep breath before I continued. "The gym was shut down today. The police came in and said while they were investigating the stolen funds, they found an account that has been sending money to the Codicia cartel for over a year."

Suddenly, Ellie started coughing and spluttering as she lowered her water glass back to the table. Landon gave her a few pats on the back until she stopped. "Sorry, went down the wrong way," she said, taking another sip of water to clear it.

"You're saying my dad has been sending money to a drug cartel?" Landon asked, his brows furrowed in confusion.

"Not only that, but there could be a very good chance he's a member, too," I added. "They're closing down the gym to further investigate."

Landon sat back in his chair and went silent. He was still frowning, and he was now chewing on his lip as if he were deep in thought.

"Did you know anything about this?" Brody asked him. "Were there any signs that your dad was working for a drug operation?"

He shook his head. "I don't think so, no. I mean there were times when he'd disappear randomly, sometimes for days at a time, but I just assumed he had gone out with friends and didn't bother to tell me. And then there were times when people I'd never seen before would show up to the house—like Victor did last summer. But I also assumed they were friends, or I thought Victor was an employee at the gym at the time, but maybe he was also part of the cartel. I really don't know."

"Wait—Victor!" I sat up straight in my chair. "He's still in prison here in Jacksonville, isn't he?"

Brody nodded. "Yeah, I think so. Why?"

"Maybe we need to pay him a visit." The room went silent as everyone stared at me.

"Why would we do that?" Allison finally asked.

"He was working with Camila and Mr. Davis. He can tell us if they were a part of the cartel, why they were taking the money, and he might also know where your dad is now. He could give us some answers."

"Even if he *can* give us those answers, Charlie, it doesn't mean he *will*," Brody said. "I'm sure members of a big operation like that, are sworn to secrecy. They would rather die than betray their leaders."

"It can't hurt to try though, can it?" I asked. "He's in prison. Worst case scenario he says nothing. At least we'll have given it a shot."

"I don't understand why we can't just let the cops handle it," Allison said. "Why do we need to risk putting ourselves in danger to find answers?"

Meeting Brody's gaze, I bit my lip as I considered telling them our theory about Mr. Davis being behind the incidents we had been experiencing. Brody nodded as if he could read my thoughts.

"Brody and I have reasons to believe that the truck accident and the incident at the restaurant were done on purpose in an attempt to harm us." I quickly relayed all our thoughts to them, including the proof that the truck had been tampered with, and the possibility that whoever broke Mr. Davis out of prison was helping him with these tasks. "It's probably only a matter of time before he strikes again."

"That's a good enough reason for me to want to go see Victor," Landon said. He had his hands on the table balled up into tight fists. "I don't want any of you getting hurt at the hands of my dad."

"Hold on." Allison held her palm up to Landon. "I agree, that if that is truly the case, then something needs to be done. But what are we going to do with any information Victor gives us? Don't you think the police have already questioned him? And they know about the two incidents—"

"But they aren't investigating those incidents any further," I interrupted. "They believe they were freak accidents."

"So, then why don't we start there before running off to prison to question a member of a drug cartel?" Allison asked, splaying her hands out in front of her like she couldn't believe what she was saying wasn't obvious. "Tell the cops what you just told us. Let them do the investigating."

"I agree," Ellie piped up. "That sounds safer."

"But that could take ages!" I argued. "What if it hits a dead end, and they give up? Then what?"

"Then maybe Mr. Davis isn't the one behind the attacks," Allison said gently.

I looked to Brody who had been quiet for a while now, but his expression gave nothing away. When he met my gaze, I silently urged him to say something.

Finally, he sighed and rested his elbows on the table. "Look, I don't know for certain that Mr. Davis is behind these attacks, but these aren't coincidences. Someone is trying to hurt us, and who else could it be? We're the reason he was sent to jail, and we're the ones responsible for Camila's death. We've given him enough reasons to want revenge, so we can't rule that out. And with all the new information we've discovered, he's obviously up to something.

"But I have to agree with Allison on this one." He reached for my hand and gave me an apologetic grin before he continued. "It was my idea to take the investigation into our own hands last time, and we nearly paid with our lives. I'm not going to be the one to put us in that situation again. I think we should tell the cops about our suspicions and let them handle it."

My shoulders slumped in defeat, but I didn't argue. As much as I wanted all of this to end, I knew he was right. It would be way smarter to let the police handle it.

Landon started shaking his head, his hands still balled into tight fists. "If they take too long or give up like Charlie said, I want us to take over."

"Landon, think about this—" Brody tried to reason with him before Landon interrupted him.

"I have thought about it. If my father is trying to hurt you—and I have a strong feeling your suspicions are right—then I sure as hell am not going to sit around and wait for him to attack again. Besides, if my dad really is a member of a drug cartel, then I have a lot of questions, and I think I deserve to get those answers."

Ellie started shaking her head next. "I don't want any part of that," she said to Landon. "I think you should listen to your friends. It would be much safer for you."

"You think I give a shit what you think?" he barked at her.

"Landon!" I warned. I understood he was mad, but he didn't need to take it out on Ellie. Both Brody and Allison looked to him with their mouths hanging open, unsure how to react to his outburst.

"Ellie, you've made it very clear to me that nothing is going to happen between us," Landon continued. "You only ever want to hang out with me if other people are around. Do you honestly expect me to believe that you care what happens to me? If you don't want to be a part of this, then there's the door." He pointed behind him.

Several uncomfortable moments of silence filled the space around us as we all waited for her response. I'd never seen Landon make an outburst like that before, and while a part of me was happy he was standing up for his opinion, it worried me too. What kind of answers did he want, and how far was he willing to go to get them?

Finally, Ellie stood from her chair. "You're making a big mistake," she said before she turned and went for the front door. A moment later, we heard the door slam and we knew she was gone.

"Hey, I know you're upset, but you didn't need to yell at her," I said to Landon. "You should go apologize."

"I'll talk to her tomorrow, she'll be fine," he said. "So, you're going to call the police, right? Then we decide what we're going to do from there?"

"I'm not going to storm out of here, Landon," Allison started. "But I think Ellie is right. We just need to let the police handle it. We could be making a big mistake by going to the prison."

"Like I said, I'll only go if the police aren't going to be any help." Landon stood up and put his plate in the dishwasher, and then went for the stairs. "I'm going to bed." We said nothing until we heard his bedroom door close.

"Charlie, you think we should have talked about the whole visiting Victor thing before Landon got home?" Allison asked. There was a hint of accusation in her tone and I didn't like it.

"I didn't even think of it until Landon mentioned his name tonight," I shot back. "I'm sorry."

Brody held his hands up between us. "Look, I'll go call the cops now and tell them our thoughts, okay? I'm sure they can have someone start digging this weekend. We're not even going to think about going to the prison until we hear back. Maybe Landon will change his mind by then."

"That sounds fair," I agreed.

"But, if the police find nothing and he decides he still wants to pay Victor a visit, I think we need to support him," Brody said. "I'd have a lot of questions, too, if I found out my dad was in a drug cartel. And if I know Landon, he's going to go look for those answers whether we go with or not, and I'd feel a lot better if he didn't go alone. Allison, I understand if you are hesitant and don't want to go with."

"Yeah, and then *I* look like the bad friend?" She rolled her eyes and stood up from her chair. "I don't think so. If he decides to go, I'll go with for support. But you better believe I'm going to try and talk him out of it first." Without another word, she turned and left the room, the front door opened and closed only a few seconds later.

"I don't think I've ever seen Allison that upset," I said, staring at the front door where she had been a moment ago. "And I've *definitely* never seen Landon that upset."

"No kidding," Brody agreed. "But everyone's emotions are running high right now, and none of us know what's going to shake out." He stood up and took his plate to the dishwasher. "Do you mind doing the clean up? I'm going to call the cops. They should have someone working tonight, right?"

I nodded. "Crime doesn't take time off. Yes, I can handle cleaning up."

He came back and kissed me on the forehead. "Thank you. We'll get this figured out. Everything will be okay."

As I watched him leave the room, I prayed with every muscle in my body that he was right.

Chapter Fifteen

Brody

Landon didn't come out of his room for the rest of the evening, and even the following morning, he waited until the last minute to come out. On the drive to the pool, he asked how the conversation with the police went last night, and I told him what the officer had told me: they'd look into the incidents, but couldn't promise they'd be able to find a way to prove it was Mr. Davis who had done it. He fell silent after that, and I decided to leave him be with his thoughts.

Since I couldn't compete at the meet, my plan was to spend the weekend talking to athletes about coming to my fundraiser. The morning was now half over already, and I was off to a good start. During warmups, I talked to a number of coaches—some I already knew, and some I met for the first time—and almost all of them said they would be happy to buy a ticket or would at least think about buying one. I would talk to several athletes today too, but right now, Charlie was getting ready to swim her first race and I wanted to watch.

Looking around, I spotted her in the team's little camping spot in the stands and I wandered over to wish her good luck. When I reached her, I wrapped my arms around her middle and pulled her close to me, kissing her hard in front of everyone.

"What was that for?" she said when we had parted. Her eyes fluttered dreamily as if she was caught off guard.

"Wanted to wish you good luck." I kissed her again.

She smiled and traced one of her fingers along my chest in teasing little circles. "If I win, how do you want to celebrate?"

"I have a few ideas," I growled. I wanted to keep kissing her and give her an idea of exactly how I wanted to celebrate, but Coach Tanner's voice suddenly reminded me where I was.

"Okay, you two, let's keep the kissing to a minimum while you're at work," he teased. "Brody, quit distracting my swimmers! Charlie, come on, let's talk before your race."

Charlie's face flushed red with embarrassment, but she giggled anyway. "Sorry, Coach."

"Kick some ass!" I called to her as they walked away.

I took a seat on the bleachers and settled in to watch her race. Allison was sitting behind me, scrolling through her phone, but Landon was nowhere to be found.

"Does Landon seem to be doing okay to you?" I turned to Allison.

She looked up from her phone and shrugged one shoulder. "Kind of quiet this morning, but that's not out of the ordinary, I suppose. Warmups were a little awkward. Ellie wouldn't even look at him."

"Where is he now?" I looked around the pool again, but still didn't see him.

"He's changing suits, I believe."

"How are you doing with the whole situation?" I asked her.

She shrugged again. "My opinion hasn't changed if that's what you're asking." She went back to looking at her phone.

I gave her a nod and turned away from her. There was no point in arguing with her right now, but maybe I could talk to Ellie. At the very least, I wanted to make sure she was okay after storming out last night. I scanned the pool deck for any sign of her.

She was standing on the far end of the pool by the timer's table with a clipboard in her hand. Leaving Allison alone at the team camp, I made my way over to her.

"Hey Ellie," I said when I had reached her side. "Got a second to chat?"

"One second," she said. She waited until the heat that was in the water finished, and then scribbled something down in her notes. "Sorry." She looked to me. "Coach Tanner asked me to keep track of each heat winner and their times, so we could compare later. What's up?"

"I wanted to talk to you about last night."

She shook her head. "I don't want to talk about that right now. I haven't changed my mind, and Landon hasn't said a word to me all morning, so I'm assuming he hasn't either."

"I take it he hasn't apologized then?" I grimaced.

She shook her head, her gaze straight ahead as she waited for the next heat to start. "Nope."

"Well, I'm sorry for him," I said. "But in his defense, I can see why he wouldn't want to sit around. He wants to feel like he has some kind of control over the situation."

"But he doesn't," she argued. "Like we've told him before, he's not responsible for what his dad does. It's not only dangerous for you to go see Victor, it's pointless. I don't think he's going to tell you anything."

"You don't know that for sure."

She rolled her eyes and faced me. "I'll be the first to admit I'm not an expert, but I also think I know more about what goes on inside a criminal's mind than all of you."

"What? How—?"

"I'm studying criminal justice, remember?"

I nodded once. "Right."

"So, since he won't listen to me, I strongly suggest you try to talk him out of it." Her gaze went back to the pool and she scribbled on her clipboard the times of the heat that just finished.

Wanting to argue, I decided to drop it instead, if only because Charlie's heat was up for the 100-yard freestyle. Taking a few steps away from Ellie, I stayed close to the pool so I could cheer her on. This race wasn't her best, so she was in the outside lane, but she was in the fast heat, so there was still a chance at her placing.

"Go get 'em, babe!" I yelled before the official blew the whistle, signaling them to get on the block.

It was silent for a few brief moments so the swimmers could hear the start. The head official called, "Take your mark!" and when the buzzer sounded a second later, the building erupted into cheers, everyone yelling for their athlete to swim faster.

Charlie had the advantage that this was our home pool, so she knew how quick it was. She was in the lead when the women came above water to start their strokes, but it didn't take long for some of them to catch her. In a 50-meter pool, they only had to go down to the other end and back, so it was a short, fast race.

I continued to yell for Charlie, who was holding her place near the front. I could tell she was giving it her all, as she didn't even take a breath until she was three-quarters of the way to the other side of the pool.

"Come on, Charlie! Kick!" I screamed, even though the chances of her hearing me were slim. In the water, all the screams and cheers only sounded like muffled noises, but she would be happy if she knew I was cheering for her, nonetheless.

On the second half of the race, Charlie was in fourth place, but closing in on third. Coach Tanner was yelling at her to pick it up as well, and over in the stands, Landon had returned and was cheering for her beside Allison. Whether she heard us or not, Charlie seemed to kick it up a notch in the last fifteen yards and was able to touch third.

"Nice job, Charlie!" I followed her gaze to the scoreboard to see what her time was. Her time was 54.67, a whopping ninety seconds faster than her previous best time. "Holy shit," I mumbled under my breath with excitement.

I ran over to her lane, and she hadn't even been out of the water a full five seconds before I scooped her up in my arms and spun her around. She was dripping with water, and I got my clothes wet, but I didn't care.

"Holy crap, girl! You dropped over a second in a 100, that's insane!"

"What can I say? I really tried to win so we could celebrate." She winked and gave me a knowing smile.

I shook my head and bust out laughing. "Keep it up, and I'm not going to be able to wait until we get home."

She leaned in closer, still breathing hard from the race. "Then let's not wait. The bathrooms over by the weight room aren't being used, and there's a lock on the door."

When I realized she wasn't kidding, I stopped laughing, and I could feel myself going hard. "You're serious?" I said so only she could hear.

She bit her lip and nodded. "I can't wait—as long as your ribs aren't in any pain, that is."

Pain or no pain, I was going to have her. Without another word, I took her hand and started leading her away from the blocks and the other swimmers. I probably should have let her recover first, but I didn't want this moment to pass. I needed to be alone with her and get my hands on her. The way she gripped my hand and followed me closely, I knew she wanted that too.

We almost made it to the door to exit the pool deck when I heard someone yell my name. Stopping in my tracks, I resisted a groan when I saw Jaxon Brown, another swimmer from Mississippi, approaching us.

"Hey, man," he said when he reached me. "You have a few minutes? I heard about your fundraiser. I'd love to know more."

Charlie squeezed my hand and gave me a peck on the cheek. "Go on," she said. She waved to Jaxon as she walked away.

Even though I kind of wanted to yell at him for ruining the moment, I smiled and shook his hand. "Of course, let's talk."

******

A few hours later, the meet was nearly over for the day, and I had talked to most of the athletes here about the gala. Tomorrow, I'd try to talk to some of the maybe's again, but otherwise, I would be able to just focus on watching my teammates.

They had done a phenomenal job today. Allison defended her title in the 200 breaststroke and took second in the 400 individual medley. Charlie swam the 200 backstroke—which she won—and took another third place finish in the 50 free.

Landon was also having a pretty good day. He swam the 200 breaststroke as well, was a second off his best time and placed fourth. He had the 200 freestyle today as well, which would be coming up in a couple of minutes. I was excited to watch his last race because even though he disagreed with me, I was pretty sure he was becoming a distance swimmer. He'd swim the 400 free tomorrow, which I was even more excited to watch.

I was sitting alone in our team's spot in the bleachers while Charlie and Allison were changing out of their suits, and Landon was warming up for his race when Ellie came to sit by me.

"So, I overheard you talking to some of the other swimmers about the gala," she started. "Can you give me a little more info about it? I think I might want to go."

"Really?" I asked in surprise. "Tickets are $250. Can you afford that as a college student? I can't promise I can give you any kind of discount. Then others would expect the same."

"What if I offered to help?" she suggested. "Would you consider waiving the fee, then?"

"You want to help?" I asked in surprise. "I mean, I definitely wouldn't turn you down."

She nodded. "I think it would be good exposure for me since I hope to work for American Swimming someday."

"For sure," I said. "Well, I'd love to have you on board. What would you want to do?"

"Do you have security set up already? I have some connections through school. I'd love to help with that."

"I hired a service already, but you can take over communicating with them and getting everything set up if you want."

My gaze drifted to the starting blocks where Landon was pressing his goggles into his eyes so they wouldn't come loose.

I cupped my hands around my mouth and yelled, "Let's go, Landon!"

A moment later, he was on the blocks and the official called, "Take your marks!" When the buzzer sounded, he flew from the block beautifully, his dive so clean he barely made a splash. A few seconds later, he was above the water, keeping up with those in the lead.

He was in lane five, which meant he was seeded as one of the faster swimmers in the heat. I told him plenty of times that the key is to keep up with the leader for the first hundred yards, and then crank it up for the second half. He seemed to be following my advice so far.

"Brody, did you hear me?" Ellie asked, taking me away from the race.

"What?" I looked back at the pool, trying to listen and watch Landon's race at the same time. "No, what did you say?"

"I said I'd be more than happy to communicate with the security service," she repeated. "Do you have their number?"

"Oh, sure. One second." I pulled my phone out and searched for the security company. In the pool, Landon was now at the halfway mark. Off the wall, he started to pull ahead to take the lead. "Go Landon!" I screamed, jumping from my seat.

"Brody, I need to leave soon and I want to beat the rush," Ellie pushed. "Can you give me the number, please?"

Fighting a groan, I pulled up the number and held my phone out to her so she could write it down. I didn't know what her damn hurry was, but I wanted her to stop distracting me from Landon's race. Landon was now closing in on the finish and still had the lead.

Allison and Charlie had come back at some point and were cheering for him on the other side of the pool. They were jumping up and down next to Coach Tanner, all three of them screaming their heads off.

The last five seconds of the race felt like they lasted forever as I held my breath in anticipation. Landon was neck and neck with the second-place swimmer, and when they touched the wall, it was too close to tell from here who had won. My eyes immediately shot to the scoreboard, where Landon's name came up as the winner.

I pumped my fists in the air and yelled loud enough for the whole building to hear. "Way to go, Landon!"

It was his first time placing first at a professional meet, and I could not be prouder of him. He had only needed to drop about half a second to qualify for Olympic trials, and he managed to drop almost three full seconds for a time of 1:49.52.

"Wow, he did awesome," Ellie said from beside me. "Can you tell him good job for me? I'm going to get going."

I nodded. "Sure—hey thanks for offering to help. I'll keep you posted on what I need from you."

"My pleasure."

I ran over to Landon's lane and leaned down to give him a high five. This was the last race of the day, so there was no need for him to hurry out of the water. He still clung to the wall, trying to catch his breath, a huge smile on his face.

"Way to go, man. I knew you had it in you!"

"Thanks, Brody," he said in between inhales of breath.

When Charlie, Allison, and Coach Tanner joined us, we helped pull him out of the water and gathered around him in one big hug.

"Way to go, kid." Coach Tanner gave him a slap on the back.

"Yeah, Landon, that was amazing!" Allison cheered. Charlie cheered along with her, and when the celebration died down, we broke away from each other so Landon could breathe.

"By the way, Ellie said good job on your race," I told him when we started walking back to the camp spot. Charlie and Allison stayed behind with Coach Tanner to figure out what time warmups were tomorrow.

His head popped up as if he were expecting to see Ellie at the bleachers. "Is she still here? I never apologized for last night."

"No, I'm sorry man. She wanted to get going. I talked to her a little bit. She's just trying to look out for you."

"Yeah, okay." He rolled his eyes. When we reached the camp spot, he started packing his bag and didn't say anything more.

"You don't think she's looking out for you?"

He shook his head and kept packing, not looking at me. "I wasn't lying last night when I said I don't think she gives a shit about what happens to me."

"Why do you think that?"

He stopped packing and turned to face me. "Because she knew I wanted to hang out with her, and she used that as an excuse to get to all of you."

"What?" I frowned, still not following him.

"She only wanted to be my friend because she knew it would give her easy access to the rest of the team. She never wanted to talk about what was going on with me or what I was going through, she just wanted to talk about you or Charlie."

"I guess I don't understand," I said, still confused. "Why would she want to talk about us?"

"I think maybe she wanted to get close to you since you're such a big name in American Swimming—Charlie is too, even as a rookie. She saw you as the opportunity she needed for getting a job with American Swimming someday. She got lucky with the coaching assistant position. She needs to know the right people if she wants to get any higher than that." He went back to packing his bag, throwing the last of his things inside. "Regardless, she doesn't care about me."

"Wouldn't she be talking about Allison too, though?" I shook my head, changing my mind. "Never mind, that's not important. I'm sorry, man, I had no idea. Why didn't you say anything? We definitely didn't need to have her at the house that often."

He shrugged. "I hoped I was wrong and she would eventually come around. But I don't know, things didn't really change."

"I'm sorry, Landon," I repeated. I put a hand on his shoulder, gave it a squeeze, and dropped it back to my side. "I wish it worked out for you."

"I don't even care about that anymore, I just wish she had been honest with me." He threw his bag over his shoulder. "I'm going to go change and then can we go home?"

I nodded and let him go. Feeling torn between confusion and anger, I didn't know what to think of Ellie anymore. Had she really been using all of us? Why hadn't I seen that?

Allison and Charlie finally rejoined me at the bleachers and I told them what Landon had told me about Ellie.

"Are you serious?" Charlie grumbled. "She was using us for her own personal gain?"

"Well, if she was, it worked," I said. "Before Landon's race, she asked if she could help with the gala. She said she wanted to be there to get her name out there. I told her she could. I should have known."

"We don't know for sure that's what was going on," Allison said. "That's just how Landon feels. There are two sides to every story. Maybe we need to bring it up to Ellie and hear her out."

"Do you think that's something she'd actually admit to doing?" Charlie asked, a hint of impatience in her tone.

Allison's shoulders sagged in defeat. "Yeah, good point."

"For now, I think we just need to tread lightly," I said. "And it's probably okay if Ellie doesn't come to the house for a little while."

Before anyone could say anything more, I saw Landon coming our way and decided to change the subject. "Hey, why don't we go out tonight to celebrate Landon's win?"

"I'm down for that!" Allison raised her hand in the air excitedly.

Charlie nodded in agreement. "Me too. Where should we go?"

"Where do you want to go?" I asked Landon.

He shrugged. "I don't know if I'm really in the mood to go anywhere except home."

"Come on, man. You won your first professional race today. We *have* to celebrate that."

"We can always order take out and I can pick it up on the way home?" Charlie suggested. "We can order from your favorite Chinese place. We can pop a bottle of sparkling cider—we've got to swim tomorrow, so can't get too crazy." She winked. "We don't have to go anywhere if you don't want to, Landon, but let us help you celebrate. It'll help you take your mind off things."

He let the smallest hint of a smile dance on his lips and nodded. "Okay, fine."

"Awesome!" Charlie gave him a high five. "Allison and I will go pick up the stuff and meet you at home."

******

Later that evening, we sat in the living room surrounded by empty boxes of Chinese food, and two empty bottles of sparkling cider. We had managed to get Landon to loosen up a little bit and have a good time and had even gotten him to laugh and joke around with us.

"Who's that one coach from Vermont who squawks like a parrot every time his swimmers are competing?" Allison asked, breaking into a fit of giggles.

"Who, Henry? Tall guy with red hair and glasses?" I asked.

"Yeah, him!" She was laughing so hard she could barely speak. "Oh, my gosh. He's hilarious. I always know when someone from his team is swimming. We should get Coach Tanner to cheer for us like that."

"I think I'd shoot myself if I had to listen to that every day," Landon laughed.

"Okay, that's true," Allison agreed, her laughter fit finally dying down. "He just wants to make sure his swimmers can hear him from inside the water just as easily as they could outside of it."

The rest of us laughed at her comment—it probably had some truth to it—and then a comfortable silence fell over the room. It was getting late, and everyone else had a long day of swimming behind them, and one more full day tomorrow. Even I was tired, and I hadn't gotten to swim today.

Allison sat up in her chair, stretching her arms above her head. "I may get ready to head home, guys. I'm beat."

Before she got up, my phone started ringing. I recognized the police station's phone number as it flashed on the screen, and I held up my finger to tell her to wait. "It's the police." I hit the green answer button and put the phone on speaker. "This is Brody."

"Hi Brody, this is Officer Carter," the voice from the other end of the phone said. "I'm sorry to call so late, do you have a few minutes to talk?"

"Sure, have you found something already? I wasn't expecting to hear from you so soon."

"We had a few of our detectives working on the case today, and we sent them to get some leads on the information you provided." He paused, and I thought I could hear him typing something on a computer in the background. "Anyway, we contacted the repair shop where you took your truck. Do you remember when you went to bed the night before the accident, and what time you left the next morning?"

"We went to bed around midnight that night, but we had some friends over who left around eleven. My girlfriend took the truck to work the next morning, and she would have left around five."

I heard him typing a bit more before he spoke again. "The repairman said it takes about thirty minutes for one brake line to empty, so really it could have been cut anytime between when you went to bed and when you left. Do you have any cameras outside your home?"

"No," I told him. Although, it probably wouldn't be a bad idea to get some. "I did hear a car alarm go off shortly after I went to bed, but I didn't get up to look. I have no idea if it was my truck, or if it was, what would have caused it to go off."

"We'll follow up with some of your neighbors to see if any of them have cameras, but even if they do, I'm not confident they'll have some pointed at your driveway."

"So, does that mean we're at a dead end there?" I asked, my stomach sinking.

"Unless we find more info from any potential cameras, then I'm afraid we might be. I do want to mention that we dusted the truck for prints, but nothing came up. Ben Davis' fingerprints are in our system, so if he had been the one tampering with it, we would have the proof right there."

"He could have been wearing gloves," I suggested.

"Yes, it's possible."

"Did you find anything with the restaurant?"

"This one was a little trickier, but based on what you said last night, I think you already knew that," he said. "We talked to the kitchen and waiting staff that worked the night of the incident, and all of them swore they had no idea how oregano got onto your plate. The waiter who served you even said he went back after you left and double checked he had put 'no oregano' on your ticket—he had. Unfortunately, there are no cameras installed in the kitchen, so there isn't much else we can go off."

"So, now what?" I asked, even though I had a feeling I already knew what he was going to say.

"We'll keep the cases open in case more information comes through, but right now there isn't enough evidence to suspect Davis. And in terms of what happened at the restaurant, I'm not sure there's enough evidence to prove any kind of foul play."

"With all due respect, sir," I said, trying to keep from yelling. "Do you really think it's a mere coincidence that these two accidents occurred so close together?"

"Stranger things have happened," Officer Carter admitted. "I know that's not what you want to hear, and I know you're worried. But as of right now, we still don't have any leads on where Davis even is. Just be careful and hopefully we'll have him back behind bars before you know it."

I knew he was doing his best, but I still felt pretty frustrated by the time I had hung up the phone. I had hoped they would have come back with solid proof it had been Mr. Davis, but that had probably been naïve of me.

"So, then we're going to see Victor?" Landon said after the phone call had ended. "You said if the police hit a dead end, we could go."

I exchanged a look with Allison and Charlie, who both looked at me expectedly. Yes, I had agreed to that, but I had also hoped more time would have passed. Don't get me wrong, I was thrilled the officers had taken me seriously and went to work right away, but now it didn't leave us with much time to change Landon's mind.

"Maybe we should think about it for a few more days?" I suggested. "Make sure this is something you really want to do."

He shook his head. "No, you're not going to talk me out of this. You agreed to go. What are we going to accomplish by sitting around?"

"We'll probably be safer by sitting around," Allison insisted. "I really do think you need to reconsider your decision, Landon."

"I'm not changing my mind," he repeated. "I'm going to go whether the rest of you join me or not."

"Why do you want to go so bad?" Allison asked, sounding frustrated.

"I just found out my dad is in a drug cartel," Landon barked, catching us all off guard a bit. "What else don't I know? My entire childhood was basically a lie. I think I deserve to find some answers."

Silence stretched between the four of us as what he said sunk in. I suddenly felt bad for trying to talk him out of going. I knew full well if I was in his shoes, I would want to find the truth, too. I pulled my phone back out and googled visiting hours at the Jacksonville prison. "They have a small window for visitors on Sunday afternoons," I said, reading off the screen. "We could go after the meet tomorrow."

"Then let's go tomorrow," Landon said. "I don't want to wait."

I nodded. "You can count me in."

"Me as well," Charlie said. She glanced at Allison to see what she would say, but another silence stretched between them.

Finally, she sighed. "Well, if there's no talking you out of it, I guess you can count me in as well."

"Then it's settled," I said. "We all go after the meet tomorrow. We'll be there for you, Landon."

Everyone nodded in agreement, and then one by one, we slowly started getting out of our chairs to throw trash away.

Allison said goodbye and slipped out the door, and Landon disappeared upstairs to get ready for bed.

In the kitchen, Charlie was wiping the counters off with a towel when I came up behind her and nuzzled my nose into her hair. I breathed in her sweet scent and held her tight.

She leaned back into my arms and sighed. "You know, despite everything that went down tonight, I still keep thinking about this afternoon."

"Is that so?" I moved her hair away from her neck and made a trail of kisses down her throat.

She turned her neck to the side, exposing more of her flesh to me. "I think I was promised a celebration if I won a race, and I don't like broken promises," she purred.

I turned her around to face me and rested my palms on either side of her face. "I would never do such a thing."

"Prove it," she dared me.

Accepting the dare, my hands dropped to her ass, and I scooped her up in my arms, wrapping her legs around me. She squealed in surprise and wrapped her arms around my neck so she wouldn't fall. "I plan on it, babe." Carrying her to the stairs, I ravaged her mouth as I went. I didn't even care if Landon saw us, I needed this woman. Now.

When we were in the bedroom, I closed the door and threw her down on the bed. We made quick work of removing our clothes, and soon I was trailing kisses over every inch of her skin. She moaned in response and clawed at my back with her fingers.

"Brody," she pleaded. "I need you."

Reaching over to my dresser, I pulled a condom out of the drawer and threw it to Charlie. She ripped it open and rolled it on in record time, her breathing coming in rapid breaths. In no time at all, I was plunging deep inside of her, and she gasped from the pleasure.

One thrust and I was about done for. Pausing to collect myself, I screwed my eyes shut and tried to hold out.

"Brody, please!" she screamed. "Keep going!"

Aiming to please, I pulled back and slammed into her, and then did it again and again until I couldn't hold it anymore. "Oh, my God!" I moaned through gritted teeth.

When I was done, I rolled over next to Charlie. We were both breathing fast. When I opened my eyes, she was smiling at me.

"What?" I smiled back.

She shook her head. "I hope you've got enough in you for another round. I'm nowhere near done." She laughed and rolled over so she was on top of me now. She straddled me and started planting kisses on my chest, working her way up to my neck.

"You're going to kill me, woman." But I didn't resist. Slowly and tenderly, she trailed those kisses along my throat, over my jaw and cheeks, and finally landed on my lips.

What was soft and tender a moment ago, quickly turned into hunger, and I knew it wouldn't be long before she'd get her way.

******

We made love until well past midnight, and finally, when we were both exhausted, we lay facing each other, still naked in the bed. Our limbs were tangled together, and I traced my thumb along her jaw ever so lightly.

"I don't think I'll ever get tired of this view." I smoothed a few locks of her hair away from her face so I could see her better. "You're breathtaking."

She giggled. "And I don't think I'll ever get tired of hearing you say that."

"Good, because you're stuck with me."

"Is that so?" she teased with a smile.

I nodded. "It's not official yet, but just you wait. It will be."

She poked me in the chest and scoffed. "Don't make promises you can't keep, mister."

"I would never do that!" I pulled her closer to me and buried my nose in her hair. "I mean it. It's coming, Charlie. And it's going to knock your socks off."

"I'll hold you to that." She planted a soft kiss on my chest and curled into me.

After a few minutes, her breathing became softer, and I knew she had fallen asleep. I continued to hold her tight and fell asleep dreaming of our future together.

Chapter Sixteen

Charlie

The next morning, the final day of the swim meet was well under way when Brody approached our spot on the bleachers with a big smile on his face.

"I got him!" he said excitedly, taking a seat beside me.

"Got who?" I asked.

"Coach Bill out of Colorado. He agreed to come to the gala, and he's paying the entrance fee for his entire team."

"Oh, that's awesome news!" I beamed. "You've had a really successful weekend, Brody. I'm very proud of you."

"I can't wait to tell Landon, too. Where is he?" His eyes darted around the building looking for him.

I shrugged. "I haven't seen him since warmups, but his 400 is coming up soon, so he's got to be around here somewhere."

As if he knew we were talking about him, Landon came around the corner and took a seat beside us. Brody didn't even wait until he was sitting down before he told him the news about Coach Bill.

"That's awesome," Landon smiled weakly, and then went silent.

Brody's gaze shot to me and then back to Landon. "Not going to lie, I thought there would be a bigger reaction out of you. Are you okay?"

Landon nodded. "Just distracted. I'm thinking about what I'm going to say to Victor this afternoon."

"Let's not think about that while we're here," I told him. "You just need to focus on your races and we'll worry about Victor later."

"Easier said than done," Landon mumbled.

"Come on," Brody said, standing up. "Let's go talk to Coach Tanner and see what advice he has about your race."

I watched the two of them walk away and silently hoped that Landon would be able to focus on his races. He had one of his best race days yesterday, and he'd been so wrapped up with what's been going on outside of swimming, he couldn't really be excited for himself.

Allison appeared a minute later, dripping wet with a towel wrapped around her shoulders. "Done for the day! And not a moment too soon. I'm exhausted."

"Me too," I agreed. "Nice swim, by the way. You make breaststroke look so damn easy."

"Thanks," she laughed. "You do the same with backstroke."

"Landon's 400 is coming up pretty soon." I directed my attention to the pool, where the first heat of the men's 400-yard freestyle had just started. "I think he's in the next heat."

She nodded. "I think you're right."

We sat in silence for a few moments as we watched the swimmers go by.

"I'm getting a little nervous about the prison visit this afternoon," Allison finally said. "What if Ellie is right? What if we are making a mistake? Landon has gotten his hopes up that Victor will tell us something, and he might not even agree to see us. If we go in there and he doesn't get the answers he wants, what is he going to do? How much more can he actually handle?"

I shrugged one shoulder. "I think he's tougher than we give him credit for. He could be taking all of this much worse. If I were in his shoes, I don't know if I would even want to leave the house. I have to give him credit for being here, and wanting to find answers in the first place."

She appeared to process that for a moment and then nodded. "Yeah, you're right. He has been through a lot, and he's handling it as well as can be expected." She pulled her bag onto her lap and started digging through it. "Shoot, I think I forgot my cap and goggles over by the cool down pool. I'll be back in a sec." She got up and made her way to the other side of the pool deck.

Behind her, I could see the first heat of the 400 free was just finishing up, and Landon had his goggles on and was ready to go. Brody was on the opposite end of the pool, ready to count his laps for him.

"You got this, Landon!" I yelled from my seat.

A few moments later, the official's whistle blew and the second heat was getting on the blocks to start.

"Charlie, do you have a second?" The sound of Ellie's voice pulled my attention away from the pool long enough that I missed the start.

"Sure, what's up?" I asked, stealing a glance at Landon as he came above the water to swim.

"How well do you know Allison?" she asked, taking a seat beside me.

"Pretty well." My eyes didn't leave the pool as I spoke. "Why?"

"I overheard a phone conversation she had. It concerns me a little bit."

I tore my gaze from the pool to see the look of concern in Ellie's eyes. "Why, what did you hear?"

"I don't know who she was talking to, but I heard her say that you all would be going to the prison today and that she would do her best to prevent it from happening." She quickly glanced in the direction of where Allison was standing and then back to me. "Then she said if she couldn't convince him not to go, she'd steer the conversation at the prison."

"Allison said that?" I couldn't hide the surprise in my voice. Stealing a glance at the pool, Landon was almost halfway through his race, and he was about a body length ahead of all the other swimmers. Allison was cheering for him alongside Brody. I turned my attention back to Ellie. "I know she doesn't want to go, but she never said anything about steering the conversation. That doesn't make sense."

"That was my initial thought too." Ellie repositioned herself so that she was in my line of sight. "But think about it. She's around Landon all the time. What if she's working with Mr. Davis and telling him all that's going on while he's hiding? She did work closely with him at the gym—"

"So did I, though," I said. "And I didn't see anything weird going on."

"Not until you were put in charge." She stared at me pointedly. "What if Allison knew about that foreign account, but didn't want to say anything? How do you think Mr. Davis would have gotten into the gym account recently to transfer that money? He would have needed someone from the inside. Someone like Allison."

I didn't respond right away. Mostly because I hated to admit that what she was saying didn't sound *that* farfetched. Allison wouldn't do any of that, would she?

Suddenly, Dr. Stevens' words came screaming back to me: *Pay attention to what your friends are doing and saying.* Was it possible it was in front of me the entire time, and I hadn't seen it?

The room broke into cheers and whistles as the heat finished, pulling me out of my thoughts. Landon had won the race, but I could barely register the excitement. I was still trying to wrap my head around what Ellie had just told me.

"If I were you, I'd play it cool," Ellie continued. "I don't know who's all involved, and I don't want to see any of you get hurt. Play it safe, Charlie. Please, I'm begging you."

I gave her a small nod to acknowledge that I heard her, and she walked away. Allison came bouncing back excitedly a minute later, seemingly unaware of my shift in mood.

"Landon is having a hell of a weekend!" she exclaimed as she resumed her seat beside me. "Two first place wins. I knew the kid had it in him."

I smiled at her but said nothing. Ellie's words still ricocheted inside my mind, and I didn't know what to think.

Allison grabbed her bag from the seat behind her once more and started stuffing her towel, cap, and goggles inside. "I'll be right back," she said as she stood with her things. "I'm going to shower and change."

When she was out of sight, I immediately got up and searched for Brody. He was still on the other side of the pool, talking to Coach Tanner and Landon. When I approached them, they were talking about Landon's race.

"Awesome race, Landon," I said, pushing myself into their circle.

"Thanks, Charlie." Landon beamed. "I'm going to go change and we can get ready to go."

"Great." I gave him a tight smile.

Coach Tanner dismissed himself and I took hold of Brody's elbow to stop him from leaving.

"Brody, I need to talk to you. Have you talked to Ellie at all today?"

He shook his head. "Not really. Why?"

"She hasn't said anything to you about Allison?"

"No." His brows furrowed, and he stared at me questioningly. "What's going on?"

"Nothing, never mind." I waved my hand to dismiss it. I'd tell him later when less people were around.

"Okay." He narrowed his eyes as if he knew I wasn't telling him something. "Then go get changed. We should get over to the prison soon."

******

After we had all changed, Brody, Landon and I piled into my car, and Allison followed close behind in hers. I considered bringing up what Ellie had told me, but Landon's mood had clearly changed since his race, and I didn't want to add more concern.

"You know what you're going to say?" Brody asked him after a few minutes of silence.

Landon shrugged and looked out the window. "I have an idea."

Looking at his reflection in the rearview mirror, I could see the fear etched on his face. "Landon, don't let anyone try to convince you this is a bad idea," I told him. "You need answers. Anyone can understand that."

He met my gaze in the mirror and gave me a thin smile. A moment later he returned to staring out the window in silence.

When we pulled into the parking lot at the prison, we all took a collective deep breath before we exited the vehicle. Allison parked beside us and fell into step shortly behind.

"Landon, are you sure this is a good idea?" she asked one more time when she had caught up to us. "I just want to make sure you know what you're getting yourself into."

"You two go on in," I said to the boys. "We'll be right behind you." They nodded and continued on without us. Something in me finally caved, and I decided to confront Allison about what Ellie had said earlier.

"Is something wrong?" Allison asked, frown lines etched deeply on her forehead.

"Allison, I want you to tell me the truth." I crossed my arms and stood my ground before her. "Are you working with Mr. Davis? Is that why you're trying so hard to convince Landon not to be here?"

Her frown deepened and her mouth dropped open. "What on earth would make you think that?"

"You worked with him a lot longer than I did. Is it possible you knew about the foreign account at the gym this whole time? Are you the insider who's helping him steal those funds?"

"What? Charlie, are you hearing yourself right now?" Her voice raised several octaves, and she cleared her throat before lowering it again. "Everything we've found out about the gym was as much a surprise to me as it was to you. I've told you nothing but the truth the entire time. Where is this coming from?"

"Ellie told me she overheard you speaking to someone about the prison visit. She said you were going to try your hardest to make sure the visit didn't happen."

"Oh, my God." A look mixed with anger and disappointment crossed her face. "I wanted to make sure he was making the right decision. I care about Landon, and I was just trying to look out for him. I didn't know that would make me a suspect. Jeezus, Charlie, I thought you knew me better than that."

"I don't know what to think anymore," I spat. "But I do think you need to sit this one out. I think you should leave."

Allison's shoulders sagged as her arms dropped to her sides. "Really? Just like that? You're not going to let me be there for my friend?"

"Until I know what's going on, I want you to stay out of this and let us handle it."

She shook her head and pursed her lips. "I thought you were my best friend. I honestly can't believe you would think this low of me."

Her words stung, and I bit my lip to avoid taking it all back and apologizing.

When it was clear I wasn't going to respond, she turned back towards her car and walked away. Before she got in, she looked back to me. "Be careful, Charlie. I'd hate to see any of you get hurt."

Chapter Seventeen

Brody

Once we were checked in as visitors, the prison guard said it would be a couple of minutes before we could see Victor. Landon took a seat in the lobby, and I stared out the window as I watched Charlie walk towards the entrance. In the background, I could see Allison's car back out of her spot and drive away.

Confused, I silently wondered what happened out there.

When Charlie walked inside, she avoided my stare, instead inspecting her toes as she took a seat beside Landon.

"Where's Allison going?" I asked her.

"She decided not to come in." Charlie's eyes still never left the floor.

"Did she say why—?"

"Landon Davis?" A middle-aged woman with short, brown curly hair appeared at the entrance of the lobby. "You all can come back now."

"We can talk about it later," Charlie mumbled as she got up and walked by me.

The three of us followed the woman—her name badge said Pam—down the long, dimly lit corridor that led to the visiting rooms. None of us spoke as we walked, but it was far from a silent journey. Beyond the cement walls, we could hear shouting, laughter, and every cuss word under the sun. Charlie and I exchanged an anxious glance as Pam guided us into one of the visiting rooms.

The room was empty, except for a table and a couple of chairs. It was the same dark, grey color as the hallway, but must have had thicker walls, as we couldn't hear the shouting as well from in there. On the far wall was a two-way mirror and I wondered how many people would be watching us while we visited with Victor.

"You can have a seat," Pam said. "The prisoner will be joining you shortly." She slipped out of the room and closed the door behind her.

All of us remained standing, too anxious to move. Only a few minutes later, the door opened again, and this time a large police officer guided a handcuffed prisoner in a grey jumpsuit into the room.

When Victor saw us, he started laughing. "Well, I'll be damned!" He continued to laugh as the officer shoved him into a chair and handcuffed him to the table. "Almost didn't believe it when they said you were here to visit me."

Once he was fastened to the table, the officer quietly left the room and we were alone with Victor, the man who had tried to kill us only a few months ago. Seeing him in the flesh again sent chills down my spine, and the scar on my shoulder from where he had shot me tingled.

"So, ya just going to stand there and stare?" he finally asked. "What do ya want?"

"Where's my father?" Landon demanded. "We know you know where he is."

"Sorry kid, I don't." His laughter from before was gone and his face was serious. "Don't know where that son of a bitch is, and honestly, I don't care. He said when they were going to break him outta here, they'd come back for me. And obviously, that hasn't happened, so the bastard is dead to me."

"Who broke him out of here?" I asked.

"The boss." Victor inspected his nails as if he had lost interest in the subject.

Landon frowned. "I thought my dad was your boss?"

"Well, he was. But *his* boss broke him out. Davis owes him a lot of money. He's not going to let him sit in prison where he's safe."

"What exactly did my dad do for a living?" Landon finally pulled out a chair and took a seat.

"You don't know?" Victor asked surprised.

"We may have heard something about a cartel," Landon whispered. "But he doesn't work for a drug operation, does he?"

Victor laughed again. "He sure does. The Codicia cartel to be exact. He's a drug lord."

Beside me, I heard Charlie gasp, and I wrapped an arm around her shoulder. Landon's mouth fell open, but nothing came out.

"Honestly, why so surprised?" Victor asked, sounding annoyed. "You were there last summer. You saw what we was doing. Fuck, you're the reason I'm back in this hellhole."

"Does that mean Camila was a drug lord, too?" Charlie asked the question we were probably all wondering.

"Not exactly." Victor shook his head. "She was living the cartel life, don't get me wrong, but she was basically a princess."

"Meaning?" I asked.

Victor leaned in closer. "Her dad is the boss. The head honcho of our district of the Codicia cartel. She did none of the dirty work but got to live off his money. And let me tell you, there was no shortage of that."

"Well, that doesn't surprise me." I rolled my eyes.

"So, how did she get wrapped into working with my dad?" Landon asked, ignoring my comment.

Victor shrugged. "I don't know the entire story, but Davis and Camila both were trying to get out of the cartel. I think her dad was trying to make her marry someone she hated, something like that. Anyway, Camila and Davis got pretty close over the years, and they agreed to help each other."

"Do you know why my dad was trying to get out? Did it have anything to do with him trying to protect me?" Landon asked, hope in his eyes.

"I don't know, it might have been part of the reason I suppose." Victor's gaze met mine, and I couldn't be sure, but it looked like there was a hint of sympathy there. Was he only saying that to make Landon feel better?

Landon did perk up a little in his chair and the faintest smile appeared on his lips for just a moment. It wasn't much, but even the slightest possibility that his father might have cared about him probably meant something to him. My heart broke all over again.

"I think he was just over it at that point, more than anything," Victor continued. "But anyway, then Camila went and got greedy. She completely drained one of her father's bank accounts and took it all with her—millions of dollars. Once you're used to living the luxurious life, I suppose it's hard to just up and walk away from it. Anyway, she shared access to the account with Davis so neither one of them would have to worry about finances. But it didn't take them long to get caught."

"When did this happen?" Landon asked.

Victor's gaze went to the ceiling as he calculated. "Hmm probably about a year and a half ago."

"That's when my dad and I moved here from California."

Victor chuckled. "Yep, you might have moved a whole country away, but it doesn't help anything when the Codicia has operations in almost every border state. It only took them a couple of months to get caught."

"That would explain why they kidnapped Roman last summer," I said. "They had to get the funds to pay back his boss."

Victor made a finger gun and pointed it at me. "Bingo."

"Do you owe money to them, too?" Charlie asked. "Or how did you get roped into this?"

"Couple years back I was working with a rookie who fucked up and got us all thrown in the clink." He rolled his eyes. "But Davis knew I was the best there was when it came to kidnappin's. He said he'd break me out if I agreed to help him."

"And now he's out free, and you're back in here." I smirked.

He shook his head. "Life can be a bitch, can't it?"

"So, how do we go about finding him now?" Landon ran his fingers through his hair in frustration. "According to you, he's out there coming up with some grand scheme to get a bunch of money for this cartel."

Victor nodded. "Yeah, and if he doesn't, he's toast."

"They're going to kill him?"

"Usually how it works."

"And you have absolutely no idea where he could be right now?" I asked again.

"I mean, I have one idea, but she'd kill me if I said anything." He went back to picking his nails and avoiding our gazes.

"*She*?" Landon and Charlie said at the same time.

"There's another woman involved?" I asked, leaning forward on the table. "Who?"

Victor held up one hand as best he could while handcuffed to the table. "Oh, no. *That* I'm not telling. I've already told you way more than I should have. Jail life ain't much, but it's still livin'. If I tell ya, I'll be dead for sure." He started clanking his handcuffs against the table and turned towards the two-way mirror. "Hey! We're done. Get me outta here."

In one stride I was on the other side of the table, holding Victor by the neck of his jumpsuit. "You better spill, or so help me—"

"Or what?" he spat. "You'll have me arrested? There's nothing you can do to me that they can't do worse. I ain't afraid of a bunch of kids."

"What's going on in here?" The large police officer from before barked as the door swung open. "Sir! Get your hands off my prisoner."

I took a step back from Victor, but held my glare. He flashed a smug smile, and if the officer hadn't come between us, I would have slapped it off his face. Once the officer had Victor's handcuffs detached from the table, he guided him towards the door.

"I'd watch your backs if I were you." He narrowed his eyes at each of us, and then disappeared with the officer.

"Let's get out of here," I said, still fuming. Leaving the room, I went straight for the vehicle outside, not even looking if the others had followed me.

We may have gotten some answers, but now I had more questions than when we started.

******

Back at the house, we gathered in the living room to discuss the prison visit. Landon sat on the floor with his back against the couch, Charlie had her legs curled up beneath her on the recliner, and I paced back and forth in front of them.

"And you are certain that there were no indications whatsoever that your dad was involved in a cartel?" I asked Landon for probably the fourth time.

"Not before what happened at the gym. It's as much of a surprise to me as it is to you." His head slumped back so that he was staring at the ceiling. "Like I suggested earlier, he probably used the gym as a front so it didn't draw any attention."

"It does make sense," Charlie agreed. "The foreign bank account is just one example of proof. The place was also being run into the ground. To be honest, I'm surprised we still have as many customers as we do. He clearly didn't care about the place that much."

I nodded. "Yeah, that's true."

Landon clapped his cheeks with his palms and ran them slowly down his face. "I have no idea who this other woman Victor mentioned is. For all we know, it's someone we haven't even met. But she's obviously dangerous, or Victor wouldn't have clammed up."

"I've been racking my brain, too," I said. "I don't know who it could be either."

A couple of silent moments passed as we all tried to think of possible suspects. Eventually, Charlie broke the silence.

"I think I know who it is," she whispered, her eyes glued to the floor.

Both Landon and I turned our gazes on her and waited for her to continue.

After a few more beats, she finally looked up at us. "I think it might be Allison."

Landon and I exchanged a glance, both wondering if Charlie was being serious.

"I hope you're joking," I finally said. "Why would you think it was Allison?"

"Think about it!" She threw her hands in the air. "She was trying so hard to convince us not to go speak to Victor today.

She was probably scared he would slip up and give something away."

"Or, she was just worried about a friend," I argued.

"Okay, but what about the account at Fit Happens?" she continued. "How do we know Allison wasn't the one helping Mr. Davis smuggle money out of the business? And that she wasn't the one that stole the money recently?"

Landon and I remained speechless as we listened to her.

"And the close-calls we had: the car accident, the oregano. She was there both times. She has access to our schedules and our every move. If someone wanted to keep us quiet or take us out of the equation, she'd know exactly what to do. She's the strongest woman I know. She could definitely hold her own in a drug cartel."

Landon shot me a sideways glance, and I just shook my head. Taking a seat beside her, I took her hand in mine. "Charlie, I sincerely hope you realize the kind of accusation you are making right now. Allison is your best friend. Do you actually think she would do this to us?"

She stared into space for a long moment and then shrugged and shook her head. "I don't know."

"Do you have any proof that would indicate she was responsible?" Landon asked.

Charlie shook her head again. "No."

"Then I think we hold off on saying anything until we know for sure," I said. "She's our teammate. We don't need to create a situation that isn't there."

Charlie sank further into the recliner and grimaced. "That might be kind of hard to do …"

"Did you already say something to her?" I asked.

She nodded. "That's why she left when we got to the prison."

"Shit." I dropped my head into my hands and pulled on the ends of my hair. "No offense, but that was pretty dumb."

"I'm sorry. I—"

"I'm going to give Allison a call," I said before Charlie could finish. "There's no reason she needs to be mad at all of us." I got up and went upstairs, leaving the two of them in silence.

"Hey, Brody," Allison said when she answered the phone. "How did the visit go?"

"Hey. We got some answers, but we also have more questions." I walked into my bedroom and closed the door behind me. "Listen, Charlie just told us about what she said to you at the prison. I wanted to make sure you knew we don't think you're working with Mr. Davis."

There was silence on the other end, and for a moment I thought she had hung up. Finally, she said, "Well, thank you for letting me know."

"I think we are all on edge right now, and obviously we all are thinking of ways to help Landon. She's just trying to look at every possibility."

"I see."

I waited a couple of moments to see if she would add anything else, but she didn't. "It's hard to gauge what's going through your mind right now, Allison. Are you okay?"

"No, I'm not okay," she said with a little more anger in her voice. "You guys are my teammates, my best friends, and you think I'm helping a criminal. You want to look at every possibility? How did I even become a suspect?"

"Well, you were trying really hard to convince us not to go to the prison, and you were there on the nights of the car accident and the incident at the restaurant."

There was laughter on the other end of the phone. "On those accounts, then all of you would be suspects, don't you think?"

"Allison—"

"You've said enough, Brody," she interrupted. "I'll stay out of your way if that's what you guys want. All I can say is that I hope you know what you're getting yourselves into."

"Allison, wait!" I said quickly, but the line had already gone dead. I dropped the phone onto the bed and cursed under my breath.

Part of me was upset because I hated that we had hurt her feelings. Another part of me felt relieved. As much as I hated to admit it, I couldn't help but think Charlie had made some valid points.

Could Allison be behind all this?

Chapter Eighteen

Charlie

When I arrived at practice the following morning, I was prepared to avoid Allison at all costs. Brody let me know how the phone call went, and I had a feeling she'd still be upset with us—rightfully so. As much as I hated suspecting my best friend, I thought it was okay if we gave each other some space until I had an opportunity to do a little more digging. I sincerely hoped I was wrong, but I couldn't shake the weird feeling in my gut.

After I had been stretching for a while, Allison still wasn't on deck. Brody had been cleared to start practicing again, and stretched with Landon a few feet away, and Ellie sat on a bench scribbling in her notebook. Coach Tanner emerged from his office a moment later and asked us to gather around.

"I've got a few things to go over before we hop in the pool this morning," he told us once we were in a half circle in front of him.

I tried to exchange a glance with the others to see if they were also wondering if Coach Tanner realized Allison wasn't there, but they were all focused on him.

He uncapped a marker and turned to start writing on his dry-erase board. "Now, the main set is a little confusing, so I just want to clarify a few things—"

"Coach," I interrupted. "Shouldn't we wait for Allison?"

He turned to face us. "Oh, that's right. I should have mentioned, Allison will be taking a few days off. She's going to go visit her parents and do her workouts from home for a little while."

The strange feeling in my gut deepened. "Did she say why?"

He shook his head. "Family matter is all she told me."

This time Brody did exchange a look with me, and I wondered if he was thinking the same thing as me.

"Anyway, let's focus on the set." Coach Tanner brought me back to the task at hand, and I tried to shove Allison out of my mind for the time being.

When he had finished explaining, I still wasn't totally clear on what we were doing—probably because I couldn't keep my focus—so I knew it was going to be a long practice.

I went up to Brody as I pulled my swim cap over my head. "Do you think it's just a coincidence that Allison left town?"

He shook his head. "I don't know, Charlie. We'll have to pay attention to what's going on around us and see if anything else seems suspicious. And maybe this is a good time to dig a little bit more into what Victor told us."

"You think we'll find out anything?"

"Won't know unless we try."

******

Over the next week and a half, Landon, Brody, and I used all the free time we had to search for clues that might show Allison was working with Mr. Davis—or better yet, to find evidence that she *wasn't*.

With Landon in school, and Brody back to working out full-time, plus photo shoots, it turned out I had the most available time to research. And so far, my efforts had provided very few rewards.

Even though the police had already questioned the mechanic who had worked on Brody's truck, I called and asked him if there was any way to tell how long the brake lines had been broken before I went into work that morning, but he told me the same thing the police had said: that it takes roughly thirty minutes for one brake line to empty. Considering I left shortly before five in the morning, the brakes could have been emptied anytime between then and when Allison had left almost six hours earlier. With still no leads from our neighbors who did have security cameras, there was no way to prove that it had been her. But on the plus side, the mechanic did say the repairs on Brody's truck were now finished, and he was able to have his vehicle back.

As for the restaurant, the police had already determined it was a dead end since there were no cameras installed in the kitchen. And unless Allison had snuck into the kitchen when she had gone to the bathroom, there was nothing to go off—I couldn't prove anything.

Digging into the stolen funds also didn't provide much information. I reached out to Officer Carter to ask for an update, and he said they discovered the login came from the IP address of the front desk computer at Fit Happens. So, we knew the theft did take place at the gym, but since the cameras had been disabled, we couldn't prove if Mr. Davis himself had logged in to the computer, or if someone had logged in on his behalf.

I asked him for a list of fingerprints found on the computer in question, even though it wouldn't necessarily prove Allison did anything wrong. She used that computer daily, her fingerprints were obviously going to be on it. But I was curious to see if Mr. Davis' turned up on it—that would leave me with a whole new batch of questions.

However, Officer Carter still hadn't gotten back to me on that, so for now, it was another dead end.

To prevent me from going completely insane over the whole thing, I did take some time every day to help Brody finalize details for his upcoming gala. It was now only two days away, and there was still plenty to do. Ellie was helping as well, and she and Landon apologized to each other, and put everything behind them to help get some things done together.

Allison still hadn't returned from visiting her parents, and at least for now, that was okay. If she was guilty, I was having a hell of a time trying to prove it. And if she wasn't, then I'd have to do a lot more than just say I was sorry.

A loud crash snapped me out of my thoughts.

"Shit! Please be careful!" Brody snarled from the other side of the dining room. "Those centerpieces are expensive. I can't keep replacing them."

It was late Thursday afternoon, and Brody and I were at the Omni Amelia Island Resort getting all the final touches put in place. Landon and Ellie were still at practice and would finish helping tomorrow.

I placed the last of the silverware on the table I was prepping, and stole a glance over at Brody. It was obvious he was stressed and needed a break. I went to the kitchen and asked the chef for a sample of everything, and he filled three large plates full of food, put them on a tray, and handed it to me.

Walking back out to the dining room, I placed the tray on a table that hadn't been set up yet—I didn't want to risk getting any of the tablecloths dirty—and called Brody over.

He held up his finger to indicate that he needed a minute, but instead of giving it to him, I went over and guided him to the table.

"Charlie, I've got a million things to do," he said, sounding flustered.

"Yes, and we have all day tomorrow, and most of Saturday to get all the final touches put in place," I assured him. "You need a break, and you need to eat something."

He sighed and took a seat. "Fine, but only a few minutes and then I need to get back to work."

"I'll take it," I chuckled and popped a piece of shrimp into my mouth. "Mmm, this is really good."

"It should be," he said, tossing some into his mouth too. "I hired the best chefs in Florida."

I smiled. "Of course, you did."

"So, hear anything from Allison yet?" he asked in between bites.

"No. Do you think she'll be back for the gala?"

He shrugged. "I don't know. If she's up to what you suspect, it'd be an easy way to have us all in one place. And we'd be surrounded by rich people."

I grimaced. "I didn't think of that. Do we need to increase security?"

He shook his head. "Ellie took care of all that. She wouldn't be able to get away with anything under their watch."

I folded my hands in front of me and rested them against my chin. "I don't even like talking about Allison this way. I know I'm the one who brought it up, but I still don't want to believe she would be helping Mr. Davis."

"I don't either. When she gets back, we'll sit down and talk to her. Clear the air. But I want to focus on getting through this weekend first."

"What about Mr. Davis?" I asked him. "Security knows to watch for him specifically?"

"Yes, it'll be fine," he said. He took my hand in his. "I'm serious, Charlie. Let's just cool it until this event is over. I've got enough to stress about without having to keep thinking about one of my best friends being out to kill one of my other best friends."

I put my hands up in surrender. "You're right. You're right. I'll take a break from the investigation for a few days."

"Thank you." He wiped his mouth with a napkin and stood up. "Alright, I need to get back to work."

"It really does look lovely in here, Brody." I took another glance around the room, where crystal chandeliers hung from the ceilings, nearly every table was covered in maroon tablecloths, and had floral arrangements in every color towering two feet high. In the far corner, a space for a string quartet was being set up with twinkly lights. "It's going to be a magical evening."

"Yes, in more ways than one." He winked and walked off without elaborating.

I felt my face blush. I didn't know what exactly he was talking about, but I had a feeling he had something special planned for the two of us this weekend.

******

I worked for another hour at the resort, and then took off to go pick up Landon from practice. Brody was so busy, I was barely able to get a few words in with him before I left, other than I would see him at home.

The drive back to Jacksonville was nearly an hour, and the whole way I daydreamed about what Brody had planned

177

for us. Did he set us up with our own private table? Did he invite someone he knew I would be excited to meet? The party was going to be *filled* with professional athletes, after all. Or maybe, he had something much more romantic planned. I was giddy just thinking about what the weekend had in store.

When I arrived at the pool, Landon was sitting outside by himself, scrolling through his phone. He stood up when he saw me drive in and made his way to the passenger side door. Suddenly, all romantic daydreams left my mind, and thoughts of Mr. Davis came rushing back in. As stressed as I was about the whole thing, I could only imagine how Landon was feeling. It was bad enough that his father was never around to guide him, but then to find out he was in a drug cartel too? I had no idea how I would react if I were in his situation.

Then, almost as quickly, something Brody had said a few weeks ago popped into my mind: *One of these days, we should teach the kid how to drive.*

Unbuckling my seatbelt, I opened the driver's door and got out of the car. I may not have been able to control how Mr. Davis raised Landon, but I could control what happened now. Someone was going to teach him how to drive.

"What are you doing?" Landon stopped in his tracks when he saw me come around to the other side of the vehicle.

"You're going to drive us home." I smiled, opened the passenger door and climbed in.

He didn't move for several seconds as if he were making sure he had heard me correctly. Once I was inside the car, I got situated in my seat and then rolled down my window.

"Are you coming? I want to go home."

Landon nodded slowly and made his way to the driver's side. Once he was seated, he turned towards me. "You know I've never driven a vehicle before, right?"

I nodded. "I do."

"And you trust me not to crash and kill us both?"

Laughing, I nodded again. "Yes, I trust you. I'll tell you what to do. Just make sure you drive the speed limit—you don't have a license. Do you know what all the letters stand for on the gear shift?"

"Yes."

"Okay, so put your foot on the brake, and put it in drive. Don't lift your foot until you're ready to move."

He did as I said, and we slowly made our way out of the parking lot. When we reached the main road, he stopped before turning into traffic.

"I don't know about this." He gripped the steering wheel so tight his knuckles were turning white.

"Landon, relax." I placed a hand on his arm. "Take a deep breath. Good. Now, put on your blinker and go."

The drive was slow, but I was in no hurry, and I wanted Landon to take his time. I didn't need to scare him off from driving ever again.

"Good. Yep, stop here," I said when a light had turned red and we pulled up behind the car in front of us. "Don't want to get any closer than that."

We sat in silence for a moment as we waited for the light to change. Out of the corner of my eye, I saw Landon shift in his seat.

"Did Brody tell you to teach me to drive?" he asked softly.

I turned to face him, but he kept his eyes on the road in front of him. "Well, we can't be your chauffeurs forever, right?" I joked.

"I suppose," he mumbled, still not taking his eyes off the road.

Sighing, I got more serious. "Landon, after everything you've been through, I just feel bad that you've missed out on so many things that a child should experience with their parents. You probably barely remember your mom, and your dad—"

"I know what my dad was like, Charlie." He snapped his attention to me for a brief moment before the light finally turned green, and he slowly started driving again. "I'm tired of everyone pitying me."

I opened my mouth to argue, but remained silent instead.

"Yes, my childhood was less than ideal," he continued. "But I'm not broken, and I wish everyone would quit tip-toeing around me."

"You're right," I agreed.

We sat in silence for a few moments, and he continued to drive on through the darkness. As he grew more comfortable behind the wheel, I could feel the vehicle accelerate to the actual speed limit.

"Do I turn at this light, or the next one?" he asked.

"This one. Don't forget your blinker."

He flawlessly made the turn and drove on like he'd been driving for years.

"I'm sorry if I sounded ungrateful," he mumbled after a while. "I really am glad you're teaching me."

I turned away from him and smiled so he wouldn't be embarrassed. "You're welcome."

The rest of the drive was mostly silent, except for the question here and there Landon would ask. It was almost hard to believe he'd never driven before. Once he got past the initial nerves, he settled right in and seemed to know exactly what he was doing. It helped that it was after eight o'clock, and the roads weren't as busy, but regardless, he did very well.

He pulled into our driveway a few minutes later, threw it in park, and sat back in his seat with a smile on his face.

"You did awesome!" I told him. "You'll be out driving on your own in no time."

"Thanks again, Charlie."

"Don't mention it," I said. "Come on. Let's go inside. I snuck a couple of desserts from the kitchen at the resort."

Chapter Nineteen

Landon

"I think that about does it!" Brody stood with his hands on his hips as he took in the scene before us. Everything had come together the way we had hoped it would.

All the tables were covered in satin tablecloths, and the most beautiful flower arrangements towered over each of them. Every seat was covered in cream linens, and the crystal chandeliers made the light dance around the room. The corner dedicated to the string quartet overflowed with more flowers, there were four fully stocked bars on every side of the room, and the center stage was raised slightly higher than all the other tables with the Children Without a Voice logo hanging above it.

"Brody, is it what you pictured it would be?" Charlie asked, wrapping her arms around him. Ellie and I stood a few feet away, taking in the view as well.

Brody gave Charlie a kiss on the forehead. "It's perfect. I wouldn't change a thing. I think we need a round of champagne to celebrate." He disappeared into the kitchen and returned a moment later with a chilled bottle and four flutes.

"Thank you for all of your help," he said, raising a glass. "I couldn't have finished it without all of you."

We clinked glasses and downed the cool liquid.

"Oh, that's actually pretty good." This was my first time trying champagne, and I lifted the glass to inspect it.

"Don't go crazy now," Brody joked, giving me a nudge on the shoulder.

"You're trying all kinds of firsts this week!" Charlie laughed.

We quickly finished the last of the champagne and started turning off lights and gathering our things to head out. I threw my jacket over my shoulder and stood by the door waiting for Charlie and Brody when Ellie approached me.

"Hey, I never did ask how the prison visit went," she said.

"Oh." I shrugged. "It was interesting. Found out some stuff I didn't really want to know, but I guess it explains a lot."

"Like what?"

"I don't know if I need to burden you with that."

"Landon," she placed a hand on my shoulder. "We're still friends. You can talk to me."

I hesitated for a moment and then decided to just tell her. "Well, I guess my dad is in a cartel, and he owes his boss a lot of money. That's why he tried kidnapping Roman last year." I chuckled to myself as a thought came into my mind.

"What?" she asked, furrowing her brows.

"It's probably a ridiculous thought, but what if my dad tries to show up to the gala tomorrow?"

Her frown deepened. "Why do you think he'd risk that?"

"The money," I said. "There's going to be a lot of money there. And he's desperate."

She chewed on her lip and then nodded. "Well, it's a good thing we hired the best security then."

"Oh, that reminds me. Brody asked me to call them and give them a few last-minute updates. Do you have the name of the security company? I can get that taken care of first thing in the morning."

She shook her head quickly. "No, don't worry about it. I can call them."

"Did Brody tell you the updates?"

"Not yet, but I'll ask him." She gave me a tight smile.

"Seriously, I don't mind. I already have the info—"

"No," she insisted. "It's my job, I'll do it. Goodnight." She side stepped me and took off towards the parking lot.

"Ellie, I didn't mean to upset you," I tried calling after her, but she kept walking.

"What was that about?" Brody asked, appearing out of nowhere.

I shook my head. "Nothing. Are you ready?"

Following Brody and Charlie out of the building, we piled into Charlie's car—she let me drive again—and pulled out of the parking lot a few minutes later.

"I can't believe we pulled it off," Brody said from the passenger seat. "Tomorrow is going to be great. Just a couple of minor things left to take care of in the morning, and we'll be good to go."

"Do you remember the name of the security company?" I asked, my eyes glued to the road in front of me.

"Yes, it's …" he paused while he thought about it. "Ugh I'm blanking on the name. Ever since Ellie took over, I haven't talked to them much. I can ask her."

"I did just now, and all she said is she would take care of the changes."

"Well, if she doesn't mind, I guess I can give her the info to pass along." He pulled out his phone and started typing away.

"I think you should get me the name anyway," I insisted. "I'd like to look into them myself."

"Sure, that's fine." He nodded, still typing away.

I probably had no real reason to be worried, but ever since I mentioned the gala would be a hot spot for my dad, I couldn't stop thinking about it. I just wanted to make sure we were covered if he did happen to make a visit.

******

The following morning, my alarm went off at seven o'clock, but I was already wide awake. My brain was buzzing all night, and I don't think I slept a wink. For some reason, I had an unsettling feeling in my gut that I couldn't shake.

Something bad was going to happen tonight. I just knew it. What exactly that was, I had no idea, but I had a feeling it would involve my father.

"Landon!" Charlie yelled from downstairs. "I made waffles if you want any!"

Attempting to push the bad thoughts to the back of my mind, I pulled myself out of bed and wandered downstairs.

"Hope you're hungry," Charlie said as she plopped two waffles on a plate and handed it to me.

"Smells really good." I took the plate and sat down, but wasn't sure if I had much of an appetite.

A moment later, Brody came rushing down the stairs, furiously typing out a message on his phone. "We've got to get down to the resort ASAP. There was some kind of electrical issue last night and half the building is without power."

"Oh, no." Charlie turned from the stove with wide eyes. "Did they say how it happened?"

Brody shook his head. "They're looking into it now. But we may need to do some rearranging. Can you be ready to go in a couple of minutes?"

Charlie gestured towards the mess she made with the waffle mix. "I just made breakfast for us."

"I don't think I can eat right now if I'm being honest," Brody said. "I'm too stressed about tonight. And this electrical issue isn't the only thing we still need to work on today. We have plenty of final touches to add before doors open at five."

"I'll clean it up," I offered.

"You're not coming with us?" Brody asked.

I shook my head. "No, I don't feel the best." It wasn't a total lie, as I definitely felt sick with worry. "I'm going to get some rest and get a ride in later with Ellie or Coach Tanner."

"I feel bad for making you clean up my mess," Charlie pouted.

"It's fine," Brody said before I could open my mouth. "We need to get going."

A few minutes later, Charlie and Brody were pulling out of the driveway in Charlie's car, and I was home alone. I quickly cleaned up the waffle mess, throwing my barely touched food in the trash.

When that was done, I sat back down at the table and pulled my laptop out. Hoping to find out any piece of information I could, I typed my father's name into Google and started searching.

Unfortunately, Ben Davis was a pretty common name, and a majority of the information I found was about every other Ben Davis but the one I was looking for. Finally, I typed in: "Ben Davis and drug cartels" and one article caught my eye.

Missing Prisoner, Ben Davis, Associated with Mexican Cartel?

A member of the Codicia cartel—currently being held in police custody—has recently opened up about missing inmate, Benjamin Davis. The informant mentioned in this article neither confirms nor denies working closely with Davis, and wishes to remain anonymous.

When asked about the missing inmate, the informant became disgruntled, making it clear to our journalists they didn't have a positive relationship. When we promised to keep the informant's identity secret, he shared the following information:

"He [Davis] grew up in the cartel. His father was a member, and he was raised to take over for him someday. To the leaders, Davis was a model of how they wanted us all to be. He did what he was told, no questions asked, and he was indifferent to the crimes he committed—meaning he didn't hesitate. He just went for it.

"But when he fell in love and got married, he began to make slip ups. He started thinking about others and what

would happen to them if he was caught. Long story short, this landed him in a bunch of trouble, and they executed his wife right in front of his eyes."

My eyes bulged at the last sentence. "He told me she was sick!" I yelled at the computer, tears threatening to escape. Standing, I paced around the kitchen, attempting to keep my emotions at bay.

It was his fault she died.

Honestly, why did that surprise me? My father was cold. Heartless. Evil. And now I knew that I grew up without my mom because of him, and if it was possible, my opinion of him went down even further.

He should consider himself lucky I didn't know where he was.

I sat back down and skimmed through the rest of the article, until I saw Camila's name mentioned:

The informant was then asked about Davis' relationship with recently deceased, Camila Hale, and if she was in any way related to the Codicia as well.

"Yes, she was. In fact, she was one of the district leader's daughters. She had tons of access to everything the cartel did. Davis worked for her father, and the two families were close. I don't know all the details, but something went down between Camila and her father. Something about a guy. I don't know, but it tore them apart, and she tried to run off with her daddy's money. Davis saw the opportunity and went with her. He was still pissed about what they did to his wife, and he wanted out. Didn't take them long to get caught though."

The "anonymous informant" was obviously Victor, as a lot of the next few paragraphs talked about the same thing he said when we had visited him at the prison.

We then asked the informant if they had any idea how Davis had escaped, and if someone had helped him. Unfortunately, despite several attempts at ensuring their identity would not be known, our informant refused to give us a straightforward answer.

What we did gather from this conversation was that the suspect in question is most likely female, blonde, and significantly younger than Davis, who is fifty-two. She is also believed to still be in the Jacksonville area.

My jaw dropped. When Charlie told us she thought Allison was the one working with my dad, I didn't want to believe her. Allison wouldn't hurt a fly. And obviously the description in the article wasn't a lot to go off, but it sure could be her.

I needed to find out.

Opening a new tab, I quickly searched for the visitor hours of the prison where Victor was being kept. Visiting hours didn't start for another hour, but maybe they'd make an exception? This was urgent.

In record time, I packed a bag full of everything I would need for the gala tonight—just in case I didn't have time to come back home before I'd have to make the hour-long trip to the resort. I had everything together, and was reaching for the front door when I suddenly realized I didn't know how I was going to get there.

I was in too big of a hurry to wait for the bus and I didn't have money for an Uber. I couldn't just call Coach Tanner or Ellie and ask for a ride to the prison either. Then suddenly, I got an idea. I stuck my head outside the door and there it was: Brody's truck. He'd probably kill me if he knew I took it, especially since I didn't actually have a license yet, but I knew how to drive now. This felt like the best option.

Running back inside for the keys, I found them buried in the junk drawer in the kitchen and sprinted back outside. I

took a deep breath, and went for it. There was no going back
now.

******

Almost two hours after arriving at the prison, I was finally
taken back to the same visitor's room as when we were here
last time. Despite my begging and pleading, the prison staff
would not let me back before visitor hours started, and even
after they started, Victor refused to let me in until it was
apparent I wasn't going to leave.

When an officer escorted him into the room, he looked as
annoyed as I felt. He scowled when I met his gaze, and
when he was handcuffed to the table, he slouched deep into
the chair, making it evident he didn't want to be there.

"You can't take a hint, can you kid?" he grumbled when
the officer had left.

"I saw the article," I said. "And I have more questions."

He rolled his eyes. "I knew that was a bad idea."

"Tell me how my mother died."

"Like I said in the article, she was executed."

"Why?"

"Because your father fucked up. That's what happens
when you upset the boss." He said this like it was common
knowledge.

"Was she a member of the cartel too?" The question
burned inside me ever since I found out the truth. I didn't
remember a lot about my mom, but I had a hard time
believing she would be a part of something like that.

Victor shook his head. "No, she wasn't."

"Did she know my dad was?"

"Not at first. He started to plan his way out when she
threatened to leave with you. But the thing about the cartel
is: there is no way out. The only way out is death. Once
you're a part of it, they're not just gonna let you leave and
spill all their secrets."

188

"So, why did he leave with Camila then?" I asked.

He chuckled. "Hell, if I know, kid. We all knew he'd get caught. But you met Camila. You knew how manipulative she could be. I'm sure she said something to convince him to join her. She wouldn't have been able to do it without him."

I frowned, confused. "Why not?"

"I didn't tell you before, but your dad is one of the best damn hackers I've ever met. That's why the boss liked him so much. He could hack into just about any account imaginable, and wouldn't ask questions. That's how he and Camila were able to run off with all that money, and that's how we were able to break into that Roman guy's company. The first time anyway."

The gala floated to the front of my mind, and I suddenly felt sick. If he was a hacker, he didn't even need to physically be there to get the money. "Did he say how he was going to get the money once he was out of here?" I asked a little more urgently.

"No, but I imagine it would be something pretty similar. A big event or company."

"A gala, maybe?"

He shrugged. "Sure, why not?"

My heart began to race and the bad feeling from this morning only intensified. I needed to get to the gala and warn Brody and Charlie. But then I remembered the main reason I had come here.

"I need you to tell me who broke my father out of prison," I said. "You told the journalists that she's blonde, and younger than my father."

"I shouldn't have said anything." He shook his head and sat up straighter in his chair. "She sees that article, she's going to know it was me."

"Please," I begged. "I need to know. Is it Allison Benson?"

Victor frowned. "I don't even know who the hell that is."

Relief washed over me for a split second, but panic soon took over again. "Then who is it?"

He sighed. "If she finds out I told you, I *will* find you."

I didn't say anything, but nodded.

"Camila's younger sister."

"Camila had a sister?" I asked.

"Well, half-sister. They have different moms, but the same daddy. Look an awful lot alike though."

"How old is she?"

"I don't know. Twenty-four, twenty-five, maybe?" he guessed. "Looks young for her age though, which plays to her advantage. She's been pretending to be a college student for the last few months."

Almost immediately, I felt my heart drop into my stomach. Everything that had happened over the last month and a half came rushing back into my mind and it all made sense now. How did it take me so long to notice?

Instead of waiting for Victor to say anything more, I flew out of my chair and ran out of the room.

I had to warn Brody.

Chapter Twenty

Charlie

"How do I look?" I stood in front of the mirror in the girl's bathroom, admiring my royal blue sequin dress. It went all the way to the floor and fit looser around my curves, so that it flowed elegantly when I walked.

"It's beautiful!" Ellie's eyes widened when she saw me. She wore a black jumpsuit with one arm covered in a tiered sleeve. Her blonde hair was slicked back into a low ponytail. "Are you going to wear any jewelry?"

I shook my head, looking down at my bare shoulders. "No, I was going to since my dress is strapless, but I still can't find the necklace Brody gave me. It's like it just disappeared."

"Definitely weird," Ellie said.

"But hopefully with my hair down, it'll cover my shoulders and I'll be fine." I combed my fingers through my hair a few times, and tossed my hair and makeup bag into my purse. "Let's go put this stuff in the car and see if Brody needs anything."

When we re-entered the ballroom a few minutes later, I smiled once again at the sight before me. Luckily, the electrical issue from this morning had been resolved, and we didn't have to do any rearranging. The lights sparkled off all the chandeliers, the musicians were tuning their instruments and practicing some songs, and the announcer for the evening was doing a sound check on stage. Kitchen staff scurried all about the room, making sure all table settings were in place, and some began piling dishes onto the buffet table.

I spotted Brody standing near the stage with a clipboard in his hands, scanning the room and scribbling a note every so often. He was already in his tux, and he had actually combed his hair—he looked incredibly sexy.

"I'll be right back," I told Ellie.

"Yeah, that's fine." She was typing away on her phone and barely looked up. "I'll be here."

Making my way over to Brody, I tapped him on the shoulder when I reached his side. He turned towards me and did a double take when he realized it was me.

His face lit up as he checked me out from head to toe. "Charlie, you look stunning." He took my hand and gave me a twirl to admire every view. "Damn, I'm going to be fighting men off you all night."

I felt my face blush. "Well, I think maybe you should wear a tux more often." I reached towards him and straightened his bow tie. "You look very handsome."

He leaned in and kissed me. "Come with me." He set his clipboard on the stage and led me towards the exit.

"Where are we going?" I giggled.

"I want to show you something."

He led me out of the ballroom and towards the elevators. Once we were inside, he hit the button for the top floor. As soon as the doors closed, he took me in his arms and smashed his mouth against mine. Our breaths came quicker, and I clung to him like my life depended on it. His hands roamed across my back, down to my ass, and back up to my chest. He swept over every inch of me, and I felt my body melt under his touch. I literally groaned out loud when the elevator doors swung open and Brody broke the kiss—I didn't want him to stop.

"Come on." He smiled. "We have to take the stairs from here."

I had no idea where he was taking me, or what we were doing, but I would follow this man off a cliff. I clung to his arm and let him lead me up a short flight of stairs to a door that said, *Staff Only*. He swiped a hotel key card into the slot and pushed the door open.

"Where did you get that?" I asked in surprise.

He chuckled. "I'll be asking the questions from here on out."

Although suspicious, I refrained from asking him anything else and followed him through the door.

"Oh, my gosh!" My mouth dropped open. We were now standing on the roof of the resort, the ocean in the distance, the setting sun beyond that. The clouds swirled different shades of purple and pink, and there was a cool saltwater breeze blowing my hair away from my face. "Wow, this is beautiful."

Brody led me further still, until we reached an awning with twinkling lights dangling from all four sides, and a blue rug was sprawled out in the middle. My heart stopped beating for a moment as I realized what was happening.

"Are you doing what I think you're doing?" I asked breathless. My nerves were suddenly tingling, and I felt butterflies in my stomach with the anticipation.

He smiled so wide I thought for sure the corners of his mouth were touching his ears. "What do you think I'm doing?"

"I'm afraid to say in case I'm wrong," I giggled nervously.

When we reached the center of the rug, he stopped and turned so that we were facing each other.

"Charlie, I know we haven't known each other long," he began, taking both of my hands in his. "But I've never doubted for a second that you're the one I want to share my life with. My life is better with you in it, and I feel as though a big hole in my heart has been filled. I'm ready for the next step, and I want to begin our lives together."

Happy tears began to fall from my eyes, and I choked out a sob when he lowered himself to one knee. Releasing one of my hands, he reached into his pocket and pulled out a shiny diamond ring.

"Will you take this next step with me?" he asked, holding the ring towards me.

I smiled and nodded like a crazy person, afraid if I opened my mouth, I'd start crying harder. He slipped the ring on my finger, stood up and wrapped his arms around my waist, lifting my feet off the ground. I clung to him and was so overjoyed, I couldn't do anything but cry softly into his neck.

When he set me back on the ground, he used his thumbs to wipe away my tears. "I hope these are happy tears, and you're not already regretting your answer," he joked.

I laughed in between sobs. "Yes, very happy tears." Taking a deep breath, I pulled him close to me and kissed him. Lost in the moment, I could've stayed up there kissing him all night, but his phone started ringing, and he reluctantly broke the kiss.

"Sorry, it's Landon." He looked at me as if waiting for permission to answer it.

"Go ahead," I chuckled.

"Landon, what's up?" he said once he had answered. "Woah, woah, woah, slow down."

My smile disappeared immediately. "What's wrong?" I asked, but Brody shook his head and mouthed *I don't know*.

"Landon, what are you trying to say?" he repeated into the phone. "Yes, we're at the resort, guests are starting to arrive. Where are you? ... How are you— ... What the fuck, are you sure?"

One of my hands shot to my mouth. I couldn't tell what Landon was saying, but I didn't like how it sounded.

"Okay, we're on the roof. We'll get down there now and find her. Call 911 if you want to play it safe." He hung up the phone and directed his attention back to me. "Landon went back to the prison to see Victor."

"Alone?" I shrieked.

"Yes, but he said Victor told him who was working with his dad. It's—"

A clapping sound stole our attention and we turned to find Ellie standing a few feet away, slowly clapping her hands.

"Ellie," Brody said, looking back at me. "It's Ellie."

Panic bubbled in my gut, but I remained silent.

"Ellie, I didn't think you'd come up here," Brody said, forcing a smile back on his face. He took my hand that he had placed a ring on only minutes earlier, and held it towards her. "She said yes! I appreciate all your help setting this up."

My mouth dropped open in shock. "Wow, I had no idea you were both planning this. Uh, thank you." I tried like hell to keep my voice from wavering.

She stopped clapping and folded her arms across her chest. Her expression wasn't one I would expect given the circumstances. She wasn't smiling, and she wasn't exactly scowling, but it was close.

"Is something wrong downstairs?" Brody asked.

She pursed her lips and shook her head no. She didn't say anything, but instead, started laughing.

Brody and I exchanged a look, wondering what the hell was wrong with her. We waited uncomfortably while she continued to laugh to her herself.

She stopped laughing and heaved in a big sigh. "No, there's nothing wrong downstairs. In fact, everything is going exactly the way I planned it would."

Brody took half a step in front of me so that he was between me and Ellie. "Tell me what's going on," he demanded.

"Oh, Brody." She smirked. "Sweet, sweet, innocent Brody. Think about what's going on here. Did you really think that I wanted to help you put this crap fest on out of the kindness of my own heart?"

"You're working with Davis, aren't you?" he asked, sounding much calmer than I felt.

"You catch on quick!"

"Is he here?"

"Unfortunately, he is." She rolled her eyes. "Your little electrical issue this morning destroyed all the malware we had in place, so he had no choice but to come in and manually direct all the online donations into our account."

"How did he get past security?" I asked.

She snickered. "I was put in charge of security, remember?"

My stomach literally flipped inside of me. *Shit.*

"It really was too easy to convince Brody to let me take over," she continued. "See, in the event that we did run into issues, I needed a way to make sure we could get in and do our business without being caught. And you were so consumed with everything else going on, you didn't even realize I fired your original team."

"So, who's down there now?" Brody sounded agitated. "I was talking to them just a little bit ago!"

"Only the best of the best." She winked. "But like I said, they're not as worried about preventing bad people from getting in, as they are more concerned about making sure we leave with what we came for."

"Money?"

"Bingo." She pointed a finger gun at us.

"Why are you doing this?" I asked. "Why are you doing Camila and Mr. Davis' dirty work for them? What's in it for you?"

"Vengeance." She narrowed her eyes. "I agreed to help break Davis out of jail and help him get the money he owes my father. In exchange, I knew he would know how to get to you."

"Why do you—"

"Hold on, Brody," she interrupted, holding up her pointer finger. "Don't interrupt. Anyway, as I was saying: getting the money wasn't easy at first. I couldn't do anything that would draw too much attention to myself. If I got caught, they'd find Davis, too, and we'd both be screwed. So, I stole small things here and there."

"You stole my suit a few weeks ago, didn't you?" Brody asked, as realization washed over us both.

I frowned. "And my necklace?"

"Hell yeah, I did." Ellie grinned. "Turns out you can get a pretty penny for a professional athlete's swimming attire. And your necklace? I sold it for probably three times the amount you paid for it, Brody." She said it like it was something to be proud of.

"Why would you do that? I thought we were friends?"

Brody gave me a sideways glance as if telling me to let it go. It was obvious at this point that we were never friends.

"I stole other things, too," Ellie continued. "Davis was even shifting money out of his business to the cartel. He gave me his login information, so I could attempt to get a little more, but it was all too slow."

"*You're* the one who broke into Fit Happens at three in the morning?"

"My dad wanted that money sooner rather than later," she continued, ignoring my comment. "We started scheming up some ideas, when what do you know? You give us this wonderful opportunity, and the rest was just too damn easy." She started laughing again.

Suddenly, I remembered something from when we had talked to Victor. "Your dad is Mr. Davis' boss?" I asked.

"That's what I said, wasn't it?" she spat.

"Victor told us Camila's dad was the boss. Does that mean Camila was your sister?"

I felt Brody reach for my hand and give it a squeeze when he had connected the dots.

"She was my sister," Ellie said. "And that's why I want revenge."

"Did you ask Brody if he'd go out with you, so you could get him alone?" I asked.

"Yep." She nodded. "And when that didn't work, I had to take a different approach. I had to force my way into your lives some other way, but I sure as hell wasn't going to date the kid."

Brody's hand tightened on mine again, and I knew he was angry.

"You just wanted to know where and when to come after us," I said it more like a statement than a question. "All those near-death experiences we went through?"

"Yeah, that was me," she admitted.

"Brody's truck?"

"Cut the brake lines. I waited outside until I was sure you were all asleep. Didn't intend for you to get in and drive it though Charlie, I had other plans for you." She shot me a wink.

I shook my head, trying to ignore that comment and the intensifying sickness in my stomach. "And the restaurant?"

"I snuck into the kitchen when I said I went to the bathroom. Loaded Brody's plate up with oregano."

"Good God," Brody mumbled under his breath.

"Obviously, none of my plans worked out, and that's why you're both still standing here." She rolled her eyes again. "And then, to make matters worse, you all started getting nosy and digging into things you had no business digging in. And don't even get me started on going to see Victor. My dad should have killed that fucking moron when he had the chance."

"So, then what stopped you?" I asked, still focused on the fact that she wanted us dead. "It's been weeks since the restaurant. If you wanted us gone so bad, why didn't you try something else?"

"I wanted to make you squirm a little bit." She pinched her lips together and appeared to take a deep breath before she continued. "Besides, another plan came to mind. After we had already set up the plans to get the money from your guests this evening, Brody asked me to help set up this proposal." She pulled up one of the legs of her jumpsuit and pulled a gun from a hidden holster. A wicked smile spread across her lips as she extended her arm and pointed the gun towards us. "I decided to keep this plan a little simpler and straight to the point. Any last words?"

Chapter Twenty-One

Landon

After I had called Brody to warn him of what Ellie was going to do, I called 911 and told them as well. Instead of staying on the line, though, I got off as soon as I reached the resort.

I wasn't sure if my father was even there, but I had to get in there and put an end to whatever he and Ellie were trying to do.

The place was packed with cars and people as guests were beginning to arrive. In order to waste less time, I left Brody's truck almost half a mile away, and ran the rest of the way to the entrance. Once inside, I stopped in my tracks. I had no idea where to start looking, or even what I should be looking for.

Scanning the room, I noticed Allison almost right away. Dressed in a simple floor-length red gown, her blonde hair flowing down her back, she stood out from the crowd. I don't know when she got back to town, but I was glad to see her— even though she was probably still upset with us.

Not sure what else to do, I ran up to her and immediately tore her away from the couple she was conversing with. "I need to talk to you right now."

"Landon, I was having a conversation." She turned to address the couple. "I'm sorry, I'll be right back."

"I need your help," I said once we were a comfortable distance away from other guests.

She put her hands on her hips impatiently. "With what? I'm the bad guy, remember?"

"I'm so, so sorry about that. It was a huge misunderstanding, but I can explain it later. This is urgent. Ellie is working with my dad. It's possible he's here."

Her eyes widened and her mouth dropped open, but she didn't say anything.

"My dad owes a lot of money," I continued. "Almost all the donations that will be made tonight will be virtual, and I'm pretty sure he's hacked the systems here to steal them. As for Ellie, I have reason to believe she's dangerous, and Brody and Charlie could be in danger."

"How do you know this?" she asked.

"Like I said, I can explain it later. Right now, I need you to get people out of here. Block the entrances, announce a fire drill, I don't care. They're going to start spending money as soon as they get in here, and it'll be easier to just keep them out."

She nodded. "I can do that."

"I'm going to find the servers and shut everything down. Then I need to find Ellie and my dad. I have my phone on me. Call me if you need anything."

Again, she nodded.

I turned to leave, but she grabbed my arm and stopped me.

"Please be careful, Landon," she said with worry in her eyes.

"I will. Thanks for being here. I'm sorry for everything."

"I know." She gave me a soft smile and then we both took off in different directions.

Running out of the ballroom, I searched the halls for some kind of maintenance room. I had no idea if shutting down the servers would actually do anything to help the situation, but I figured it was a good place to start.

Finally, I found a door labeled *maintenance* that was left open a crack. Pushing it open, I went inside and took a look around. One side of the room was basically a wall of wires and flashing lights. Not knowing what anything in this room did, I started pulling out every wire I saw.

"What the hell do you think you're doing?" A familiar voice boomed behind me.

Startled, I stopped what I was doing and turned to face the voice. The room was poorly lit, but I could still make out my father's shape a few feet away.

"I know what you've done!" I yelled to him. "I know you're working for a cartel, I know Ellie is the one who broke you out of prison, and I know why you're trying to steal all this money."

"Landon, get out of here before you get hurt," he growled.

I laughed. "Since when have you been concerned about what happens to me?"

"Just do what I say!"

Ignoring him, I turned back towards the machines and resumed pulling at the wires. I kept pulling as fast as I could until I was grabbed by the neck of my shirt and pulled back, hard. My body hit the ground with a loud thud and the wind was knocked out of my lungs. Sucking in huge gulps of air, I attempted to roll to my side and prop myself up.

My dad stepped over me and frantically tried to put the wires back in place.

Once I had some of my breath back, I pulled myself off the ground and ran to the other side of the computer system and started pulling at the wires from that end.

"God dammit!" I heard my father's heavy footsteps only moments before he whipped me around and his fist connected with my jaw.

I stumbled back from the blow, but ignoring the searing pain in my face, I snapped out of it and threw myself against my dad's back. Wrapping my arms tightly around his neck, I squeezed as hard as I could.

"Get off me, boy!" His hands pulled at my arms, attempting to loosen my grip, but I held tight.

"Give it up, Dad!" I yelled. "You're not going to get the money. I don't care what they do to you, you're not getting it."

Finally, he slammed me up against the wall hard enough that I was forced to loosen my grip and I fell to the floor.

Leaning against the wall, I attempted to massage the pain out of the back of my head. My dad now towered over me.

"Did you finally grow a pair of balls or something?" he cackled.

I glared at him. "It's high time I start fighting back. I've let you stomp all over me my entire life, but not anymore." My legs were a little shakier, but I pulled myself to my feet once more. "I'm not going to let you get away with this."

Before I could take a step towards him, he pulled a gun out from somewhere behind him and held it towards me. "That's enough, Landon."

I stopped in my tracks and held my palms up in front of me instinctively.

"I really don't want to have to do this, but if you don't knock it off, you're going to leave me with no choice." His voice shook as he tried to catch his breath.

"You killed mom, might as well kill your kid too, right?" I shot back.

"*They* killed your mom! And they're going to kill me too if I don't get them their money."

"So, you'd rather off your own kid than risk being killed for your own stupid decisions?" I shook my head. "You're fucking scum. I'm ashamed to be related to you."

"Shut up!" He clicked off the safety and loaded the barrel.

I squeezed my eyes shut and prepared for the worst. A loud crash made me jump, and I took a deep breath when I realized it was the door crashing open, and two police officers stood in its frame. Allison was behind them, pointing her finger in our direction.

"I told you he's here!" she yelled.

The two police officers drew their weapons, and pointed them towards my dad.

"Drop your weapon!" the shorter one yelled.

My father didn't drop it though. He turned his attention back to me. "If I die, they'll come after you next," he said. "They'll stop at nothing to get their money."

"He said drop the gun!" the other police officer yelled, each of them taking a step closer to my dad.

"I need to make sure that doesn't happen," my dad said softly. It was hard to tell in the dark room, but he almost looked sad.

A split second too late, I realized why. Then there were several loud bangs and the room went dark.

Chapter Twenty-Two

Brody

Charlie gasped at the sight of the weapon in Ellie's hand, and I took half a step forward, extending one palm like that would stop her from shooting us.

"Ellie, hang on," I said. "I'm sorry about what happened to your sister. She was going to kill Charlie if I didn't do anything."

"You think Charlie means anything to me?" She scowled, tightening her grip on the gun. "My sister was my best friend and confidant, and now she's gone. I can't let you get away with that."

"Killing us is not going to bring her back," I tried to reason with her. "There has to be something we can do. I have money. You can have it, just let us go."

She huffed. "After we get the rest of the money tonight, I'll be free as a bird. I don't want your money. I want to personally make sure you meet the same sticky ending my sister did."

Suddenly, there was a loud bang on the door to the roof that made us all jump. Shouts came from the other side: "Fernandina PD, open up!" Ellie had obviously blocked the door after she had followed us up there.

More banging came, and Ellie turned to face the noise in response.

"Run!" I told Charlie, taking her hand and running in the opposite direction.

"Where are we supposed to run—?"

Gun shots sounded behind us, and we instinctively ducked and covered our heads. "Get back here!" Ellie yelled.

The roof was littered with various electricity boxes and AC units we had to run around until we got to the edge on the opposite side. The wall surrounding the edge came up just above our waists, and we had to lean over it to peer over the side.

Panic was written all over Charlie's face. "What do we do?"

I scanned the side of the building, and saw a fire escape a few yards down to the right. I pointed to it and the two of us ran to it.

"There's nowhere for you to hide up here!" Ellie shouted from behind us. "I *am* going to get you."

"Charlie, take my hand," I demanded. "I'm going to help you over the edge."

"Are you going to come down after me?" she asked, taking my hand.

"I'll hold Ellie off until you're safe."

She ripped her hand out of my grasp. "No! I'm not going to leave you behind."

"We don't have time to argue about this." I took her by the shoulders and urged her towards the fire escape. "You need to go, now!"

Reluctantly, she agreed and carefully lifted herself over the edge and down the ladder to the fire escape stairwell. There were unshed tears in her eyes, and I could tell she was terrified.

I made sure she reached the stairwell, and then I quickly ducked behind one of the giant AC units nearby. All I had to do was keep Ellie busy for a few minutes until the police broke down the door, right?

I could hear Ellie's footsteps as she neared my hiding spot. I had no idea what I was going to do, but I had to decide fast. Holding my breath, I waited until she reached the edge. She placed her hands—along with the gun—on the wall, but before she was able to peer over the side, I bulldozed into her and took her down to the ground where she landed with a loud thud beneath me. The gun flew from her hand and landed a few feet out of her reach.

"Get off me!" she growled. She swung her arms and kicked her legs ferociously, attempting to wriggle out from underneath me.

"Give it up, Ellie!" I squeezed my eyes shut as she clawed at my face and tried with all my might to keep her held down.

At some point, she managed to get her nails deep into my skin, right over my left eye. I screamed out in pain and instinctively reached for my face with both hands. She took the opportunity to land a punch to my gut, and I fell over sideways trying to get my breath back.

While I gasped for air, she scurried to her feet and ran to where the gun had landed. I was able to see her holding the gun at me from my good eye. Holding out a hand in front of me, I tried once more to reason with her.

"Ellie, please. You don't want to kill me."

"Yes, I do!" she screamed through clenched teeth. "My life has been a living hell for as long as I can remember. My sister was the only good thing I had, and you took her from me."

"She did that to herself. What if she couldn't ever get the money back? Do you honestly believe your dad wouldn't have punished her the same way he's punishing Landon's dad? What would you have done then? Killed your own dad?"

"I would have tried!" Her lips started trembling, and I could tell she was holding back sobs. "She would have done the same for me."

"Would she though?" I asked. "Did she even tell you what she was planning before she ran away? Make any indication of you going with her?"

"She … she said it would have been too risky for us both to leave," she stammered. "She said she needed someone from the inside to have her back."

"So, even though she knew you were both miserable, she decided to leave you behind. That doesn't sound like a good sister to me."

"You don't understand!" she cried. Tears were streaming down her cheeks now, but she still held the gun pointed at me.

"No, I don't," I agreed. I was still sprawled on the ground below her. If she wanted to shoot me, she easily could. I needed to keep her talking. "I'm not even going to pretend like I know what you went through, Ellie. And I never knew Camila like you did. But I knew her well enough to know that she was only looking out for herself. She would use everyone around her for her own benefit, and when she was done with them, they were gone."

"She wouldn't have done that to me," she whimpered. "She loved me."

"If she had really cared about you like she should, she would have taken you with her. Gone to the police, went into witness protection—I don't know. Something! She wouldn't have left you there alone to figure it out for yourself."

Suddenly, there was a loud crack, like the sound of snapping wood from the other side of the roof, followed by at least half a dozen footsteps. Within seconds, a line of officers was standing nearby, their weapons drawn and pointed at Ellie.

"Put the gun down, or we'll shoot!" one of them yelled.

Ellie didn't move. She stayed frozen to her spot, the gun still in her hands, tears still flowing.

"Ellie," I pleaded. "Please, do the right thing. You can get your life back. You don't have to do this."

"Put down your weapon!" another officer repeated.

Finally, I saw the defeat in Ellie's eyes. She lowered the gun to the ground and lifted her hands above her head. "I don't want to die," she said. "But I don't want to live this life anymore."

She lowered her gaze to the ground as one of the officers approached her and put her in handcuffs. Another officer knelt beside me and helped me sit up.

"Can you stand?" he asked.

I nodded, and he helped me to my feet.

"We're going to have to take a look at that eye," he said, pointing to the scratches on my face. "You might need stitches."

The officer who had handcuffed Ellie proceeded to lead her back to the roof entrance, and the rest of us followed closely behind.

When we had reached the ballroom where the gala should have been held, I saw a totally empty room. All the guests and employees had been rushed outside. Some tables where guests had started gathering had half-filled glasses of wine on top of them, and half-eaten plates of food.

What a shame this night turned out the way it did. All of those months of planning and preparing, ruined in the blink of an eye. Part of me wanted to take a look around and see what could be salvaged. Maybe we could postpone and still hold the event at a later date. But the larger part of me wanted to get outside and find Charlie.

Running ahead of Ellie and the officers, I burst through the main doors and was once again welcomed by the cool night air. Outside, hundreds of guests stood huddled in bunches, all looking confused and frustrated. Pushing through the crowd, I ignored questions as I rounded the corner to where I was certain the fire escape had been located.

There, I saw several police cars, a firetruck, and a couple of ambulances all flashing their lights. Charlie was among them, wrapped in a blanket, and anxiously staring at the sky as if she were expecting something to fall from it.

"Charlie!" Relief filled me as I ran towards her.

When she turned her gaze towards my voice, she immediately broke down in tears and opened her arms for me.

Crashing into her embrace, I held her tight as she sobbed into my shoulder. "Oh, my God. I'm so happy you're okay."

She broke the embrace and held me at arm's length as she inspected my body. "Did she hurt you? What happened to your eye?"

"Ellie took a swing at me. Officer said I might need stitches." I shrugged. "It doesn't hurt that bad."

"Bullshit." She glared. "You have blood dripping down your face. You shouldn't have stayed behind."

I smiled and pulled her into me again. "I'm fine. It's over. She's in police custody now. She went willingly."

"I still can't believe she was the one working with Mr. Davis," she said into my shoulder.

"Speaking of him, did they find him?" I asked. "Have you seen Landon at all?"

She stepped out of our embrace once more. "I don't know. I haven't seen him."

"We should go look for him."

She held me in place. "You should have the paramedics look at your eye first."

Wrapping an arm around her shoulder, I shook my head no. "It can wait. Let's go."

Holding her close to my side, we went back towards the main entrance of the resort. We kept our gazes held forward, scanning the crowd for any signs of Landon or Mr. Davis, and ignored the dozens of questions and remarks thrown our way. We kept going until I heard a familiar voice calling my name.

Charlie and I turned towards the voice and saw Roman Howard approaching us.

"Trouble seems to follow you around, doesn't it?" he said when he had reached us.

"Roman, I wasn't expecting you," I said as I shook his hand.

"Yes, well I had half a mind to stay hidden until they caught Davis, but I couldn't not come to your event." He cleared his throat and adjusted his black tie. "Not after everything you've done for me."

"I appreciate it. I am sorry that it turned out the way it did."

He shook his head. "I guess we shouldn't be that surprised, should we? While he was out, something was bound to happen. Do they have him in custody now at least?"

I shrugged. "I don't know. That's what we were trying to find out as well."

"Right. I'll leave you to it then," he said. "If you ever need anything, Brody, don't hesitate to ask."

"Thanks, Roman."

He disappeared back into the sea of people, and Charlie and I once again proceeded towards the entrance. Two police officers were guarding the door, and next to them Allison was in hysterics as she attempted to speak to them.

"Allison, what's wrong?" I asked when we reached her.

"Oh, there you are!" She jumped when she saw us and wrapped her arms around me and then Charlie. Tears were gushing from her eyes, and I could barely understand her through her violent sobs.

"We're okay, Allison," I assured her. "Everything's going to be fine."

She shook her head furiously. "No, everything is not fine," she cried. "It's Landon."

"What happened?" I asked. Dread suddenly filled my gut, and I felt like I was going to be sick. "Is he okay?"

Allison's lip trembled as she attempted to hold in another sob. "He killed him."

I blinked several times, not sure I had heard her correctly. "Who killed him?"

"Mr. Davis." The sob she had been trying to hold back broke through and tears started streaming down her face again. "Come with me." She turned back towards the main doors and indicated to the officers that we were with her.

Beside me, Charlie's face had gone white, and she too looked like she was moments away from vomiting. We followed Allison down a long hallway out of the ballroom until we reached a small room where several more police officers were gathered.

"I'm sorry, I can't let you in here," a tall, female officer said. She held one hand towards us, and the other held a camera. "We're collecting evidence."

"Please let them through," Allison begged. "They won't touch anything. They were the closest thing to family he had."

"He lived with us," Charlie added. Her breathing had picked up, and a look of pure panic was etched on her face.

The female officer seemed to think for a moment, and then nodded solemnly. "Don't touch anything."

I took Charlie's hand in mind and silently walked forward through the door of the small room. My knees nearly buckled when I saw them. In front of us were two bodies with police tape surrounding them. On the end closest to us was Mr. Davis, and the other was Landon.

"Oh my God, no!" Charlie screamed. Both of her hands flew to her mouth, where she attempted to stifle heavy sobs.

I wrapped my arms around her and held her close to me. Staring at the scene before me, I completely froze. I kept thinking any minute I would wake up from this nightmare and this would all be a lie. But I kept blinking, and nothing changed. Landon was still lying on the floor in a puddle of his own blood, unblinking, his skin already turning a light shade of blue.

"What happened?" I whispered.

"His dad held him at gun point," Allison explained. "Landon had been trying to deactivate the servers. I showed up with the police, who told Mr. Davis to drop his weapon or they'd shoot." She started to cry again as she retold the story. "Mr. Davis said they'd come after Landon next if he was killed, and then he pulled the trigger. The cops opened fire immediately after, but it was too late. I watched the whole thing."

Releasing one arm from Charlie, I wrapped it around Allison to comfort her. "Fucking bastard," I mumbled under my breath.

Mr. Davis had actually killed his own son and made it sound like he was doing him a favor. If he didn't do it now, the cartel would just do it later, right? He was lucky the cops got to him when they did. If he was still alive, I'd be sure to kill him myself.

"Brody, who's the 'they' he was referring to?" Allison asked after a few moments.

"I'll tell you later," I said. "Are you alright?"

She shook her head lightly. "I don't know. I can't get the scene out of my head. I just keep seeing him die in front of my eyes."

Charlie unlatched herself from my hold and took Allison in her arms. They were both crying and they held each other tight. "Allison, I am so, so sorry for everything I said to you," she sobbed. "I don't expect you to forgive me anytime soon, but know I am here for you whenever you need someone."

Allison didn't respond. Instead, she squeezed her eyes shut and clung to Charlie like she was afraid she'd lose her, too.

"Let's get out of this room," I said to them. "We need to find Coach Tanner and tell him what happened."

Leading the girls away from the scene, I took one last look, and said a silent goodbye to Landon.

Chapter Twenty-Three

Charlie

Several hours later, after finding Coach Tanner, answering a million police questions, and making arrangements for Landon, we were finally back home. It was after midnight, and I was completely exhausted. Heading straight for the stairs, I started getting ready for bed, even though I was certain I wouldn't be able to sleep a wink tonight.

Once I had changed out of my dress and into an oversized t-shirt and some sweatpants, I felt a bit better. Looking in the mirror, I saw streaks of makeup running down my face, and my eyes were red and swollen from all the crying. Afraid I'd start again, I washed my face as quickly as I could and left the bathroom expecting to see Brody getting ready for bed as well, but he was nowhere to be seen.

"Brody?" I called. Stepping out of the bedroom and into the hallway, I called his name again. "Brody? Are you coming to bed?" I listened for his response, but heard nothing. I was about to walk back into the bedroom when I noticed Landon's door was open.

I went to the door and peeked inside. There, Brody sat on top of Landon's bed, his elbows resting on his knees, his face buried in his hands. The sight broke my heart, and made me want to cry all over again.

"Are you okay?" I asked softly from the doorway.

"I should have told him to stay away," he said without moving. "He'd still be here if I had just told him to go home."

Rushing to his side, I sat on the bed beside him and placed a hand on his arm. "Brody, you can't blame yourself for this. We didn't know this was going to happen."

His head shot up from his hands to face me. "But we knew there was a good chance his dad would be there tonight. I should have never let him out of my sight." His eyes were wet with tears that had refused to fall until now.

"He's an adult now, Brody. You know as well as I do that we wouldn't have been able to shelter him forever."

"Well, we could have tried," he sobbed. He buried his face in his hands once more and I wrapped my arms around him, resting my cheek on his shoulder.

Gently massaging his arms with my thumbs, I let him cry it out. His body shook with each sob, and it took every ounce of will power to fight back my own tears. Eventually, the sobs grew quieter, replaced by heavy breathing and lots of sniffling.

"Brody?" I asked quietly. "Do you think Mr. Davis was right?"

"About what?" he sniffed.

"If he hadn't killed Landon himself, would the cartel have come after him?"

He shrugged. "I don't know."

"Don't take this the wrong way," I paused as I tried to put into words what I was thinking. Brody lifted his face out of his hands and looked at me expectedly. "Do you think it's a good thing Landon doesn't have to live in fear anymore?"

He stared past me as he thought about my question. Finally, he met my gaze again. "Maybe. But Davis shouldn't have put him into the situation to begin with. Once he knew he was a father, he should have separated himself from his wife and Landon. They might both still be alive if he hadn't been so selfish."

"That's true." I nodded slowly.

"God, he had so much life to live yet." He ran a hand through his hair and pulled on the ends. "It's not fair."

"We just need to focus on the good times we spent with him," I said, trying to think positively. "Remember last fall, the swim meet up in Ohio when Landon found that stray cat on the way back from dinner?"

The tiniest hint of a smile played on Brody's lips at the memory. "He smuggled it into the hotel and wanted to take it home with him until Coach Tanner found out and made him take it back where he found it."

"The kid had a heart of gold," I said, smiling to myself. "Those are the kinds of memories we need to hold on to. His memory will live on through all of us."

Brody took my hand in his and gave it a tight squeeze. Leaning towards me, he rested his forehead against my own. We stayed like that for several minutes as silence stretched between us. Finally, he pulled back, stood up from the bed, and guided me to the door, my hand still in his.

"Come on, let's try to get some sleep," he said.

We walked out of Landon's bedroom and closed the door behind us. Trapping all our memories of him inside, for us to revisit later.

******

Bright and early the next day, after not being able to sleep a wink, I stood at Allison's front door, ringing the bell. After everything that happened over the last couple of weeks, I owed her a big apology. I told her I was sorry last night, but with emotions running so high, I also felt like I needed to sit down and talk to her now that everything had settled down some.

Staring at my toes, I let out a long breath in anticipation. Finally, she answered the door with a small smile on her face. Her cheeks were red, and her eyes still puffy from all the crying she undoubtedly did overnight.

"Hey, Charlie," she said. "You know you don't have to ring the bell. You can always just come right in."

I nodded. "I know. I just wanted to make sure we were still friends after all the things I said to you."

She opened the door wider. "Do you want to come in and talk?"

"That'd be great." I followed her inside, ditching my shoes at the door.

"Can I get you anything to drink?" she asked, leading me into the living room. The room was slightly smaller than Brody's, but much cleaner. Her white carpet was flawless, and her grey recliner and couch looked brand new.

"I'm okay, thank you." I took a seat on one end of the couch, while she took a seat in the chair across from me. There was a short silence as the two of us tried to decide what we would say.

"Charlie—" Allison said at the same time I said:

"Look, I want to say—"

Allison smiled. "You go first."

"I'm really sorry about everything." I realized I was staring at my feet as I spoke, and I forced myself to meet her gaze before I continued. "I shouldn't have been so accusing. It's just that you seemed so adamant about Landon not going to the prison, and then Ellie had said some things about you, and when you left for a few days … it felt suspicious."

She bit back a laugh. "Shoot, I didn't think about how that looked."

"What do you mean?" I asked, confused.

"Charlie, I didn't leave town because of what you said, or because of anything to do with Landon going to talk to Victor," she said. "My grandmother passed away. I went home to be with my family and go to the funeral. Geez, I realize now that probably did seem a little suspicious. I would have said something, but y'all were mad at me, so I only told Coach. I'm sorry."

I shook my head. "No, you had every right not to tell us. You have nothing to apologize for. I'm sorry for what I said. I got wrapped up in what was going on. I should have just talked to you first."

"Apology accepted," she said quietly. "I know you were only trying to look out for Landon. I would have been tempted to think the same thing if the roles had been reversed."

"You should at least yell at me a little bit or something." I pouted. "It might make me feel a little better."

She laughed harder this time. "Trust me, Charlie, I was upset about what you said, but I'm over it. It was a misunderstanding. That's it. Let's just pretend it never happened."

I nodded. "It's forgotten."

Her smile faded and she looked as though she were fighting back a new batch of tears. "Besides, it kind of pales in comparison to what happened at the gala."

"How are you handling it?" I asked, even though I was pretty sure I already knew the answer.

She shook her head as if searching for the right words. "I can't stop seeing it." The tears she had been trying to hold back broke through hard and fast.

Rushing to her side, I put my arms around her and held her close.

"Every time I close my eyes, that's all I see," she sobbed. "I keep seeing him die over and over again."

I remained silent as I held her shaking body. Her sobs shook her to the core, and every couple of moments she'd have to take in a huge gulp of air in order to breathe. I ran a soothing hand across her back while she cried and tried like hell to be strong. After several minutes, her cries became softer, and the only sound was her sniffling nose.

"I'm sorry," she said, breaking out of my hold and sitting up. "Every time I think about it, I breakdown."

"That's to be expected unfortunately," I said, trying to keep my voice steady. I cleared my throat before I continued. "Brody and I didn't sleep well last night either. We couldn't stop thinking about it. I can't imagine how much worse it would be if we had actually been there when it happened."

She bit her lip, forcing back more tears. "It was awful. I don't know when I'm going to be able to get the image out of my mind. Like I said, I see it every time I close my eyes. What if I'm never able to get a good night's sleep again?"

"If I give you the contact info for Dr. Stevens' office, will you go talk to her?" I asked. "She's helped me so much over the last couple of months. I think she could help you, too."

She nodded. "I think I'll need to give it a shot. Thank you."

I wrapped my arm around her, pulled her towards me again and she rested her head on my shoulder. "You're not alone, Allison. Please come to me or Brody, Coach Tanner—somebody—if you need to talk. We are never too busy for you."

"Thank you." She stayed nestled into my shoulder and we sat in silence for several minutes, both of us lost in our own thoughts. Finally, she sniffed one last time and spoke up. "Can you tell me something good? I need to talk about something else."

Racking my brain, I tried to think of something positive to tell her. After a moment, I perked up when I remembered what else had happened last night. "Brody and I are engaged," I told her.

She bolted upright in her seat and gaped at me. "What! When did that happen?"

I pursed my lips. "Before shit hit the fan last night."

Her shoulders sagged. "Oh, Charlie. I'm sorry that such a momentous milestone was tainted for you. It's not fair that that had to overshadow your big day."

I shrugged. "I'm trying to separate the two memories from each other. The proposal really was beautiful. He brought me up to the roof of the resort."

Her eyes softened. "I knew Brody was a romantic. Let me see the ring."

I held my hand towards her to show her the large, princess cut diamond.

"It's beautiful!" she gushed. "He did a good job."

I nodded as I held my hand closer to admire it myself. "He did."

"Oh, you know what?" She sat up straight again like an idea had just come to her. "I need to keep myself busy to keep my mind off Landon. Planning a wedding might help, if you'd like some assistance? I don't have much experience in wedding planning, and I totally get it if you're not okay with that—"

I held my hand up to stop her and smiled. "Allison, I would love your help. I have no idea where to even start. It'd be a great project to work on together. We might even let Brody in on it," I joked.

She laughed. "This could be fun! Thank you."

"What are best friends for?"

Chapter Twenty-Four

Brody

A week after the attempted gala, we laid Landon to rest. There wasn't much of a ceremony or funeral for him, but Allison, Charlie, Coach Tanner, and I were at the cemetery when he was buried. We had a priest join us, he said a few words, and that was that. It wasn't much, but I wanted to believe that's how Landon would have wanted it. Surrounded by the people he cared about most.

Following the burial, the four of us met up at the pool with beers and wine bottles in tow. We spread out on the bleachers, the whole place to ourselves, and talked about our favorite memories with Landon.

"I remember his first day with us." Allison was staring straight ahead as she took a swig from a bottle of wine we were sharing. "He looked like a little lost puppy. He had come such a long way in the short time we knew him."

"I'll never get that look of pure, innocent joy on his face the first time he qualified for Olympic Trials," Coach Tanner added. He had to avert his gaze when tears threatened to fall.

"He would have gone far, that's for sure," Charlie said quietly. She sat upright on one of the benches, while I laid down with my head resting in her lap. After a long moment of silence, she looked down at me. "Brody, you've been pretty quiet. Anything you want to say about Landon?"

Instead of responding, I closed my eyes and let my thoughts run free. Did I have a favorite memory with Landon? He was basically a little brother to me. From the moment we met, we had an instant connection, almost as if we had met each other before. Instinctively, I had looked over him, and when I found out about his father, I became even more protective of him.

Maybe not intentionally, but in a way, he looked out for me, too. He made me want to be a better role model for him. I never blinked an eye when I used to get in all kinds of trouble with my old friend, Chase. It wasn't until Landon came along and started making his little remarks about him that I realized what we did *was* pretty stupid.

We were each other's support system. I had no family, and his family didn't give a hoot about him. We both knew what it was like to feel alone, and maybe that's why we connected so easily.

"Brody?" Charlie asked, snapping me back to the present. "Are you okay?"

"Here." Allison held the bottle of wine towards me. "Take a drink."

Reluctantly, I sat up and took the bottle from her, taking a long drink. "I loved every memory with him in it," I finally said, leaving it at that.

Silence stretched between us once more, as if every one of us were in some kind of trance. The only noises were the buzzing of the lights, and the soft flow of water through the pool filters. It was quiet for so long, I almost expected the others would start getting up to leave. I, on the other hand, was perfectly content sitting here and remembering all the good times we had in this building.

"I have something for Landon," Coach Tanner finally said, breaking the silence. "Maybe you all could help me put it up?"

He stood up and took off towards his office, and the rest of us exchanged confused looks. A minute later, he came strolling back out of his office with what looked like a giant, rolled up tarp thrown over his shoulder.

"I have a buddy who owns a print shop," he said, laying the tarp in front of us. "I asked him to make this for us to remember Landon by. I was hoping to have it ready for his memorial service earlier today, but it wasn't finished until after. Picked it up on the way over here."

"What is it?" Charlie asked.

"Well, how about all of you come help me unroll it, and we'll check it out."

He grabbed one corner of the tarp and the rest of us took hold of the other corners. As we unrolled and spread it out, I had to keep myself from tearing up again.

Allison laid down her corner and brought her hands to her mouth. "Coach, it's beautiful."

The tarp was actually a big banner. It had to be at least four feet wide, and probably twice as tall. A picture of Landon took up the entire top half, and the words, *'Sometimes we're tested not to show our weaknesses, but to discover our strengths,'* was written underneath. At the bottom, *Landon Davis, Forever in Our Hearts*, was in bolded letters.

"I thought maybe we could hang it up on the far end of the pool," Coach Tanner said. "That way it's like Landon is always here with us."

I gave him a tight grin. "I think that would be a great idea. Charlie, let's see if we can find some ladders."

While Charlie and I searched for a ladder or two, Allison and Coach Tanner found some nails and a hammer and were planning the perfect spot to hang the banner.

It took some digging, but we managed to find two ladders in different custodial closets across the building and brought them into the pool. Coach Tanner and I each took one end of the banner and climbed on the ladders, while the girls gave us directions on where to hang it. It was definitely a team effort, but with the four of us working together, we managed to have it hung up in only a couple of minutes. Once we were satisfied with its placement, we stood back and admired it.

"It's perfect," Charlie whispered. She glanced at me, and we smiled at each other. Taking my hand in hers, she gave it a squeeze.

"Good work, team," Coach Tanner said softly. "He's looking down at us, and he'll be cheering you on at every practice."

We stood in silence for a few minutes more, and I once again let memories of Landon wash over me. All the carpools, the swim meets, the friendly competition at night practices when it was just the two of us, even all the crap that went down with Camila last year. There were plenty of things I wish I could have changed about what happened, but one thing was for sure: Landon died a hero. He stood up to his dad in Atlanta when he had held Roman Howard hostage, and he had stood up to him once more last week at the resort, trying to protect all the guests at the gala. Landon was selfless, he would have done anything to protect the well-being of others, and unfortunately, that ended up being his demise.

If I couldn't go back in time or change the outcome of what happened, I only wish I could see him one more time to make sure he knew I was proud of him. Lifting my chin, I closed my eyes and prayed he was watching us at this very moment, hearing my thoughts.

"Well, it's getting late everyone," Coach Tanner sniffed. He wiped at his eyes, and I knew he had been fighting more tears. "We do need to get back to practice tomorrow, so I suggest all of you get home and get some sleep."

We nodded in agreement, and silently gathered our things to leave. Holding the door open as the others filed out, I stayed back a moment to take one more glance at Landon's photo.

"I'll see you tomorrow, buddy," I said out loud. His picture smiled down at me, and I couldn't help but smile back. For the first time since his passing, I felt hope that he was in a better place, hanging with my parents looking down at me.

This wasn't goodbye forever. We'd see each other again someday, and I looked forward to that time.

Epilogue

Allison

Three months later

"I think things are finally starting to feel a little more normal. I only woke up once last night." I was sitting across from Dr. Stevens as she nodded and took notes while I spoke.

It took me a couple weeks after Brody's attempted gala to finally crack and beg Charlie to give me Dr. Stevens' information so I could make an appointment with her. I tried so hard to deal with it on my own, but after so many sleepless nights, I was on the verge of a mental breakdown. Not to mention my appetite just wasn't there anymore, and as a professional swimmer, I needed to eat a lot in order to train at the intensity that I did.

In fact, one day, I had eaten so little, and was so exhausted, I passed out while I was brushing my teeth and hit my head on the vanity in the process. I was home alone at the time, so I was very fortunate that I came to on my own and wasn't too badly injured. But it was a wake-up call for sure. I decided that night I needed help. Ever since, I've been meeting with Dr. Stevens twice a week to work out my problems.

"My appetite still isn't where it should be, though. I've lost a lot of muscle weight."

"How many meals are you eating a day?" she asked, glancing up from her notes.

"I am eating supper and lunch every day," I told her. "But I'm still struggling to make sure I eat breakfast."

"It's still an improvement." She smiled. "It will take some time to get back into those normal eating patterns. You don't want to go from eating very little one day, to eating thousands of calories the next. That wouldn't be healthy either. I think you're on the right track, and it will continue to get better."

I nodded to show her I had heard her, but didn't respond.

"Everything else going okay?" she asked.

"I guess." I shrugged. "I don't know, it's been different for a while now."

"Since Landon has been gone, you mean? Or is there more?" She started scribbling in her notes again.

"I'm sure it's because of Landon and everything that happened," I said. "I told you they closed Fit Happens, and I had to get a new job at a different gym. It's been hard to adjust. Charlie isn't working with me anymore and I don't know anyone. They all know about the gala and that I was there, and it's like that's all they care to talk about with me. I get they're probably curious, but I don't want to talk about it. I'm afraid I'm being off-putting and I'm not really making any friends."

She nodded in agreement. "It's only natural they would be drawn to the details, but the event is still somewhat fresh in everyone's minds. I'd give it a little more time. Eventually, they'll lose interest in the tragedy and maybe you will have a fresh start."

"Yeah, maybe," I mumbled.

"You're not doing anything wrong, Allison," she said. "You believe that, don't you?"

"I suppose."

She leaned forward in her chair and gave my knee a pat. "Anyone in your shoes would do the same thing. If they can't understand that, that's their problem. Not yours."

I gave her a tight grin. "You're probably right."

"I am right, honey," she chuckled. "Alright, should we call it a day?"

Glancing at the clock, I nodded. "Yeah, I should get back to the pool. We have some new swimmers starting today."

"How exciting! You'll have to tell me about them next week."

We said our goodbyes and I took off for the pool. Coach Tanner recently signed a pair of twins to join our team, and today would be their first day. The two ladies, Natalie and Nicole Coleman, had both just graduated from college last Spring—Florida State, if I remember correctly—and were both incredibly gifted swimmers. Coach said he'd never signed on a pair of twins before. I found it just as amazing as he had. How many twins did *you* know that were both incredibly talented in the same sport? I was eager to meet them and see how they'd do.

Pulling into the parking lot, I grabbed my bags out of the passenger seat and stepped out into the hot and humid air. Summer had only just officially begun, but we had had a warmer-than-usual spring, so it had been dreadfully hot for a while already. I was thankful the walk to the building was short, and that I would be getting into the cold water soon.

When I opened the pool doors, a small boy immediately jumped into view. "Boo!" he yelled, his hands held up in front of him for extra effect.

"Oh, shi—" I covered my mouth with my hand to avoid saying the expletive in front of the little boy. He couldn't have been older than five or six.

"Oliver, I told you to sit down and wait for your dad over here!" A young woman with light brown hair came running over to me. She was dressed in a blue TYR one piece, with a pair of black athletic shorts over the top. "I'm so sorry, his dad is coming to get him, I told him it could be a while yet."

"That's okay," I laughed, stepping inside and letting the door close behind me. Who were these people? I thought the little kid practices had been moved outdoors for the summer.

"I'm Nicole, by the way," the girl said, sticking her hand towards me. "You're Allison, right?"

My eyes lit up as realization washed over me. "Oh, hi!" I took her hand and gave it a shake. "Sorry, yes. I'm Allison. Welcome aboard. We've heard so many great things about you and your sister."

She blushed. "Thank you. We're both very excited to be here. Natalie is just getting changed. She'll be out soon." She walked with me to the bleachers where we normally set down our stuff. "Oliver, sit here and stay put, please."

"Is this your little guy?" I asked, trying to do the math. Coach Tanner hadn't mentioned anything about either of them being a mom, but I suppose one of them could be.

"Oh, no!" She laughed. "He's my nephew. My brother lives in Jacksonville, too. His daycare lady is sick today, and he had to run some errands this morning. Natalie and I said we'd watch him for a few hours. He's supposed to come pick him up soon."

"You've got some pretty nice aunts, buddy," I said to Oliver. He smiled and his cheeks turned red, but he didn't say anything.

Charlie came walking out of the locker room a moment later with who I assumed was Nicole's sister, Natalie. They weren't totally identical, but they did have the same hair color, and were roughly the same size and shape. Upon closer examination, I noticed one had green eyes and the other had blue. That would probably be the easiest way for me to tell them apart moving forward.

Soon, Coach Tanner and Brody joined us on deck, and we were lost in introductions and small conversation. Brody shook hands with the girls as he said hello, and I noticed Nicole blush ever so slightly at the sight of him. Feeling protective for Charlie, I felt it was a good time to tell them he was taken—just in case they didn't read the news.

"Brody and Charlie are engaged!" I said excitedly. "They'll be getting married in a few months, and they have graciously allowed me to help plan their wedding."

Although Nicole's face fell just a touch at the news, she rebounded quickly and congratulated them.

"Have you planned a wedding before?" Natalie asked.

"No, this is a first for me," I said. "It's been a learning curve so far."

"You'll have to chat with our brother." Natalie looked to Nicole who nodded in agreement. "He works as an event manager at one of the resorts here in town. He helps plan tons of weddings every year."

"I'll have to keep that in mind." I smiled.

Suddenly, the side door opened, and a tall man dressed in khakis and a blue polo rolled in. His dark hair was combed back, and it was clear the man hadn't missed a workout in a while. He had a dark beard that matched his hair.

He was drop dead gorgeous.

"Oh, speak of the devil," Nicole chuckled. "There he is now."

"*That's* your brother?" I asked before I could catch myself. I couldn't tear my eyes off him.

"Daddy!" Oliver jumped out of his seat and ran to the man, who caught him in his arms and squeezed him tight.

"Hey buddy!" He laughed, setting him back down on the ground. "I hope you were good today." He glanced at his sisters, who nodded. "Excellent. That's my boy." He tussled the boy's hair gently.

"Everyone, this is our older brother, Rhett," Natalie introduced him.

We all mumbled hellos and gave little waves. Coach Tanner walked over to him and shook his hand.

"We're very excited to have your sisters join the team," he said. "I think they'll both go far."

"I'm super excited for them both," Rhett said. "I know they've wanted this for as long as I can remember. But I don't want to keep you from getting practice started. I just came to get Oliver, and we'll be out of your hair."

"Can you stay for a while?" Nicole asked him.

Rhett looked to Coach. "Is that allowed?"

"Of course!" Coach nodded. "Stay as long as you'd like."

"Well, alright! Oliver, let's hang out for a bit." He took the boy's hand and made his way over to the bench his son had been sitting on minutes earlier.

"Perfect," Coach Tanner said. "The rest of you, let's get moving. Get in and stretch your muscles for ten or fifteen minutes, while I write the rest of the warmup on the board."

While everyone started getting their caps and goggles on, I couldn't resist the temptation to go talk to Rhett. Obviously, he had a kid and was more than likely married, but I still felt drawn to him. I had to say hello.

"Hi," I said shyly, walking up to him. I cleared my throat and tried to sound like my usual bubbly self. This guy was actually making me nervous. "I just wanted to introduce myself—"

"That's Allison!" Oliver said before I could.

"Allison?" Rhett repeated, chuckling at his kid. "I see you two must have already met?"

I laughed. "Yes, he thought I was you when I walked in. Tried to scare me."

Rhett made a face. "Sorry about that. Oliver, did you apologize to Allison for scaring her?"

"Oh, no! That's okay," I said quickly. "It was all in good fun."

"His daycare lady said the boys have been taking turns trying to sneak up on her and the other kids, too," he said. "Must be a phase they're going through."

"That must drive your wife crazy," I said, seeing my opportunity to find out if he was married. It wasn't subtle, but I didn't care.

"Ex-wife," he said, and I tried like hell not to break out in a wide grin. "Long story. I'll spare you the details, but he hasn't seen her in a few weeks. She's been spared from it."

"Oh, I'm sorry to hear about that."

He waved it off. "Nothing to be sorry about."

I looked over my shoulder to see that almost everyone else had gotten in the water and started their warmup. I probably only had another minute or two before Coach would yell at me to get in as well, but I didn't want to stop talking to Rhett.

"So, listen, your sisters said you work as an event manager?" I asked.

"Yeah, I work for Hilton. I get to help plan all kinds of events."

"Maybe I could pick your brain sometime?" I tried to shoot my shot. "Charlie and Brody—my teammates—" I said, pointing to the pool, "are getting married soon, and they've asked me to help plan their wedding. I could use all the help I could get."

He smiled wide at me, and I couldn't help but smile back. "I'd love to help you out sometime."

"Great—"

"Allison, let's get going!" Coach Tanner called to me.

"I'll be right there!" I yelled back, and then turned my attention back to Rhett. "Maybe I can get your number from one of your sisters? We can set something up?"

"Absolutely." He was still smiling that big, gorgeous grin. "Anytime you'd like."

I bit my lip and folded my hands together like I was praying. "Thank you."

"Of course. I look forward to spending time with you."

Waving goodbye, I turned towards the water, smiling the entire time. For the first time in a really long time, I felt butterflies in my stomach. I liked Rhett, and I looked forward to spending time with him, too.

Please visit my website to view my weekly blog and stay up to date on what books I've got coming out. https://meganreiffenberger.com/

Also, join me on Facebook: https://www.facebook.com/SwimmingThroughLyfe. I love to hear feedback from my readers!

If you enjoyed *Below the Surface Vol.2*, please consider leaving a review! Reviews are critical for other readers to discover my books.

Thanks for reading!

Megan Reiffenberger

Author Bio

Megan Reiffenberger was born in 1994 in Watertown, South Dakota, and has lived there most of her life. She graduated from George Mason University with a Bachelor's Degree in Marketing, and she currently works at NATE: The Communications Infrastructure Contractors Association as the Member Services Coordinator. If she's not working or writing, you can often find her going for a run or a swim, as regular exercise is of the utmost importance to her. In fact, inspiration for Megan's novels, *Sink or Swim* and *Below the Surface,* were drawn from her sixteen years of competitive swimming experience.

If you want to know more about Megan, or when her next book comes out, please visit her website at https://meganreiffenberger.com/ or follow her on Facebook (Swimming Through Life), Twitter (@Megan_Reiff22), and Instagram (reiffenberger22).

9 781736 988435